We Know Where You Live

A Maggie Garrett Mystery

Jean Taylor

Seal Press

Library of Congress Cataloging-in-Publication Data

Taylor, Jean M.
We know where you live / Jean M. Taylor
I. Title.
PS3570.A935W4   1995   813'.54 — dc20   94 – 37238
ISBN: 1-878067-62-1

Printed in the United States of America
First printing, March 1995
10 9 8 7 6 5 4 3 2

Distributed to the trade by Publishers Group West
In Canada: Publishers Group West Canada, Toronto, Ontario
In the U.K. and Europe: Airlift Book Company, London, England

Cover photography by Elizabeth Mangelsdorf
Cover and book design by Clare Conrad

Acknowledgments

Thanks to Bob Crocker and Jim Mitulski for many kinds of spiritual support, shared hopes, thoughtful literary critiques ("*too precious!*"), and endless trips on the Bernal bus. To Jill Goodman for your friendship, your eyebrows, your willingness to read and reread a book outside your normal interests. To Jaem Heath O'Ryan for those sessions that bring me back to who I am. To Janja Lalich, Rebecca Gordon and Jan Adams for making me believe I could do this. To Bob D'Arcy, Suzanne Dumont, Bill Hellendale, René Richard, Sharon Stover, Ayanna Flechero, and Jill Sizemore, for reading early drafts without scoffing, or for examining late drafts and finding those telltale glitches. Special thanks to Barbara Wilson and June Thomas of Seal Press for sensitive and intelligent editing.

THE CHARACTERS

Maggie Garrett, sole proprietor, Windsor and Garrett Investigations, sole support of Pod and Fearless, overindulged cats.

Ricardo Galvéz, Maggie's assistant, high school junior and computer hacker.

Liam O'Meara, Maggie's best friend, AIDS activist, owner of Loba the wolfhound.

Jessie Giuliani, Maggie's other best friend, cancer activist, matchmaker.

Tate Pritchard, Maggie's friend, psychotherapist, Jessie's lover.

Kristin Chase, attorney, rapidly becoming Maggie's ex-lover.

The Pride Lesbian and Gay Democratic Club

Lynnette McSorley, member Executive Committee, freelance termagant.

Betty Hastings, member Executive Committee, club president.

Miranda Post, member Executive Committee, club treasurer.

Stephen Leong, member Executive Committee.

Tom Ng, member Executive Committee.

Warren Coleman, member Executive Committee.

Miguel Alvarez, member Executive Committee.

David Lindley, member Executive Committee.

Geoffrey Lawrence, ex-president, now Mayor's "official gay."

Mavis Baker, ex-treasurer, successful realtor, troublemaker.

Larry Gross, ex-treasurer, down but not out with pneumocystis.

Marc Romano, ex-treasurer, Geoffrey's ex-lover.

Joe Leslie, ex-treasurer, Geoffrey's confidant.

Jolie Krawczyk, Mavis' ex.

The Police

Sergeant Diana Hoffman, Homicide Section.

Detective Earl Desmond, Burglary Section.

Chapter One

Six years ago, when I was a law firm drudge by day and a post-punk girl rocker by night, I nearly got fired for refusing to work weekends. I stood my ground because, I said, "I have a life."

Now I had my own business as a private investigator, but sometimes I wondered if I still had a life. It was a sunny Saturday morning, and I was at work, in my two-room office "suite." Two hours earlier I had stopped off to check the mail for the overdue payment a client had promised would be there—it wasn't. There was also a nagging doubt in my mind about whether my assistant Ricardo Galvéz had remembered to turn off the coffee maker—he hadn't. The sickly sweet, burnt caramel smell assaulted my nostrils from half-way down the hall.

Cleaning up the charred coffee led to sponging down the counter and tiny office fridge, which led to reorganizing the supplies and making a list of what we needed.

In other words, I didn't want to be at home, ordinarily my favorite place. My lover Kristin was vacationing in Maine—without me—to think about "where our relationship is headed." That was assuming we still had one to contemplate. My house was full of reminders of better days, and it was not the place I wanted to be, even if the tradeoff was cleaning refrigerator scum at the office.

Midway through, I made a new pot of coffee, took a break and read the *San Francisco Chronicle*.

The headlines were the usual: another thousand layoffs, another endangered species standing in the way of a development project, a crackdown on prostitutes in the Tenderloin District. Buried inside was the report of a gay bashing, the ninth incident of extreme violence against lesbians and gay men in the past month.

Even before the latest attack, the Stop the Bashing Coalition had planned a demonstration to protest the lack of any response from City Hall. My friend Jessie Giuliani was one of the main organizers of the demonstration, and we'd stayed up late the night before making signs and banners. I felt a personal need to raise hell, because I knew one of the bashing victims, a long-time survivor of HIV. He had also survived being beaten with tire irons by three men, but since that night his T-cell count had fallen precipitously.

As I was making my weekly vow to quit reading the paper on weekends, someone pounded on the outer door of the office. The translucent glass door to the office usually gives enough clues for me to guess the identity of callers, but it failed me now. Today's visitor was short, but vastly wide. He/she/it looked like a purple and brown haystack.

"Open up, Maggie! I know you're in there—the guard downstairs told me you were!"

I opened the door. You endure earthquakes and killer fogs to live in San Francisco, and you submit to the vagaries of Lynnette McSorley to live here as a political lesbian. She's six inches shorter than me and weighs in at under 150 pounds, but people remember her as big. Local officials have ignored

4

her at their peril. She simply will not go away.

"Hi Lynnette! You got me, come on in. Want some coffee?"

Lynnette appeared to have come directly from bed. Her tangled brown ringlets were flattened in back, and she was wearing what might have been loose leggings or tight pajamas in red candy stripes with a wrinkled brown turtleneck. Two woven Guatemalan knapsacks stuffed full of various articles of clothing and other possessions crossed her chest, over the fuzzy lavender poncho I'd mistaken for a haystack. Lynnette carries a lot of responsibility for the stereotype of no-style lesbians.

"How come you didn't answer your door? This is the smallest office I've ever seen! How much does it cost? Phew, it smells toxic in here—don't you know about using eco-friendly cleaners?" Each new comment was punctuated by a gasp. Lynnette talks much faster than she breathes. "Have you seen the latest SNEWS?"

Knowing she'd wind down eventually, I half-listened while I poured her some coffee. "I can't remember what the first few questions were, but no, I haven't seen the SNEWS." The *San Francisco News*, one of the least socially useful of the local gay (no, not lesbian and gay) newspapers, specialized in nasty rumors about local organizations. SLEAZE would have been a more accurate nickname.

Lynnette pulled a copy of the paper from one of her bags and gestured with it. "If they could dig up something on Mother Teresa they would! I don't get it. The paper is mostly ads for phone sex services, but they act like they're avengers from God whenever they get hold of a new rumor about a community organization!"

"So, what is it this week?"

"That egomaniac Morris Drake wrote an editorial he had the gall to call 'Democracy in the Democratic Clubs.' Listen to this: 'Sources from within the Pride Lesbian and Gay Democratic Club, who asked to remain nameless for their safety, claim that money raised in political campaigns has been siphoned off for other purposes. Some assert that funds have gone into the pockets of the club leadership.' It makes me so mad!"

"Why let Morris Drake upset you? You're probably one of three people who read editorials. Everybody else just reads the personals."

"And those other two people who read it will add a few twists and tell two more people, and then they'll tell a few more, with a few more enhancements. Believe me, by this time tomorrow, it'll be all over town that the Pride leadership is about to be hauled off to jail."

"But, none of it's true, is it?"

"It doesn't have to be true! Are you just pretending to be so dense? Theft at nonprofits makes even better gossip than whether some football player is gay. In the last three months there've been four big scandals about money getting lost or stolen from groups. Remember when the president of Friends of PWAs got arrested for embezzlement at that ceremony where he was about to get an award? The media loved that one. After the last few years, our club doesn't need any more bad PR!"

"I haven't read anything, good or bad, about the Pride Club since your big election upset a few months ago, and that was all smiley photo opportunity stuff."

"Exactly! We finally dumped Geoffrey Lawrence and his groupies, and the community is taking us seriously again. But all it takes is gossip like this to bring back everybody's doubts about us."

"Why don't you organize Pride members to write to the 'Letters to the Editor' column at the other gay papers? They love to publish stuff that makes the competition look scummier than they are. You know, something scathing but dignified, socking it to old Morris."

"Well, actually, it's not as simple as that . . . ." Lynnette sank back into the chair and inspected the interior of her coffee mug.

"What do you mean? It's not true, is it? Who's the treasurer now, anyway?"

"It's Miranda Post, but she just got elected. As a matter of fact, the club has had three treasurers in the past year and a half, before Miranda. Of course the transition each time has been pretty bumpy, and sometimes people were bitter when they left, but I never thought it would come to open attacks like this."

"Either I'm missing some subtle point or you're holding back. What's the problem?"

"Well, there might be money that's not accounted for. You know about slate cards, right?"

"Not much. It would be safest to assume that I'm pig-ignorant."

Lynnette rolled her eyes but launched in. "Right before every major election, Pride puts out slate cards with our recommendations and then distributes them through our volunteer network. Half the political clubs in the City do it. Pride never charged a fee for its endorsements, like some groups, but we always have accepted donations for club projects, or maybe to help with printing expenses for the election materials. Got it?"

I nodded.

"Some people in the club believe more donations went

through the club to pay for cards and other election materials than what our current records show. Plus, there's talk about contributions from political action committees and candidates, big donations, but there's no record of them."

"How could that happen?"

"We had a lot of treasurers, none of them lasted very long, and they all used different accounting methods. Some of them did fancy computer spreadsheets that nobody could understand, and some only kept handwritten records. Then every time one quit or got kicked out, they weren't exactly great about turning things over to the next one."

I was getting restless. I'd already blown half the morning, and my house needed big-time maintenance. There was the refrigerator to excavate, and the shower was moldy again. The cat box didn't bear thinking of. Torn between being a good hostess and wanting Lynnette to leave, I promised myself I wouldn't offer her any more coffee.

Suddenly I noticed the silence in the room, and gulped. Lynnette was staring at me expectantly.

"I'm sorry, could you repeat that?" I could feel myself blushing. One of the tribulations of being a pale-faced redhead.

"Honestly, I do not see why you have a reputation as an investigator if you can't follow a simple conversation! I said, how long would it take you to track down what's going on?"

"You want to hire me? Whoa, I thought you'd just dropped by to vent. From what you've said, you need to do an internal audit, and to drag the old treasurers back in to put the pieces together."

"If you had paid any attention to what I said, you'd understand that the ones who used to be treasurers are probably the ones spreading rumors now! Besides, most of the original records don't exist anymore. They burned up in the fire at Joe Leslie's building last year."

"How convenient!"

"Yeah, a lot of people said that. Last night the Executive Committee had an emergency meeting, and we voted to bring in an investigator from the outside. We picked you, on Bill Freidel's recommendation. Even though you're not into electoral stuff, you do know your way around the community. Bill said you were very low-profile when you worked for him. What did you do for him, anyway?"

Mantra for the day: I have invited this person into my life to help me learn patience.

"Lynnette! I wouldn't have even mentioned Bill's name to you, and I certainly won't tell you anything about what I did or didn't do for him. It's like a priest or a doctor. What my clients tell me stays with me, period."

"Like a doctor. . . well, that's good, it's what we need, somebody who can keep her mouth shut. Do you think gossiping is genetic, like sexual orientation? Anyway, we want to hire you to get to the bottom of this and report to us. That way we can stop all the loose talk."

"Okay, you've convinced me you need somebody from the outside. But you should get someone to wade through bank records, and that's not me. Ask the woman who does my taxes! I know several good number-cruncher types. I could recommend one."

"We need someone who knows the lesbian and gay political community. An accountant wouldn't ask the right questions. When we get all the records from all the banks in one place, you can have one of your numbers people total them all up. But we don't even know where all the accounts are. They kept opening new ones with different people autho-

9

rized to sign checks. Somebody has to dig up all the bodies, so we know at least as much as Morris Drake does."

I offered her more coffee to give myself time to think. Did I need work badly enough to take on what might become a miserable quagmire of blaming and counter-blaming? What to do? Stall for time.

"Lynnette, I need to think about this, and I wish you'd think about it, too." Good, good, maybe she'll change her mind! "Let me give you my standard contract. You can take this copy back to the Executive Committee to read over. Here's my rate formula. I would need a retainer fee." I pulled a set of forms out of a drawer and handed them to her.

She glanced at the forms and blinked at me accusingly. "Why are you suddenly talking as if you'd never met me before?"

"I didn't mean to hurt your feelings, but if I do accept this job—and I haven't decided to accept it yet—it has to be on formal terms. I need to know who'd get my reports, how much time you want me to spend, who's off limits to approach. What you have to decide is whether you want to pay me to find out ugly stuff about the wrong people. That kind of thing happens all the time in investigations." I glanced at her out of the corner of my eye, to gauge the effect of this.

She was getting out her checkbook.

Chapter Two

After Lynnette left, I headed for home and performed triage on my house: vacuuming, cleaning the cat box and removing the green nuclear waste in the refrigerator vegetable bins.

It was the fourth weekend that I hadn't got around to washing my car, and some smart-ass had written "Help, I'm being held hostage by a slob" on the back window. I took a hose to that spot and the pigeon droppings. It's a six-year-old off-white Toyota that looks just like millions of other cars, which is of course the point for a P.I. The body is a little dinged up, but it's got a killer engine. I bought the car from the sister of a drug-dealer who had finished customizing its engine a week before he was blown away by a competitor, and I'm fanatical about keeping the inner workings maintained. My physical safety has depended on it.

If I didn't run into anyone I knew, detoured around the earring stores and ran past the bookstores without stopping at the bargain racks outside, there was enough time to do grocery shopping. I took my two-wheel cart down the hill to Real Foods. As usual, the purple cauliflowers, carrots shaped like beets and tiger-striped tomatoes transfixed me. I bought enough food for seven farmhands, and had to rush home.

It took considerable rearranging, but I got everything

jammed into the fridge. I was on my way out when I noticed the envelope stuck under the door. It was the plain white dollar-a-box variety, with nothing written on the outside.

Inside was a sheet of white paper, clipped to five hundred-dollar bills. Centered on the page were the words "DON'T TAKE THE JOB. THERE'S MORE OF THIS."

I felt an immediate urge to call Iowa and tell my dad. He's always going off about how agribusiness giants get paid billions by the government not to grow crops. I could inform him that I'd been invited to join their ranks and profit by not working. Then it sank in. Whoever left the envelope at my door could just as easily have fired a shotgun through the door or torched the house. The note wasn't funny anymore.

"The job" had to be the Pride Club investigation. But who knew about it or, for that matter, cared enough about it to leave this message for me?

With a pair of chopsticks I plucked up the note and envelope and sealed them in a zip-lock bag. Later I would take them to be fingerprinted by my ex-cop buddy Marcia, who for reasons known only to herself maintains a mini crime-lab in her basement. There was little hope for getting any useful information. After decades of TV cop shows, everyone knows enough to wear gloves. The text had been word processed and laser-printed in the standard Courier typeface used in a million offices. Finding the printer would be a CIA endeavor. I put the bills in a clean envelope and stuck it in my sock drawer.

Now I really was late. By taking every short cut I knew and exceeding the speed limits, I got to Jessie's place only ten minutes after she had expected me. When I pulled up in front of the Potrero Hill house she shares with her lover Tate, Jessie was waiting next to the stack of picket signs and banners I'd helped create the night before. As always, she looked ready for a garden party. Her pale violet jumpsuit, embroidered with flowers on the collar and across her chest, matched the tint of her eye shadow. One of her famous big-brimmed, flowered numbers was perched on her wild salt and pepper curls.

Jessie is an executive secretary at the law firm where I worked part-time for over a year. Her ultra-feminine appearance has sometimes led new attorneys to underestimate her intelligence, abilities and toughness. Jessie never forgets, though as a practicing Christian she does try to forgive.

When I'm on a difficult case or just need to rant about a trying client, Jessie is my confidante. She's a terrific listener and frequently gives me a new perspective when I get stuck. At the mention of the Pride Club, she rolled her eyes.

"Those people can make you crazy. Tate did a mediation for them and another club a couple of months ago—some dispute over who had prior dibs on a mailing list. She kept their confidence, of course, so I didn't hear details, but she made me promise not to say 'oppression,' 'community' or 'internalized homophobia' in her presence for a month!"

"What's your take on the rumors about missing funds?"

"In general, I'm inclined to give groups the benefit of the doubt. Look at how many AIDS organizations get in trouble over spending their money on great things that didn't happen to be on their grant proposals. Maybe it's just a matter of bad bookkeeping. On the other hand, there must be chunks of money going in and out of a group like Pride, and the temptation to skim would be powerful."

I didn't tell her about the bribe money. Jessie would consider my possession of it a moral dilemma to be explored at length. I wanted to leave it be for the moment and see what developed in the case.

Hundreds of demonstrators were milling around the Civic Center in front of City Hall when we arrived. We unloaded the car, and I spent fifteen minutes searching for a free, legal place to park before giving up on the legal part. When I returned, Jessie was chatting amiably with Louisa Burke and another woman. This was remarkable because Jessie and Louisa are ex-lovers who would not generally share the same side of the street.

Jessie's motivation became plain when she introduced Louisa's friend Elise. Jessie made a point of telling Elise, a wiry, wary-eyed woman in a Northwest Women Composers Festival sweatshirt, that I'm a musician. Then she announced that Elise planned to move from Seattle to San Francisco—perhaps I could share some rental hints with her? Elise and I flashed each other sickly smiles, acknowledging the awkwardness of it all. Then she and Louisa drifted away.

I turned on Jessie. "When are you going to stop with the matchmaking? Until you hear different, I'm in a relationship!" Jessie loathes Kristin and considers finding me a more suitable partner to be her responsibility. She's always introducing me to women, the most astounding variety of women, in the hopes that one of them will "take." Like all the matchmaking I've ever heard of, it's been a disaster. We can laugh about the ones from last year, but I haven't forgiven her yet for the one from January (a member of a nine-person Maoist sect) or Ms. April, a goddess worshiper who wanted me to join her at a lunar rite that featured songs in celebration of menstrual blood.

"Well, you certainly don't do well on your own," she said, mildly embarrassed. "I'm going to go light a fire under those people at the microphones. They were scheduled to start ten minutes ago! Everyone's going to take off for the beach if they don't start soon." It was one of those perfect San Francisco days that we get twice a year, warm with a slight breeze, and some sunbathers had spread-eagled themselves on the few patches of grass.

A long-time survivor of breast cancer, Jessie is co-founder of Cancer Rising, an activist group of women who appropriated the ACT-UP! model of creative protest. Cancer Rising was the uniting force behind the demonstration, as one of the few groups in the community commanding enough respect to bring together such widely divergent groups. Jessie organized the speakers. I could see her hold up five fingers to each one ("You have exactly five minutes. Thirty seconds over and we haul you off bodily!"). Soon chants demanding action from City Hall echoed on the streets and walls of the Civic Center.

The crowd in the plaza continued to grow. It was a great day for people-watching. We looked more like the annual Lesbian/Gay Pride Parade than a militant demonstration. People had agonized over what to wear. Most of us had settled for jeans and t-shirts, but there were the usual drag costumes, the habits of the Sisters of Perpetual Indulgence and the strategically placed strips of leather on some of the biker women. Gay and lesbian parents pushed babies in strollers. Collectively we were a thing of beauty. But we were also righteously angry. This was not a celebration of our sexuality but a demand for action in the face of murderous attacks on us.

Besides the broadly defined queer community, there were the usual hawkers of Stalinist, Trotskyist and Maoist newspapers, trying to shoehorn the issue of homophobia into their analyses. Petition circulators paid by the signature plied their captive audience—no one could say she didn't have time to sign. An immigrants' rights group had joined the demonstration to protest Mayor Rawlings' plans to deny health services at city clinics to "freeloading aliens." A welfare rights group was using street theater to dramatize the administration's plans to cut assistance to families.

Demonstration organizers circulated among the crowd giving out STOP THE BASHING stickers in a variety of garish shades. Nearly everyone seemed to have at least one of them stuck on a bag, a hat, their clothing or their skin.

The SFPD had sent a large contingent to keep things orderly. They stood on the edges of the crowd, talking among themselves. Word was that the cops agreed with us. A month earlier, police at the Mission Station had even circulated a petition requesting more foot patrols on the street. The petition had been politely acknowledged and filed away.

I wandered over to the speakers' stage to find Jessie. She and two other demonstration leaders were in heated discussion with Geoffrey Lawrence, former Pride Club president and now the Mayor's liaison to the lesbian/gay community. Geoffrey, dressed in beautifully tailored linen the shade of French vanilla ice cream, towered over Jessie.

Though I couldn't hear most of the words, the gist of the conversation came across. Geoffrey's perfect tan was assuming an unattractive reddish hue. He pointed at some of the signs (depicting the Mayor wielding a baseball bat, his foot planted on a bloodied victim), and gestured in Jessie's face. Jessie shrugged and gave her most charming smile, to the effect that she couldn't be held responsible for the actions of headstrong youth. In fact, Jessie had painted the raunchiest ones herself.

Finding no support for his outrage, Geoffrey turned on his heel and stalked over to a knot of suited figures. I almost felt sorry for him. It would be hard to act as front man for an administration that took the lesbian/gay vote for granted to the point of ignoring us. Still, Geoffrey must have known what he was getting into when he took the job. It was commonly agreed that the gay/lesbian population, like the working poor in the housing projects, people of color and women of all races, had not voted for Sam Rawlings as much as they had voted against his opponent, a racist Republican homophobe.

I returned my attention to the speeches being blasted across the plaza. The main speaker of the day was Margaret Tharpe, a retired high school teacher and president of the Castro Neighborhood Association. She chided City Hall for its condescension in dealing with a group of "old people and homosexuals—and worst of all, old homosexuals." Several TV news crews were filming, and I hoped she'd make the six o'clock news. With her snowy white hair tied up in a bun, she looked like everyone's favorite teacher—and she was out as a lesbian.

In a breathtaking display of cooperation, the four local lesbian/gay Democratic clubs had drawn lots for which club would speak for all of them. Betty Hastings, president of the Pride Lesbian and Gay Democratic Club, was that speaker. She was a slim African-American woman in her mid-forties. She commented on her choice of apparel for the day (a conservative suit), "I continue to hope that Mayor Rawlings will join us, and I dressed for the occasion." I'd heard that her father was an influential Baptist minister in Oakland. A childhood listening to good preaching no doubt contributed to the fire and eloquence of her message. Although Mayor Sam Rawlings was a Democrat, Betty made it clear that the Pride Club was willing to take him on if need be. Fist upraised, she finished to wild applause.

Geoffrey Lawrence followed Betty, speaking as the

administration's Official Gay. Geoffrey couldn't criticize the man whose favor was worth $80,000 a year, and the Mayor had done nothing that Geoffrey could praise. So he said nothing, at considerable length. Using the royal "we," he thanked the planners of the demonstration and the participants for everyone's "spirited but peaceful presence." There were retching noises all around me. However, I noticed that four TV cameras were grinding away.

That evening I ate dinner at Jessie and Tate's house while we watched TV reports on the demonstration. To our delight, CBS carried a brief segment on its national news, including a clip of Margaret Tharpe. We rated it an 8 out of 10.

The local stations gave the demonstration extensive coverage, since there hadn't been any hostage takings, floods or forest fires that day. As we clicked from channel to channel, we groaned as Geoffrey Lawrence's telegenic smile filled the TV screen again and again. Toward the end, Tate had to restrain Jessie from lunging at the set every time a camera zeroed in on Geoffrey.

Jessie went into the kitchen to make tea, and I followed. To distract her, I picked her brain about the Pride Club job.

"I admit I'd like the villain to be Geoffrey Lawrence," I said. "There'd be the side-benefit of embarrassing Sam Rawlings for hiring him as a 'special assistant.'"

"Do you have any basis for picking Geoffrey?"

"It's obvious! He's a smarmy rich-boy jerk, he'd step on your face if it meant he could get closer to a camera, and he's making a career for himself off of decades of other people's work, people like you and Margaret Tharpe."

"Now, Maggie, you're letting political value judgments interfere with your objectivity—again! True, Geoffrey is a disgusting opportunist, but that's not the same as being a thief.

Just because someone is rich, it doesn't mean they'd commit a crime. They're the ones who don't need to! Look for someone with access to funds who's also hurting for cash."

The reference to cash reminded me of the anonymous note and bribe money. When I told her about it, Jessie launched into a tirade about my taking risks that should appropriately be allocated to the police and the justice system, and for such low pay, besides. I said she sounded like my parents, and she praised their wisdom. She swore that she would now have to find me a worthwhile girlfriend *and* employment that didn't throw my loved ones into fits.

Chapter Three

Sunday morning I was having a disturbing dream about Kristin—the kind that makes you wish you were in therapy because you could devote a whole session to what it means—when the doorbell rang. It was only 7:10. Nobody I knew would drop by at such an hour, and the likelihood of Ed McMahon bearing millions of dollars was as remote as the likelihood of Jehovah's Witnesses bearing scriptures was high. I pulled the covers over my head.

The bell rang again, and again. I threw on a robe and stumbled into the living room. By the fourth long ring, the cats were nose-down at the door, sniffing and scowling, and Loba, an Irish wolf hound, had assumed her Protector bearing, eyes on me for her cue.

I peeked around a shade in time to see Lynnette McSorley, even more heavily burdened with ponchos and bags than yesterday, stomp around the side of my house. A few seconds later she was back, examining the windows (for a way to climb in?).

I gave up. At least she wouldn't stay long, being highly allergic to animals. I turned to my premier defenses, the furry creatures arrayed at my door. "Company's coming!" I hissed. "Everybody welcome Auntie Lynnette!"

"Doesn't your doorbell work?" she said by way of greeting. "Get away from me, fur-ball!" Fearless, a graceful black part-Siamese, dodged Lynnette's swipe at her, but didn't go very far. "If cats are so smart, why don't they know I'm allergic and I hate them? How can you keep all these animals in this little place?" She punctuated her remarks with a sneeze, and swatted at fat, long-haired tabby Pod, who was attempting to climb into one of the shopping bags she had set down.

"Lynnette, do you know what time it is?" I was now sufficiently awake to be incensed that I was in fact awake at this ridiculous hour.

She looked at her watch, and moaned. "God, yes, I'm going to be on a radio talk show this morning, and I go on in fifteen minutes! I brought you a bunch of materials on the club, so you'll be ready for the meeting tonight. Sorry I can't stay to go over them with you—"

I opened my mouth to tell her where she could go with my blessing.

"—but you have to realize that I can only be in one place at a time!" She frowned at my persistence in trying to keep her and slammed out the door.

Her going left a profound silence. The animals were staring at me again. "Don't ask me," I said.

I crawled back into bed, glorying in my reprieve from another lengthy Lynnette ordeal. The purring cats settled themselves on either side of me, and we were all dozing off when the phone rang.

"Hi, Baby. Missing me?" It was Kristin calling from the family summer house in Bar Harbor.

I started awake and rolled back the covers, spilling Pod onto the floor with the comforter. Fearless neatly sprang onto a chair and out of his reach, having learned that Pod punishes witnesses to his embarrassments.

"Maggie, are you there?" She sounded impatient.

"Hi, darling, I'm here, we just had a little cat circus going on. How's life at the old home place?"

"Hot! Every day Laurel and Jennifer and I sit around at the beach rubbing lotion on each other and teasing the lifeguards. We've got a contest going for who can make one of them fall out of his chair. Laurel keeps cheating by taking off her top. You won't believe how brown I am. Even my tits are brown."

Kristin never says words like "tit." Who was discussing (and what else?) her breasts with her? I tried to think of something upbeat to say.

"Well, I'm still sunburned from yesterday's demonstration. Did you see us on TV last night? Over five thousand people—of course the cops said it was only a thousand. . ."

"What demonstration?" Now she sounded bored.

"You know, the Stop the Bashing group I told you about."

"Don't you think it would make more sense to tell those guys they're asking for it when they go cruising in the park at two a.m.? If everybody could manage to keep it in their pants until they got home, none of this would happen." Getting towed for illegal parking is the worst thing that's likely to happen in Kristin's everyday world.

"Kristin, you're sounding like the right-wingers. 'It's your own fault—you bring violence on yourselves.' Why should we have to worry about holding hands, or even wearing a Silence Equals Death button? That's what got one woman beaten up, a damned button!"

No response. I'd done it again.

"Kristin? Let's not fight long-distance. We always have a harder time talking when we can't see each other's faces." I could hear her take a deep breath and exhale before she spoke.

"This is typical of your behavior, Maggie. You attack me, I get angry, and you say 'oh, puleeze, Kristin, let's not fight,'" she sneered. "And just who do you think is going to thank you for running around screaming in the streets—your clients?"

Now there was silence on my end. I was furious with her, but this was no way to end a conversation. Why had I brought up the damned demonstration, anyway?

"You're right, I started it, and I'm sorry. I want to share what's happening with me. But then I end up attacking you. . . ." The words tumbled out. I didn't mean much of what I was saying, but if I kept saying it, maybe she'd take that hateful condescension out of her voice.

"Fine. Let's just drop it." Now she sounded truly bored. "I'll call you in a couple of days to let you know what time I'll be getting in. You can still pick me up, can't you?"

"Of course. I'll be waiting at the gate with a rose in my teeth."

Feeling like a double loser—I'd groveled and been ridiculed for it—I wanted to crawl under the covers and die, or at least hide. However, the aroma of coffee from my timer-driven drip persuaded me that life might be worthwhile. I sprinted to the kitchen (ten feet away in my doll-sized cottage) and was back in bed, coffee in hand, in fifteen seconds flat. If there were an Olympic bed to breakfast competition, I'd be a medalist.

Sunday morning breakfast in bed had been a tradition for Kristin and me: jam smeared on more than muffins, and butter licked off each other's fingers. This brought memories of recent mornings: awkward silences, layers of anger and resentment, slammed doors. Bed no longer felt like a refuge, and I got up.

I went for a quick run in a nearby park with Loba, a pure-bred wolf hound. She belongs to my friend Liam O'Meara, but he can't keep her at his current place, so she's staying with the cats and me until he figures out what to do with his life. She's the size of the pony I had as a child, and she needs exercise the way I need coffee. Usually the rush that goes with the run keeps me from brooding, but it didn't work today.

Early in my relationship with Kristin we laughed about opposites attracting. She's a corporate attorney, closeted at work, on the partner track. I'm out to the world, and I've only had a full-time P.I. practice for a year—until then I still some-times had to work as a temp in law firms. She's East Coast old money. I'm from a long line of Midwest dirt farmers. Her friends are from college or her law firm. Mine are a ragtag assortment from political groups, past temp jobs, members of rock bands I've played in, cops and other P.I. scum like me.

We did, as they say, make a striking couple. Kristin's me-dium-height, with delicate features, small bones. Her hair is that dark blond shade that only rich girls seem to have. She's often described as looking "like a porcelain doll." I'm tall and rangy, look better in clothes than out of them, and my low-class red hair is so bright that I have to cover it up for surveil-lance work. I inherited Grandma Bessie's heavy eyebrows, which, even though I prune them, make people think of Frida Kahlo. I've never been likened to any kind of doll.

Back at the house, I poured myself a cup of coffee and dived into the Pride materials, to a chorus of crunching cat and dog kibble. In spite of the manner of their delivery, the archives promised to be a big help. I sorted everything chro-nologically, to get the flavor of each era. The cats assisted with enthusiasm, teasing out loose clippings and serving as paper-weights on the tallest stacks.

For several hours I read articles from the local press, as well as newsletters, campaign materials, promotional puff pieces about the club on glossy stock, hastily compiled hand-written financial reports, club minutes, correspondence—and copies of the few treasurers' records that hadn't gone up in smoke at Joe Leslie's apartment. There was a striking differ-ence between the seamless, trouble-free image the club lead-ership sought to portray and the stormy debates that were suggested by the minutes, and sometimes pointed out by the media. This immersion helped me identify the men and women who had been and, in a few cases, continued to be the leaders of Pride.

Only when I took a break to eat did I replay the conversa-tion with Kristin. Why did I keep trying to bridge the chasm that widened every day?

Kristin had told me that only her achievements brought so much as a smile from her parents, and that sarcasm was the family mode of communication. Following a long phone conversation with her mother two months ago, Kristin with-drew into her job and her old East Coast friends. When the crisis passed, she refused to discuss what she called "changes I have to make in my life."

Lately we'd fought nearly every time we'd been together, and even our sex life was combative and tense. Kristin at-tacked what she considered to be my political naiveté, my shoddy business and associates, my lack of ambition and child-ish demand to be "out" to the world. I spent hours analyzing each exchange, convincing myself I was still smart, attractive and funny. Meanwhile Kristin simply assumed that she was right. She would be the reasonable party in the impending split.

Thinking about Kristin and her family made me feel ganged up on by the rich and beautiful. I decided it was time to call in reinforcements and phoned my alter ego Liam. We know the absolute worst things about each other, those irrational fears, those politically incorrect fantasies of bloody revenge on your enemies, those hideously embarrassing events you can't share with just anyone. All of which makes the unabashedly partisan support we give each other the more precious.

We arranged to meet for coffee at our favorite spot in the Castro, which has nothing to recommend it except that it's where we always go, and the counter people know us. Truth to tell, they know Liam.

It's a standing joke between us that waiters take my order while staring at Liam. He's very handsome with a presence that makes strangers stop him on the street to ask if he's a model or a rock star. This makes him acutely uncomfortable, since he longs to have his looks ignored in favor of his beautiful soul. I try to sympathize with this, the way I sympathize with friends whose rich parents torment them by throwing money at them. It's simply outside my experience. Furthermore, it would be easier to swallow Liam's "beautiful soul" protestations if he didn't wear red pants and teal suede jackets with ten-inch fringe.

Liam was waiting for me at a table by the window when I arrived, with the self-satisfied smile of the chronically late person who for once is early.

"All right, get ready to say 'I told you so,'" I sighed, settling into a chair.

"You kicked her out? It's about time!" He watched my face for clues. "Maggie, please tell me you didn't let her kick you out?"

"She's not back yet, but while she's been away, I've had time to realize how bad things have gotten over the last months."

"I could have told you that. As a matter of fact I have told you that, several times. For example, last month, when you went on and on about her bringing her briefcase along whenever she comes over, and what she said about the birthday card your mom sent her, and then there's how she condescends to Jessie . . . ."

"I told you that you could say 'I told you so,' and now you have, okay?"

"At least let me rub it in a little. I always have to listen to you telling me what terrible taste I have in men."

"Only because it's true. Leo, for example. Or the one with crystals, what was his name? Or the amazing disappearing Wayne."

After I told Liam my theory about Kristin discarding me along with all her other objectionable baggage, he made me enumerate the traits that she found "objectionable." As I already knew, these included everything he and I held dear. However, sometimes you need to have these things repeated. And I was finally admitting to myself that the qualities Kristin despised in herself were the very ones that had attracted me to her.

As usual, our conversation soon started veering off on tangents. And as usual, we laughed too loudly and disturbed the more sedate customers. We rehashed the demonstration of the day before: how Geoffrey Lawrence had managed to say absolutely nothing about the series of bashings in his TV interviews, why more straight people hadn't participated, why the TV cameras always found the "Truly Strange People for

Peace" at any event. By the time he left for the AIDS organization where he works, I felt like my old spunky self. It still hurt to remember how things used to be with Kristin and me, but it was no longer overwhelming.

Yes, love is a splendid thing, but if it wasn't for friendship, I think the world just might end.

Chapter Four

I went home to give the Pride materials my full attention, and became so enmeshed in the past that I lost track of time. When Liam arrived, there was no time to change out of my grubby jeans and sweater. He was borrowing my car for a hot date and showed no mercy for my unreadiness. He dropped me off at Metropolitan Community Church and gunned the engine. I sighed for the energy of early passion and watched him take the hill and disappear. It was unusually warm for a June evening, perfect for being outside—if you had someone with you. I sighed again and went into the church.

It's always the same story when I enter this building, even though I've been inside it dozens of times for meetings, a couple of same-sex weddings and too many memorial services. I have to tell myself over and over, "It's all right, it's a queer church." Church was an important part of my life and value system growing up. When the pastor of my hometown church led prayers condemning my "sinful and perverted lifestyle," I put organized religion out of my life, and my spirituality went underground.

Now when I hear the MCC pastors speak of a loving mother/father God, I feel old stirrings. But even in this friendly place I feel like a half-wild dog, abused in its first encounter with humans, watching people at a campfire. I long for the warmth and companionship, but I'm unwilling to be hurt again.

There were still about twenty minutes before the meeting was scheduled to start. I located the room and was surprised that so many others had arrived early. The phrase "operating on gay time" is based on reality, but two dozen people already were in the room, arguing, gossiping and networking like crazy.

As usual in political organizations, most of the members were men, but there was a higher than average percentage of people of color. I recognized Betty Hastings, the president. Smaller up close than she had looked at the demonstration, she maintained the somber, no-time-to-waste-on-frivolities demeanor I had seen the day before and on her TV appearances. At the moment she was huddling with Stephen Leong and Tom Ng, both members of the Executive Committee. I recognized several other club members from the demonstration or the archive materials.

Lynnette, as we had agreed ahead of time, loudly welcomed me as an old friend writing a book on gay and lesbian political movements of the nineties. My line of work demands an elastic attitude toward the truth. Uncovering information that people have taken pains to conceal frequently requires lying. If I told anyone here that I'd been hired to sift through dirty financial dealings, they'd refuse to talk to me, or slant their comments to punish their enemies. Luckily, one of my natural gifts is the telling of plausible lies. For this case, research for a book held the greatest probability of getting me interviews with everyone concerned.

Lynnette introduced me to Betty with a broad wink, to signify that we all knew why I was actually there. I congratulated Betty on her speech at the demonstration, and asked for a time to discuss the club with her. She was polite enough, but her grim countenance left no doubt about how she felt about the investigation and my involvement with the club. I thought about the anonymous note, and fervently hoped Betty wasn't involved in leaving it at my door. Lynnette asked her about an agenda item, and I left them.

There was a modest spread of coffee and sweets across the room, and I headed toward it. My immersion in the club archives had meant missing dinner. I was shamelessly stacking more than my share of cookies on a napkin when a massive woman swooped down on me, hand extended.

"You must be Maggie! Mavis Baker, of Baker Realty. Lynnette told me about your book. Glad you could come." Mavis was taller than me and twice as broad, with a "Been there, done that" quirk to her mouth. I briefly imagined how fine she'd look in jeans and a flannel shirt or a uniform—she was wearing a badly made doubleknit suit like the farm women of my childhood wore to church. After thoroughly checking me out, she took my elbow in a firm grip. "Let me introduce you to some people you'll want to interview."

"I've already talked to them—you're the one I've been hoping to meet." I gave her my best big-green-eyes-through-lowered-lashes glance. "I've heard so much about you. Do you have a few minutes now?" She gave me a second appraisal, making no secret of weighing whether my charms merited sticking around instead of working the room. I lost out to politicking.

"Sorry, I've got to talk to some other folks before the meeting. I just came back from a Professional Women's Club meeting, and I need to get some time on the agenda tonight. We're going to do a joint candidates' forum in the fall. Let's see, I have plans for after this is all over, but I could get together sometime this week." We pulled out appointment books and negotiated an interview for Wednesday. Then Mavis spotted Betty, and was gone without a good-bye.

I made my way back to the refreshment table. All the good cookies were gone. I was snagging a couple of Oreos when Lynnette loomed on my right, another woman in tow. I ignored her until my styrofoam cup was full of weak coffee. By that time Lynnette was tearing up the carpet with the toe of her Birkenstocks.

"Maggie, this is Miranda Post, our treasurer." She lowered her voice slightly and spoke out of the side of her mouth: "She knows why you're here."

Miranda radiated the peppy energy of a high school cheerleader. A short, compact woman with frizzy blond hair, she looked about fourteen, although I knew she was only a couple of years younger than me. She had a luminous smile that lit up her face. When she let down her guard, though, her wattage was rather uneven. There was a dark smudge on her cheek and a long scrape on her hand and wrist. A large, bulky bandage covered much of her arm.

"Was it an accident or a fight?" I asked.

"Two nuts in a car nearly hit me on 18th Street. They must have been going at least sixty, and they ran right through the stop sign! I landed on my elbows and got this to show for it."

"Did you see a doctor?"

"I didn't need to, it's all superficial. One of the club members is an R.N., and he took a look at it. Besides, I don't have any insurance, and the Emergency Room at San Francisco General is not my idea of health care."

"Did you get their license number?"

"No, their license plate had even more dirt on it than their car did. Just another day in the big city." She smiled and dismissed the topic. "I was hoping I'd get a chance to talk to you. For the past week I've been wondering what to do with something I found in Joe Leslie's treasurer stuff."

"What is it?"

"Well, it's some kind of list. Part of it's like a code. But there are dates, initials and what look like amounts of money on it."

"That could have a simple explanation. It doesn't sound especially strange."

"That's what I thought at first. Then Joe started leaving messages on my machine that he had to talk to me. One night he showed up at my apartment with this lame story about how he was worried that some important personal paper of his might've gotten mixed up with his treasurer stuff."

"What did you do?"

"Joe's no friend of mine. I've heard what he thinks about women, especially Betty and me as leadership. He made it impossible to piece together the club's finances after he left. I figured that, whatever it was, it must be really important for him to try to buddy me out of it. That's why I told him I hadn't seen it. He seemed to believe me."

"Have you told anyone else on the Executive Committee?"

Miranda glanced nervously around the room before speaking. "I didn't think that was a good idea until I had more to go on." She smiled at me and her shoulders fell as she relaxed. "That's why I'm so glad to have somebody from outside the club working on this. I can trust you to—"

Betty's voice interrupted, announcing that the meeting was starting "now." We hurriedly arranged for Miranda to come to my office on Tuesday.

Meanwhile, Betty made two more announcements about starting the meeting, each at increasing volume. Finally the networking frenzy subsided and the membership sat down. As I took a seat near the refreshments table, I caught former Pride President Geoffrey Lawrence staring at me from across the room. He flashed me a resplendent smile. Someone must have told him I had media connections.

Again I thought of the anonymous note at my door. Geoffrey came from a wealthy background, and now moved with big-time Democratic Party contributors. He might assume that throwing hundred-dollar bills around got the quickest results. Besides, if money was missing from the club, the automatic suspects were the officers serving when the money disappeared. Treasurers came and went, but Geoffrey had been the club president for the entire two years before the upset election in March.

The chief agenda items were committee reports and plans for a fundraiser. When Betty asked if there were any additions to the agenda, a woman stood and asked for discussion of the rumors about mismanagement of club funds. Murmurs and head nods from several in the room showed that she wasn't alone in her concern. However, Betty was ready for this. She announced that while the Executive Committee members believed there was nothing to the rumors, they were doing a thorough investigation, and would give a full report at the next club meeting. The woman who raised the issue sat down, grumbling to her companions. Betty shot me a look that told me I'd better produce something useful out of all this, and the meeting proceeded.

Another of the Executive Committee members, Warren Coleman, reported that club membership had increased by twenty-five percent since the last election. Warren came across as a slightly lower-budget version of Geoffrey: not quite as handsome or polished, and the clothes might not come from designers, but the assurance in his smile was the same. Maybe they shared other things, like a history of stealing the Club's money?

Miranda, as treasurer, reported that dues from the new members had stabilized the club's finances, and even dues payments from long-time members had picked up. It reminded me of Lynnette's comment about the community's regained faith in Pride.

Miguel Alvarez, one of the Executive Committee members who had been swept into office on the Diversity Slate, reported on a City Task Force on AIDS in Communities of Color. I assessed him as bright, competent and humorless. I wondered if research had been conducted on the inverse proportion of political activism and humor. Of course, it had been suggested to me that I was humorless about some topics, and I knew better....

Ten minutes into the meeting and already my attention was drifting. You're on a case, Garrett, surrounded by potential perpetrators. Wake up!

I tried Miguel on for size as the sender of my get-lost bribe. If he thought a project that he considered important was put in jeopardy by my investigation, I bet he'd favor the end over the means of stopping the investigation. He was a definite maybe.

Mavis reported on plans for the congressional candidates' forum. All the candidates had agreed to come, another promising sign for the prestige and credibility of the organization.

The fundraiser, a community service awards ceremony with entertainment, turned out to be the controversy of the evening. David Lindley, another Executive Committee member and chair of the fundraiser, outlined the plans so far. Immediately he was accused of renting a hall so expensive that its cost would absorb all the proceeds—this much I'm sure of. Most of what was really going on in the ensuing debate escaped me.

A man with creatively buzzed blond hair asserted that the owner of the hall should have been pressured to donate it, the way he had for ACT-UP! A Latina in business dress claimed that the hall-hiring had been motivated by personal ambitions (but didn't say whose). Miguel Alvarez retorted that, because of her ties to a Marxist party, the Latina had her own axe to grind about fundraising. I watched Mavis approach the Latina and the woman next to her. Then they all laughed and cast derisive looks at Miguel, who flushed and gave Mavis a poisonous glare.

Miranda was passing notes to Betty, probably ideas for getting the meeting back on track from the way the two exchanged glances. I found myself thinking about Miranda's close call earlier that evening. Had it been an accident, as she thought? Before I received the anonymous note, I would have thought that, too.

Mavis moved on to stand behind the chairs of two preppy-style men. She bent and whispered what must have been a funny if inappropriate remark. The men laughed loudly, then glanced around guiltily, like little boys sharing a "dirty" joke. After that, I kept an eye on Mavis. She took no part in the debate, but she was all over the place, influencing the discussion by whispering innuendos and goading long-time enemies to go at each other. Mavis rose several places on my list of those who deserved special attention. She'd been treasurer in Geoffrey Lawrence's day, she was savvy, and judging from her behavior this evening, she didn't appear to be bothered by principles.

Betty was trying valiantly to chair the discussion, but each new speaker responded to the attacking remarks of the previous one. Warren Coleman made a well-phrased if self-contradictory comment about internalized homophobia that was met by equal proportions of vehement agreement and disagreement amongst the participants. The corner of the room where Mavis had been standing erupted in catcalls. Warren ignored Mavis' antics.

One more trip to the refreshments table. I picked up some more coffee and cookies to clear my head. This discussion reminded me of spending time with the family of Ricardo, my sole employee. The Galvéz family members speak English with varying proficiency and I do my best with Spanish. But when a difference of opinion arises, it is argued in rapid Spanish, and events from generations back get mixed in. This meeting reminded me of those disputes: I understood on a literal level, but without years of context it made no sense.

Now a self-important man who had to be an attorney was sharing his concern, in extensive detail, that the location of the event might be a problem because of the wave of gay bashings—it was not near public transit. He was right, of course. I hate it when I find myself supporting the views of obnoxious people.

David Lindley responded that club members could pick up people at the Muni station seven blocks away and drive them to the event. Lynnette hopped on this, accusing him of causing extra work and risking women's lives.

Ten o'clock and they hadn't discussed who would recruit the entertainers, plan and cater the food, determine the honorees. I convinced myself that I wouldn't learn anything more about old dirty business tonight and quietly made my exit.

Chapter Five

I stood in front of the church for a full minute trying to remember where I'd parked before I realized that Liam had the car. So much for a quick getaway. As I poked through my bag for my elusive transit pass, I became aware of the woman lounging on the steps to the building. Her long legs were extended in close-fitting jeans and she wore a sleek leather biker's jacket over a t-shirt. She bent over her cupped hands lighting a cigarette, and I didn't think she was aware of me until she spoke.

"Had enough P.C. politicking for one night?"

"It was my first meeting and I didn't understand half of it. I don't remember seeing you inside." She smiled. I cringed at my own words. How obvious. Well, I definitely would have remembered this woman. She'd stick out anywhere because of her height and model's carriage. Her features were sharply defined, all a little exaggerated: strong nose, heavy brows, thick lashes, full lips. I found myself staring at her lips.

"I wasn't at the meeting. I've got a coffee date with someone who's in the meeting, Mavis Baker. She promised she'd leave at 9:30 whether it was over or not." She checked her watch and rolled her eyes. "Guess she hasn't changed."

"It's pretty hot and heavy in there, and she's in the middle of it. She might be a little while longer."

"It's not one of *those* dates. She'll say the hell with me and stay to the end. Mavis would never miss the chance to get in the last word. My name is Jolie. You look familiar. Who are you?"

"Maggie Garrett. Hi, like I said, this was my first meeting. It's hard to tell what it's like on one visit. Are you a member?" That's right, act like a P.I. Remember you're working tonight, not cruising.

"Oh, for a couple of years I was very involved, with Pride and with Mavis. But when Mavis and I broke up, she got to keep Pride and I got to keep the VCR." It had the brittle ring of a frequently told joke. Keep it light, it's no big deal.

I couldn't think of anything to say—me, Ms. Silver Tongue herself. I asked her for a cigarette. She produced one and lit a match, and I leaned down to get the light. She smelled like leather, an expensive perfume and her own body scent.

"What did you expect it would be like?" she asked, while our faces were still close. I was momentarily flustered, then realized she was talking about the meeting.

"I guess . . . more politics and less politicking. Betty and some of the members want to make Pride an independent political force. But other people just seemed to be there to attack the club leadership, or to promote themselves or their own agendas." Thinking out loud is one of my worst habits, and I was digging myself in deeper and deeper. This was the ex of Mavis, whom that very evening I had named as a back-up suspect for looting the Pride Club.

"Maggie, you're an idealist! You must be disappointed a lot of the time." She accompanied this with a look that turned it into a high compliment. "You should have been around in the bad old days of Geoffrey and his clique."

"Well, tonight it was almost as if there were two clubs— one that wants to stir things up and get in the face of City Hall, and another club that wants to be curled up in City Hall's lap." Hmm, speaking of curling up in laps . . . Stop it! I was probably blushing again. My former boss Jack Windsor had deep contempt for male P.I.s who "lead with their dicks." What would the female equivalent be?

"You might be right about two clubs. For club members from the Geoffrey days, the priority is getting on the right side of the right people, and staying there. Some of them are trying to get into office themselves someday, or at least get to work for someone who does, like Geoffrey."

"But do they manage to get elected, or appointed?"

"Yeah, a few of them do. Especially when Geoffrey was in charge, being from the Pride Club gave you an inside track— if you were a white man and a friend of Geoff's. The problem is, they end up with those nasty politician qualities we all know and love." She blew out a stream of smoke with disgust. "It affects how they see everything. Look at Mavis."

"Only Mavis isn't a man."

"She's not in office, either, is she?" Jolie gave me a long, assessing look. "I'm gonna stand up Mavis and the horse she rode in on. Why don't you come with me? I'll tell you all the dirt about Pride. . . ."

"Only if you let me bribe you with a beer, or a cup of coffee."

"Come on." She motioned her head toward the motorcycles arrayed in front of the church. "You can be the first passenger on my new bike."

Jolie pulled a pen and a scrap of paper from her jacket pocket, wrote a few words, then folded it and scrawled Mavis' name on it. Using one of the many tacks on the scarred surface, she stuck the message at eye level on the front door of the church.

We walked to her huge Harley, which didn't have a scratch or nick on its gleaming surface. She maneuvered the bike faster and more recklessly than her skill warranted. At least she'd given me the helmet to wear. I noticed that I'd been holding my breath for the last couple of turns when we got to The Raven, a mostly women's, mostly dykes' coffee house in lesbian land on Valencia Street, a strip between the gay male Castro and the multinational, mostly Central American, Mission District.

We settled in with decafs and pastries at a table next to a couple of off-duty women cab drivers who were entertaining each other with scathing impressions of their customers. Jolie told me she was an artist and sometime model. I added the writer-of-lesbian/gay-history-books story to my standard half-truth about being a free lance legal assistant and playing guitar in local bands.

"Of course, that's where I've seen you," she said, laughing. "At Grigo's with that thrash band. They stank, but you were hot. I won a bet with a guy who swore you had to be a man. The schmuck didn't think a woman could play that well!"

We talked about music for awhile, discovered that we liked many of the same groups, and compared notes on the local scene. No matter what we talked about, there was a delicious layer of sexual innuendo, and when our eyes met we caused electrical power surges as far away as La Jolla.

I told her about Kristin. It's always interesting to hear what comes out of your mouth when you tell a stranger about your lover—trying to be objective in the telling, you end up revealing more than you would to your closest friend.

"I still love her, but I've been realizing lately that the things that I value in Kristin are the ones she wants to ditch. She sees them as weaknesses. She brings out all my insecurities about not graduating college or worrying about my 'career path,' and she hates my involvement in politics. I'm pretty sure she's planning to dump me when she gets back, and that's probably for the best. But I'm not used to being passive, and I'm tired of waiting for it to end." It had taken me weeks to reveal this much to Jessie and Liam, and I was pouring it all out to someone I'd known for an hour. Time to get back to work.

"When you and Mavis split, why were you the one who left the Pride Club—aside from custody of the VCR?"

"I was just a member. Mavis was one of the boys. She was the only woman on Geoffrey's slate when they got elected to be the Executive Committee two years ago. So naturally Mavis was the one they wanted to stick around when we broke up. I was only the slutty girlfriend."

"After you left Pride, did you join one of the other clubs?"

"No, the stuff that went down at Pride was enough for me. I hit every dyke club scene around, and every dyke's bed, too. Wonder how I missed you? I stayed drunk and sorry for myself for about six months. Then I bottomed out and started going to dyke AA and NA meetings." Was I going to get the full 'drunkalogue?' We might as well convene a 12-step meeting right here. Jolie could be the guest speaker.

"I'm weaning myself off the meetings now," she continued. "I've been seeing some of my old friends again, not just people from my groups."

"Old friends like Mavis?" I had to know if Jolie and the Amazon in doubleknits were still an item.

"No, Mavis was never a friend. We lived together, but it wasn't a relationship—it was more like a war, and every time we were together it was another battle." She smiled at me.

42

"That's taken six months of therapy for me to be able to say. When Mavis and I stopped being lovers there was nothing left. We hurt each other too much, and I couldn't be around her without using." She took a long drag on her cigarette and ground it out forcefully. "I have to make amends to her, and let go of what she did to me. That's what I was hoping to-night would be."

"That's a gutsy thing to do." I said, enjoying the possibilities that were rising around us. The weight that had been pressing on my diaphragm lifted. "You must be feeling pretty strong to do that, and to meet her at a place where you'd see people that you used to know from the club."

"I've always jumped into everything with both feet. I think you have to take what you want—don't you?" She drew another cigarette out of the pack and tongued the tip before lighting it. The burlesque sexuality was funny, but it was also highly erotic. "I decided when I saw you that I would pick you up. And I did."

"Is that what this is, a pickup?"

"Well, Maggie, what do you want it to be?" Our eyes locked, and a few seconds or ten minutes went by. Jolie reached under the table and ran her long fingers slowly, deliberately, over my thigh. I felt the course of each fingertip. Jolie smiled in triumph at my reaction.

An ash dropped from her cigarette. I gently took it from her fingers and put it out. "Later we can work out who got picked up," I said. "But let's get out of here. Now."

Chapter Six

A waitron who had been leaning on the espresso counter came over to take our money, and wished us a nice evening with a leer. As Jolie and I walked to the door, my arm in hers, I felt as exposed in my lust as if we'd been rolling around on the floor. Surely everyone in the room must be able to feel the heat we were generating.

Her bike was parked in a darkened area between streetlights, and there was no traffic on the street. For a few seconds in the silence, we could have been anywhere. She turned to me and cupped my face in her hands. The first kiss was tentative, almost shy.

"Take me home with you?" she asked, between kisses growing in heat and intensity. I slid my hands under her jacket, under her t-shirt, and found her small, hard nipples. She moaned softly and ground her hips into mine.

"Come home with me, Jolie," I answered. Ceremoniously she placed the helmet on my head. I climbed behind her on the bike and wrapped my arms around her waist.

When we got to my house, with a door between us and curious animals, it was as if we had both lost the ability to speak, and didn't care. No words were needed as we tore off each other's clothes.

Jolie nuzzled my breasts, using her teeth and lips on my nipples, bringing me to the threshold of pain. Her long fingers worked their way impatiently through my pubic hair and laid siege. I heard a sobbing kind of sigh come out of my chest.

"Do that again," Jolie commanded, and brought her lips down on mine. We moaned into each other's mouths until I started laughing too hard to breathe and moan at the same time.

I hadn't felt this kind of passion, this freedom with Kristin for months. When Kristin kissed my breasts I couldn't surrender to the moment, never knowing if she'd think of a criticism she'd been meaning to make, or simply turn away to read a few more cases to prop up a court memorandum. What was happening tonight wasn't love, but it might be a beginning.

I tried to maneuver so that I could pleasure Jolie, but she pushed me back firmly.

"I want to make you happy tonight," she said. "Tomorrow I'll tell you exactly what I want you to do to me." Jolie watched my reactions for a few seconds, with no expression on her own face, before lowering her mouth to burn a path down my chest, over my stomach, lingering in my navel.

The Difficult Moment had arrived. Thirty seconds of internal debate, stories of lesbian-transmitted HIV, Jolie's claim to have bedded half the lesbians in San Francisco while on drugs. Conclusion: Safer sex. I reached into the bedside table drawer and pulled out the roll of plastic wrap and a pair of lavender latex gloves. "These will make me happy," I said, smiling.

"You're not serious?" She was staring at me in amazement.

"Never done it with Saran Wrap? It's pretty kinky, I think you'll like it."

Afterward I lay cradled in her arms, sweating and relaxed. She insisted that my coming was enough for her, that what she wanted was to make love to me. I tried to find out more about her. I was definitely off-duty now, but work and personal interest were parking in the same spot. It fascinated me that this woman and Mavis Baker had been lovers. She didn't want to talk and responded to my questions by covering my mouth with hers. Since I wasn't feeling argumentative about anything, I kissed her back—and lost consciousness.

I woke during the night, thinking I had heard a sob, but when I spoke her name softly, there was no answer. I decided I must have been dreaming and went back to sleep.

Chapter Seven

The phone woke me in what felt like the middle of the night. The caller wasn't using the answering machine, just dialing again when the machine clicked on. My dad's heart condition? Liam in an accident? I staggered into the kitchen to answer.

Ricardo had been talking for nearly a minute before what he was saying sank in. In brief, we were well into Monday morning, over an hour past the time when I'd usually be at work, and a man with lots of money to spend had called about hiring me to investigate his employees.

"He's a major loser, but he runs Neige Verte."

"He runs what?"

"It's where big-time executives and musicians and coke dealers get their clothes. So he must have plenty of money to pay you and your assistant—that's me—to snoop around. He wants you to call him back 'at once.' I said you were at a breakfast meeting. Pretty slick, huh?"

"That was fast thinking, I owe you. I'll get there by 9:30, and call him first thing when I get in, I promise." According to the kitchen clock, it was 8:45. A perfect way to start to the week.

"But wait, there's more!" Ricardo said. He watches too

much TV. "Somebody put this weird envelope on the floor, after I got here. It's got your name on it. What should I do with it?"

"Don't touch it until I get there. Is there coffee?"

"You always ask me that, and don't I always make coffee first thing? I got my priorities down, boss!" He rang off indignantly. Had Jolie heard me, and if so, did anything on my end of the conversation sound odd coming from a clerk/guitarist? I hoped she was a heavy sleeper.

However much of my conversation Jolie heard, she was definitely awake. As soon as I perched on the edge of the bed, she threw back the covers and brought me back down with her into the pillows.

"Call in sick. I'll make us breakfast, and we can eat in bed," she whispered, her breath hot on my throat. Her deft fingers found my nipples and brought them to attention. My pulse jumped and my brain disengaged.

For a few delicious minutes I considered giving in, but reality intruded, as it often does in the light of day. My business is too close to the brink of disaster to play at it. There was also the matter of that envelope Ricardo had found on the floor. And finally there was the fact that I'd blown it again. A night of dynamite sex with Kristin had turned into months of dreary incompatibility. Now Jolie and I would need to discover whether we had more in common than sexual chemistry. Dinner together would be more likely to advance this goal than breakfast in bed.

I resigned myself and came up for air with a groan. "I'm sorry, Jolie, but I've got to go to work and I'm an hour late. My co-worker saved my butt by calling. There's not even time to make coffee."

"Yes there is. You go get in the shower and I'll put on the

coffee." She was being suspiciously agreeable.

I was just rinsing shampoo out of my hair, eyes closed, when I felt her presence behind me, her soapy hands circling my breasts and stomach, sliding downward. We stood for a minute under the streaming water, Jolie nuzzling the nape of my neck and murmuring details of what she would do to me if I would only come back to bed. I turned and kissed her deeply, taking her hands in mine. I knew if I didn't keep her hands still, we'd end up back in bed for the rest of the morning. It was time to leave.

"You're even better than caffeine, and I don't say that to just anyone. I've got to get out of here, but you can stay and sleep in if you want." I certainly don't say *that* to just anyone. Not to anybody, as a matter of fact. Jolie pouted in response.

Ready to head out the door with Loba, I gasped when I saw an envelope stuck under the door, then recognized Liam's scrawl on the outside. The envelope contained my car keys. He'd noted where it was parked on the outside of the envelope. Not a word about how his date had gone—a bad sign.

Loba showed her deep disappointment when I turned us around after two blocks. "I know, I'll make it up to you later, I promise," I said. She gave a mournful whine in response, and insisted on sniffing every tree on the way back. I have surrounded myself with highly manipulative animals.

Two doors down from my house I nodded to a man in a painters' coverall, lounging on the hood of a car and smoking. He gave Loba a nervous glance as we passed. I wondered which of my neighbors was hiring him, and whether they'd spring for one of the fancy jobs with each strip of molding painted a different, complementary color. The state of the painter's car, only a few years old but filthy, made me doubt the quality of the work my neighbor would get.

During our walk I had hung my emergency clothes in the bathroom to steam out the wrinkles. It seemed safer to put them on in there. The outfit had been expensive but it paid for itself in peace of mind: a well-cut black knit dress that's as comfortable as a sweatshirt and stays fresh-looking even when I've sat in the surveillance van all night, and a short, business-like jacket that helps me gain entry to offices. I found a clean, un-run pair of sheer black pantyhose, threw earrings and makeup into my bag to put on later, and I was ready.

I went back into the bedroom to say good-bye. Jolie sat cross-legged on the bed toweling her hair. Her still-naked body was magnificent in the streaming sunlight. She tossed the towel to the floor and threw her arms back in a catlike stretch, displaying her breasts to their best advantage. The woman did have a highly developed instinct for a seductive pose.

"It's not too late to change your mind," she said. One eye was obscured by her glistening damp curls.

"Later. Leave me your phone number, and then write down every idea you had for today, and we'll do them, in any order you choose." I bent to kiss the tip of her nose and quickly backed away to evade her reach. "Call me if I haven't called you."

On the drive to my office, Jolie crowded out all the other things I had to think about. I'd never been involved with a woman like her. To say she wasn't my type was meaningless, since experience showed that I didn't have a "type." That was one of the reasons why Jessie came up with such an assort-ment in her matchmaking. But always before, I had at least deluded myself that I shared common interests with my sex partners, known them somewhat better, if not for much longer. I didn't even know Jolie's last name! Had going to bed with her been only a way to spite Kristin? I hoped not. We'd sort it out tonight, I promised myself, and put Jolie firmly from my mind.

One advantage to arriving late was that the homeless people who sleep in the outside lobby area of the building would be awake. Frequently I step over rows of still-sleeping bodies, and I'm always afraid of treading on somebody's arm or leg. I spoke to a couple of the regulars and went inside.

Ricardo was out on an errand, but he'd made a fresh pot of coffee. After the first life-giving cup I felt prepared to call my prospective client, T.M. Neighbors. He was in a meeting, his secretary told me. I left my name and said I'd call again.

Trying not to think about what I'd be doing if I'd stayed home with Jolie, I opened the morning's mail and hit the jackpot: a couple of checks that would probably cover the insurance on my car, the garage fee for the surveillance van, and the other outstanding bills. Frequently I feel like a brief way station for money. It comes in, I deposit it, the bills come in, I pay them. I think profit is supposed to play a role here somehow, but I don't have the hang of that part yet.

I'd forgotten about the "weird envelope," so when I came upon it on the bottom of the stack Ricardo had left for me, I was unprepared. My hands shook as I pulled on a pair of latex gloves. At least I wouldn't get my own prints all over it this time. The envelope was of the same plain stock as the previous one, only this time my name was on it, in the same word-processed type as the note.

The writer came right to the point. "GET OUT BEFORE IT'S TOO LATE."

No hundred-dollar bills this time. We were at a different level of communication.

Now what? A law-abiding citizen goes to her local police

station and turns a poison-pen letter over to the proper authorities. I wasn't in any position to do that, and anyway I had no illusions about how seriously a note like this would be taken by overburdened station cops. The question was, what if anything should I do about it? For the time being, I put the note in a plastic bag for safekeeping until I could get it to Marcia.

Chapter Eight

Ricardo's music arrived before him, the bass setting of his Walkman audible from the hallway. On vacation from high school, he would be here almost every day for the next two months. Working for me keeps him out of trouble (literally— the Mission District can be a dangerous place for a seventeen-year-old Chicano), and I pay him a little. I could probably demand money from him. He comes for access to the computer, his true love.

Ricardo is the son of my old friend Alicia. As a favor to her I hired Ricardo to install the software on my computer and set up my printer when I opened my office a year ago. He never left. Although he is perfectly willing to impersonate a receptionist, run a data analysis, or print a mailing list, he lives for hacking. Never think that any aspect of your life kept in any computer system is confidential. Adolescent hackers take such data protection barriers as a personal challenge. When I can't get information through proper channels, Ricardo and his clandestine network haven't failed me yet.

He's a great-looking kid, with Alicia's glossy black hair, dark eyes, long lashes. He also has her sunny disposition. Some of my male clients have ogled him in my presence, and my guess is that they've gone further than that to make their interest known. He is unfazed by it—or the worshiping glances he gets from straight girls and women, for that matter. To my continuing amazement and delight, he seems to be without homophobia. Any allusions to my sexuality bring the same pained expression he turns on his mother when she talks about the men in her life. Since we're so old (I'm twenty-eight, she's thirty-four), it's unthinkable that we would do anything wilder than holding hands with the objects of our affection. He is also as protective of me as he is of his mother, and I feel alternately touched and irritated by this.

"Yo, boss. Big date last night?"

"None of your business, child. Come sit down and tell me about this weird envelope."

"It was on the floor in the doorway there," he said, pointing at the connecting door between his outer cubicle and my office. "Somebody put it there after I opened up. So what's in it?"

"We'll get to that, but I need you to try to remember any details you can about how the letter got here. Think about everything you did when you got in today. It's important."

"Right." He shut his eyes, "I came in, turned on the computer, opened the window in your office. Then I took the coffee-maker thing down the hall to the john to get water." He opened his eyes. "That's when I saw the envelope, when I got back!"

"Did you see anybody in the hall then?"

"Just one of the dental assistants from Dr. Ki's office—the old one, not that hot blonde—and that tax guy from down the hall—you know, Maggie, I think he sleeps here. . . ."

I gave him a rundown of the case so far, including both of the notes. He was particularly interested in the hundred-dollar bills. He was less than thrilled at the prospect of starting a data base from the few pieces of financial data that Lynnette could provide. I mollified him with the promise that as soon as I identified the villain of the piece, Ricardo could start invading his or her privacy with abandon.

He got to work, and soon the walls were vibrating from his musical choice of the day, Snoop Doggy Dogg. Our major source of friction is what to play on the office boombox. Initially I tried to pull rank as boss, but neither of us took me seriously. Now we take turns picking the radio station or tape selection. It was Ricardo's day, and rap songs echoed into the hall outside. Luckily I don't get much walk-in business.

I made a set of files for the Pride Club investigation. If I do this at the very beginning of a case, I can be highly methodical, keep everything in order and instantly retrievable. The alternative is chaos and operating from memory. For my late boss and mentor Jack Windsor, flexibility had been his watchword—except about the recordkeeping aspect of investigations. In his case the methodical procedures and accessible files were made necessary by the blackouts that came with his alcoholism. He died two years ago from liver failure at the age of fifty.

Jack left me the business and some very useful connections I could never have made on my own. Besides making me known as his "junior associate" to people in high and low places during the years I worked for him, I suspect that Jack called in some favors before he died. People not known for graciousness have helped me out unexpectedly several times.

Jack also provided the unwelcome legacy of two handguns, an official, registered .38 Smith and Wesson in his will and a nonregistered .357 Magnum, left where I'd find it. My refusal to carry a gun had been a major source of contention between us. He managed to get in the last word. I still have both guns, unable to bring myself to refuse his bequest. Although I have a permit for the .38 now and I've become a half-way decent shot, carrying it is another issue. I keep it in the office, in a hiding space under the desk where Jack used to keep a spare bottle. Every time I go into a somewhat risky situation I carry on a heated imaginary debate with Jack about taking the damn .38. I almost always win.

My other inheritance from Jack was his surveillance vehicle, a nondescript Dodge commercial van. Perfecting its interior with ergonomic seats, coffee setup and chemical toilet was the triumph of Jack's career. He took such pride in passing it on to me that even insurance and garage fees haven't persuaded me to ditch it.

After I worked for him for two years, Jack changed the name of the business to "Windsor & Garrett," and I kept it after his death, partly out of sentiment, partly because it sounded like a large, rather stuffy outfit, unless you knew either of the principals. I figured a bit of spurious respectability couldn't hurt.

When the files were completed, I poured some more coffee and drew a chronology of the Pride Club's treasurer turnover:

> Miranda Post, Elected March 7, serving for three months now
> Joe Leslie, Appointed, served twelve months, lost election
> Marc Romano, Appointed, served seven months, quit
> Mavis Baker, Elected, served four months, quit
> Larry Gross, Elected, served two years, lost election

I was already scheduled to see the current treasurer, Miranda, on Tuesday. Even though she had held office for only a short time, Miranda would likely have most of the answers Lynnette and the Executive Committee wanted. The other Committee members were, officially at least, unaware that she held the cryptic list that Joe Leslie had lost, because Miranda mistrusted at least one of them. Based on the actions of my anonymous penpal, I was inclined to agree with her.

But without knowledge of the list, the rest of the Executive Committee would see the investigation as simply a damage-control operation to quash rumors. It was no surprise that the club president, Betty Hastings, thought the investigation was a waste of time—assuming, of course, that she was telling the truth. The Executive Committee members were going to get quite a bit more than they had expected for their money, and they weren't going to like it.

"Just shut up and take the damned money! You need it, and if they don't give it to you, they'll give it to some slimeball P.I. who'll have no qualms about taking them for everything they've got." Great, now Jack Windsor's voice was coming from my checkbook. But it was true—I needed the money, and I'd be more responsible than some of the P.I. agencies the Pride Club might hire.

I started dialing my way down the list of Pride officers.

Joe Leslie, the treasurer for the last three months before the upset election, was first. His answering machine came on. I hung up. Experience had shown that dropping in was more efficient than leaving messages. I'd try him that day and take my chances.

Marc Romano proved to be reticent about discussing himself, but enthusiastic about the AIDS organization where he worked. When I told him about my particular interest in the Pride Club, he became nervous and evasive. He insisted that he had no evenings available for weeks, but conceded that yes, he did eat sometimes. We made a lunch appointment for Tuesday.

Mavis Baker and I were set for Wednesday. She had been treasurer under Geoffrey and was still a power in the club under the new regime. She had shown no reluctance to talk to me when I met her Sunday, though she also might put heavy moves on me. I hoped her initial friendliness held, regardless of its source. Would my night with Jolie change that? If Mavis didn't have anything to lose, she could make this case considerably easier. Unfortunately, everything I'd heard about her associations with Geoffrey made me suspect that she would be connected to any shady financial transactions that could be traced to him.

Larry Gross, who held the position for almost two years before a change in club leadership, had been my pick for most reliable source of background information. But when I called his home number, I learned that he had been hospitalized two days earlier with pneumocystis pneumonia. His housemate took my message, but I knew the likelihood of talking with him was slim. Answering a stranger's questions about old misdeeds would be the least of Larry's priorities.

Last on my list were the former club president, Geoffrey Lawrence, and the current one, Betty Hastings. A phone call to Geoffrey's office got me a fifteen-minute audience that day. I reminded myself of Jessie's warning. I wanted Geoffrey to be behind all the problems at Pride, plus the recurring drought the Bay Area had endured and maybe an earthquake or two. But I'd keep an open mind. Yes I would.

Betty Hastings, on the other hand, had been one of my heroines for years because of her long record of building connections between African-American organizations and feminist groups. Now she was trying to get Black churches involved in AIDS prevention efforts. It was too bad that she was against this investigation, but I still looked forward to meeting her on Tuesday.

After one last attempt to reach T.M. Neighbors, I left him another message to show my good intentions, and set out to meet the Pride leadership, past and present.

Chapter 9

My first stop was Joe Leslie, the treasurer who'd been dethroned with the rest of Geoffrey Lawrence's slate in the March election. He was self-employed as a picture framer and window installer with a workshop on Sanchez Street. I parked in an illegal spot a block away and hoped that my lucky streak would hold: no parking tickets for three weeks, a lifetime best since I'd left Iowa.

It was a mixed residential and commercial neighborhood, run down and not yet gentrified, although there was a heavy presence of coffee houses. Every flat surface was covered with the photocopy-art flyers of the afternoon, posted over the flyers of the morning by rock groups promoting their gigs at hole-in-the-wall clubs. Probably I should be collecting them. They'll be worth fortunes some day, like those psychedelic posters from the 1960s.

I crunched down on a big shard of glass, and thereafter picked my way over broken bottles on the sidewalk, cursing last year's cuts in the street maintenance budget, crackheads who throw their trash out of windows, and my forgetfulness about getting my shoes re-soled.

Joe Leslie's storefront, Great Glass, was the ground floor of an apartment building that had partially burned a few months earlier. I remembered the fire because for a few days afterward there were news headlines about evidence of arson. Joe lived in an apartment over the shop, and according to Pride Club meeting minutes, nearly all of his treasurer records were destroyed in the fire. His business downstairs didn't show much damage.

Joe was alone in his shop. He was about my height, but had the body mass of a man who devotes his life to weightlifting. His size and the semi-hostile squint of his small gray eyes gave him a sinister image. Joe was probably in his late twenties, but it was hard to tell. When he shifted his leather cap I caught a glimpse of bald scalp.

I introduced myself with the gay historian story, and he grudgingly agreed to talk to me. He didn't offer me a seat, in fact there weren't any chairs, so I leaned on the work counter and pulled out my note pad. As we talked, he cut mats for a trio of floral prints.

He seemed like the type to require flagrant flattery, so I poured it on. As an officer of a major organization in the gay capital of the country, how had he seen the democratic process reflected in Pride?

"We got Thornton Gray elected to the state legislature and we got Carson Lutz on the City Board of Supervisors. It was Pride that did that, no matter what anyone says." He looked around, as if someone might materialize to contradict him. "Those screaming radical dykes that took over the club will never be able to make things happen the way Geoffrey could. They don't know how to play the game."

He wouldn't meet my eyes for more than a millisecond even when he was speaking to me, focusing on every other point in the room. Probably not a wealth of women friends, I concluded.

"Can you tell me about the last Pride Club election?"

"What do you want me to say?" He jabbed his hooked knife into the counter, and spat out the words. "The Diversity Slate recruited a whole bunch of new members a few months before the election, and then they railroaded us out with a pack of lies about how we were racist and sexist and some other -ists I can't even remember." At this last, he did look at me, accusingly.

"Wow," I gushed. "It sounds like the club was stolen from the people who'd been making it work for years!" I'm counting on God to be very understanding about things like this when my time comes.

"You got that right. The Mayor picked Geoff to be his special assistant because Geoff knows how to get things done in the real world. These new people live in some kind of a dream world."

"How about you? How long have you been in the club?"

"Was. I *was* in the club. Not anymore. I can't take that process stuff they do now. Besides, my business takes all my time. But before I quit, I'd been in for about a year."

"So if you'd only been around for—what, eight or nine months?—the leadership must have been pretty impressed with you to name you treasurer."

"Yeah, Geoff put me in the job 'cause he knew I'd have to be good with accounts to make it in my own business. I keep all my own books, billing, collections. You've got to do it all yourself to make a dime these days."

"One of the things we're especially interested in for the book is the lack of continuity in the democratic process." He gave me a blank stare. "For example, when you took over as treasurer, did the old treasurer cooperate?"

"No. Marc Romano, the guy who used to be the treasurer, he got a fundraising job with an AIDS group. Geoff told him he should step down, because it wouldn't look right if Marc had financial positions with two organizations." He was reciting now. Someone had drilled these words into him. "Marc didn't think that it was a big deal, and said he didn't want to resign. Geoff insisted for the sake of the club, and Marc up and quit."

"Did he quit the club altogether?"

"Yeah, I think he only joined to be with Geoff. He never really was part of the club, and when Geoff broke up with him, he was out of there."

"So you and Marc never sat down together with the records?"

"Are you kidding? Marc knew Geoff was kicking him out of bed to be with me. He left me some spreadsheets he'd done at his job, but he wouldn't answer my phone calls and I had to figure out everything on my own."

"But he did turn over the checking accounts, and financial records, didn't he?"

"You'd have to ask him if he held anything back. We never talked."

"That must have been so frustrating for you! The woman who served as treasurer before Marc, Mavis Baker—she was still around, right? Was she able to help you?"

"That cow didn't understand the first thing about finances, and on top of that, the word was that she had her fat hand in the till. Her little girlfriend had a big habit. That's why Geoff sacked her as treasurer."

"That's interesting. I thought I'd heard that she quit."

"Geoff let her quit so it wouldn't look so bad for her. Now, that's leadership for you."

"So you were completely on your own as treasurer. How

about when you left office, after the election in March? Did Miranda Post ask for your help to transfer the responsibility?"

"Well, the problem was, there was a fire in this building. You can still see the smoke through the paint up there." He pointed into the corner of the ceiling. "It's a miracle the whole block didn't go. Most of the records on Pride that I had here burned up. Then there was cleaning up this place to deal with, and the insurance and all, so I didn't have any time for that stuff."

"Are you and Geoffrey still close?"

"Yeah, but Geoff—" Joe stopped mid-word, and appeared to think better of what he'd been about to say. "Listen, I've got a customer coming for these. Why don't you talk to Geoff? He's the one that could tell you what happened with the Pride Club."

And, abruptly, we were done. I thanked him for his time, but he didn't respond.

I found a working phone booth on my third try. Ricardo reported that so far he'd found "hella weird shit" (i.e., numerous discrepancies) in the Pride Club treasurers' records, and that Neighbors, my prospective client, had called again and had been very rude to him. As I was soothing Ricardo's bruised ego, I gazed without focus at the street. I almost missed seeing Joe Leslie drive by in his Great Glass van. He hadn't stuck around to work after all.

There were no messages on my home phone. So much for my hope that Kristin might call to make up.

I still had two hours before my appointment with Geoffrey Lawrence, plenty of time to visit the *San Francisco News*. The likelihood of getting kicked out of Morris Drake's office was considerably higher than his giving up the names of his sources, but maybe I could get a take on whether the SNEWS planned to make an ongoing crusade of probing the Pride Club.

The SNEWS office was located in an old brick building between a laminating company and a wholesale plumbing supplier on Folsom Street. The front desk was occupied by a scowling man who explained to each caller before putting them on hold that he was the display ad coordinator and should not be answering phones, but what could you do, the receptionist had quit. He flicked a glance over me, dismissed me and began his lament to a new caller.

I spared him the annoyance of seeing me again and slid past his desk to find Morris Drake myself. The office was one enormous room, which must have been a body shop at some point, from the paint fumes that still hung in the air. Twelve or fifteen cubicles occupied the center of the room. One of the side walls had been partly built out to create a darkroom. Nearby were banks of file cabinets, bookshelves full of books, pamphlets, crumbling cardboard boxes full of more books and pamphlets. Several offices occupied one wall.

With luck, Drake's name would be on one of the doors. No luck. They were occupied by the Publisher, Associate Publisher, Advertising Manager and Circulation Manager. Drake must have one of those anonymous, identical cubicles. Too bad I didn't know what he looked like.

I walked up to the only female I'd seen in the place, a very tall African-American woman with gorgeous braids. She peered at me suspiciously over heavy tortoise-shell glasses. Just my luck if she was one of the name-plate owning office holders and wanted to know my business.

"I'm sorry to bother you, but I have an urgent hand delivery for Morris Drake, and I'm lost. I must've misunderstood the man at the desk when he told me where Mr. Drake sits." She gave a shout of laughter.

"Child, if that scum so much as spoke to you with a civil tongue, you should call Oprah, or Donahue at the least, because you have performed a conversion! Reggie has no time for women! Morris is in the second stall past the coffee machine over there. Just follow the steam coming out of his ears. But I'd think twice if I were you. He's having a *bad* day!" She laughed again and settled in at the copier with a big stack of papers.

I approached Drake's cubicle as quietly as possible. He was at his computer terminal, his back to the opening of the cubicle, talking on the phone. His voice carried, and from what I could hear, the conversation was about his editorial on corruption at the Pride Club. I walked over to the coffee machine, and went through the motions of fixing myself a cup and then sipping at it. From where I was standing I could hear most of his end of the dialogue.

"Barry, I'm sorry you caught heat over this, but I've been covering politics in this city for twenty years, and you can't take threats like that seriously—" The person on the other end of the conversation must have cut him off. He pulled a pint of Southern Comfort out of a drawer and drank out of it while he listened.

"No, damn it, Barry, you know I can't tell you who told me about Pride! That's why people will tell me things. It's confidential!" Barry cut him off again and responded at length. When Drake spoke next, it was in an entirely different tone of voice.

"I understand, but. . . . Look, I won't write anything more on the subject. There are plenty of other problems out there to cover—" He stopped abruptly as Barry objected so loudly that I could hear his roar from where I stood. "I'm sorry, you're right, there is no problem with the Pride Club. You want a retraction? Now that's going too far, what kind of credibility would I have if I—Unpaid leave! What the hell is that, something you just made up? No, for the last time, I won't give up the names. Yes, I guess that does settle that, you son of a bitch!" Drake crashed the receiver into its cradle.

I had crept closer and closer as Drake capitulated and then rebelled, and I was only a few feet from his desk when he disconnected his keyboard and threw it across the room. Then he pushed his computer monitor onto the floor, and followed it with the files on his desk. People from the surrounding cubicles came to investigate.

"Is it an earthquake?" A paper-thin woman with spiked white-blond hair tore out of the Associate Publisher's office. When she saw the source of the noise, she swore eloquently and took a deep breath. "Morris, what's the meaning of this?"

"Your chickenshit boss Barry just fired me, that's what! One of his rich friends put the heat on him about my editorial on those little crooks at Pride. Be responsible, he says! You maligned one of the community's finest organizations, Drake, he says. Give up the names of your sources, Drake! The son of a bitch put me on unpaid leave 'til I gave in, so I told him where he could put his unpaid leave!" The woman's eyes widened but she held her ground. "Didn't you go to jail to protect a source one time, Mimi?" He stuck his face close to the Associate Publisher's. She pulled herself together and asserted her authority.

"Morris, you're drunk. Come into my office, now!" she demanded.

"No, I don't think so," Drake said. "The nice thing about being fired is that I don't ever have to go into your plug-ugly office again—or look at your plug-ugly hairdo."

"Morris, please. Don't make me have you removed." Mimi caught the eye of a large man nearby and gestured in Morris Drake's direction, and the man obligingly reached for Drake's arm. Drake dodged out of the way, and the big man stumbled over the computer keyboard.

Mimi coldly told the assembled SNEWS staff that the show was over now and they could go back to work. She noticed me for the first time and demanded to know who I was. Ever since the scuffle began, I had been edging toward the door. Now I called back to her as I sped up, "Yerba Buena Coffee Service, checking on your supply. You've got plenty, but you might want to consider switching to decaf—your employees seemed to be very stressed. Have a nice day!"

Reggie the non-receptionist didn't even look up when I exited. I crossed the street, and waited. A few minutes later Morris Drake came out, escorted by two other SNEWS staffers. He reeled toward a bus stop and slumped on one of the seats. He pulled the Southern Comfort out of the breast pocket of his jacket and gulped from it. I ran to retrieve my car and pulled up at the curb.

"Hi, need a ride?"

"Who're you?" He peered at me through dark shades. "Seen you before, in there."

"Right. My name's Maggie. I'm interested in the truth about the Pride Club. Could we talk?"

He considered it, or perhaps blacked out for a minute. Then he got up and started to stagger down the street in the opposite direction. "No," he said over his shoulder. "Already fired—or quit—not sure. All because of that shitty club. Go away! They're probably watching me. You'll just get me in more trouble. G'way, you hear me?"

I drove away. Oh well, even if I'd failed to talk to Morris Drake, one question had been answered: There'd be no more muckraking about the Pride Club from the SNEWS. What I'd heard convinced me that the club—or its past leadership— had some persuasive frighteners working on its behalf.

I needed a drink, myself, only my drug of choice is caffeine. There was still almost an hour to go before my session with Geoffrey, so I drove to Muddy Waters, one of the many Valencia Street coffee joints. Like the others, this one features strong, high-quality coffee, with the customers providing the only decor. There are always enough people with leisure to drink coffee all day to keep them in business. I always speculate about what the customers do for a living that allows them to dress fashionably, sit at pricey laptops and drink lattes in the middle of the day—and how I can get in on it.

I picked up one of the newspapers discarded by earlier patrons and noticed that the only response from the Mayor's office to the latest gay bashing had been sending Geoffrey Lawrence to Saturday's demonstration. The front page was dominated by a photo of the Mayor greeting a delegation of Japanese businessmen. Mayor Rawlings towered over the other men, who were bunched together to fit into the view of the camera. Rawlings became famous as a basketball player in the 1960s and parlayed that into elected office. His key assets were his bland affability, his finely honed media presentation and his sincere devotion to the needs of the largest corporate interests in the City. The caption under the photo quoted Rawlings: "We San Franciscans want to affirm our commitment to keeping San Francisco the tourist mecca of the world through our all-out offensive on crime."

Below the photo was a feature article on the "war against crime in the neighborhoods." By creating a round-the-clock police presence, marijuana dealers had been driven out of Dolores Park, at least for the moment. Mayor Rawlings was already running hard for re-election, and he was focusing police personnel on projects that would get positive press coverage, like the Dolores Park sweep, and on beats in neighborhoods he was courting for the next election. Unfortunately this strategy did not reduce the numbers of children killed in drive-by shootings in the projects or queer-looking men and women mauled in the Castro and Mission districts.

Seeking mindless diversion, I turned to the entertainment section and read that a rock band in which I used to play lead guitar (mostly at fraternity keggers and benefits) had just been signed by a major label. It figured that hard-edge dyke and feminist bands would be big now that I'd given up on becoming the next Chrissie Hynde. My horoscope said the day was auspicious for new financial beginnings—maybe the Fabulous Weasels would throw over their current guitar player and call me. Maybe T.M. Neighbors would hire me to solve his theft problem. Maybe I should play the horses.

The model in a full-page Macy's swimsuit ad resembled Jolie. Her hair was wet the way Jolie's had been when I left the house, and she wore that discontented pouty stare favored by photographers, again the way Jolie had looked when I left that morning. Memories of Jolie's lips, her hands, the scent she wore, how soft her face was in sleep—all made me long to touch her, to know what was behind all the personas she put forth. Who knew, maybe there had been, could be, something more between us than hot sex. Tonight, Maggie, put it away until tonight.

I quickly turned to the editorial section. A letter to the editor from three police officers who asked to have their names withheld accused the Mayor of over-policing upper-income neighborhoods at the expense of people living in the projects and neighborhoods of predominantly immigrant and non-white people. The Op-Ed page featured an economist's diatribe about the national deficit. I automatically dismissed it as worthy and dull, the kind of thing I never read. But the blown-up quote that accompanied it grabbed my attention: "People's eyes glaze over when they are presented with columns of numbers."

That was it. The problem with the Pride Club leadership, and most similar bodies, was that they hated dealing with numbers. They wanted the bottom line. If the numbers contained a potential embarrassment for the club, the Pride leaders would leave it to me to take care of the crisis, and once the crisis was over they would leave it to Miranda to worry about as treasurer. It helped explain why so many nonprofits endured nasty scandals about money and why no Pride treasurer's balance had jibed with the one before or after. Nobody but the treasurer ever paid attention.

Chapter Ten

Even with my dawdling I was early for my audience with Geoffrey Lawrence in his City Hall office. His secretary, Ms. Sims-Holden, checked her appointment schedule to assure herself that I wasn't a fraud. Had I ever wanted to know what Nancy Reagan would look like as a peroxide blonde, Ms. Sims-Holden was the living answer. She gave my appearance a distasteful inspection and wordlessly conveyed how gauche it was to arrive early, thereby forcing her to share her anteroom.

On a hard chair next to this paragon's desk, I reflected that Geoffrey's location only two doors down from the Mayor's office must give him great satisfaction. I turned down Ms. S-H's grudging offer of refreshments and wondered how she coped with the daily influx of lesbian and gay visitors, many possessing even fewer social graces than I.

Then my Midwest upbringing set in. Maybe Ms. S-H was forced to take whatever civil service job came along to support aged parents suffering from expensive illnesses; maybe she was a tireless volunteer for the homeless; maybe she pursued a hot, illicit sex life after-hours. Following a short phone conference, she announced that Mr. Lawrence would see me, and I gave her a warm smile, born of my new solidarity with her. She responded with a look of shocked disapproval.

When I entered his office, Geoffrey stood and seized my hand in both of his. He had removed his jacket to reveal a custom-tailored, perfectly pressed cotton shirt. His braces (the term preferred by corporate types for fancy suspenders) had a tiny woven design—yachts? A lock of his hair fell artlessly over his brow. His eyes shone with interest and what I would have taken for attraction in a straight or bisexual man. This guy was very, very good at what he did.

"Thank you so much for seeing me. I know how busy you must be," I murmured, feeling challenged to charm the charmer.

"Not at all. Tell me about your book."

I gave him the lesbian/gay history book story, emphasizing the magnitude of his contributions to our community, and what a large chapter his would need to be. I set up my tape recorder, and he started talking.

"I believe that gay men and women must take the same path that national minorities have taken throughout our country's history. Like the Irish, the Italians, the African Americans, we have to help each other into positions of authority and influence. It's crucial that we have gay governors, gay representatives, gay senators. And doing that means getting over our petty differences and voting as a block."

Naturally that means supporting the white men who look the most like Kennedys, I thought, smiling and nodding.

"Was that your strategy in the Pride Club?"

"Absolutely." He leaned forward, working familiar material. "We got behind winners. You put up a Black lesbian welfare mother and you may have the moral high ground, but you'll never win an election. We looked at political realities. And, Maggie, it worked. That's the main thing. It worked."

"While you were in charge of the club, mainstream politicians made a point of getting Pride's endorsements. Could you talk about that?"

"It was gratifying to have the ear of city and state officials and candidates. We flatter ourselves that we were able to influence some important legislation."

"Was there a financial aspect to that influence?"

"I've always stayed away from the financial end of things, Maggie. One person can't do everything, so I delegated those matters to qualified individuals."

"So you wouldn't know, for example, whether Candidate X had donated money to the club at some point?"

"Wouldn't know, wouldn't want to know. It might taint the process."

"When I spoke with Joe Leslie, he told me about his difficulties in getting cooperation from Marc Romano or Mavis Baker. Could you tell me a little about that?"

"I'm sure we all wanted the best for the club, we just held different opinions on how to get there. Only time will show who was right."

Time to try another approach. "One of the most troublesome things for me is how often progressive people turn on each other and focus on our differences, rather than confronting the institutions and individuals that mean us active harm—"

"I couldn't agree more. Since my becoming liaison for the Mayor, you wouldn't believe some of the scurrilous things that have been said about me—"

"That's exactly what I was going to ask you about! I've heard that the recent editorial in the SNEWS was a thinly veiled attack on you. Could the rumors about misused funds be related to past difficulties with other Pride officers—say, Mavis Baker or Marc Romano?"

"I feel confident that neither Mavis nor Marc would attack me. Aside from the fact that there weren't any improper activities, if I were at fault, so would they be, as treasurers. In any event, my work for the Mayor keeps me far too busy to keep up with the latest irresponsible gossip. I'd much prefer to talk about my current work."

"Certainly. Many people in the community are upset about what they see as the Mayor's indifference to the gay bashings. Have you been in communication with the Mayor about these concerns?" Geoffrey's smile became more forced. This obviously was not the current work he wished to discuss.

"We believe that what has been called the gay-bashing crime wave is a media creation, sensationalized out of all proportion to the facts. There are always assaults on gay men and lesbians, just as there are, unfortunately, assaults on people all over the City. As a matter of fact, the statistics show that, overall, violent crime in the City has gone down since the Mayor took office. Our administration's sensitivity workshop for police who cover the Castro district has won several community awards. And we've given out over 900 whistles in the past year. I take a personal interest in 'Operation Whistle-Stop,' since it was my idea."

"Then you agree with the Mayor that nothing further needs to be done to end anti-gay violence? Besides the whistles, that is."

"I see you weren't satisfied with my response. I'm afraid that sometimes to get to the greater good, we need to be patient about attaining favors that might appear to disproportionately reward a special interest group—" Geoffrey was interrupted by his intercom. His smile vanished, and I thought I heard him gulp. He noticed me watching, and got control over his expression as he put down the phone.

"Maggie, I'm—um, sorry, I . . . I'll have to cut this short today. The Mayor needs my urgent attention." Geoffrey arose from his chair with uncharacteristic clumsiness and gathered up my recorder. He handed it to me as he hustled me out of the room. "Ms. Sims-Holden will call you to schedule another session." His hand was icy cold when he shook mine at the door.

I stepped into a Women's Room nearby. One of the downsides to a caffeine habit like mine is that I've been forced to develop a mental data base of all the tolerable public restrooms in San Francisco. This one was a genuine original: high ceilings with plaster garlands and arched windows. It was a spacious "ladies' retiring room" from the days when couches could have been provided without concern that homeless women might attempt to sleep there. Alas, no hot water was available in the marble wash stand and there were no towels. Back to the austerity of the 1990s.

When I came out, shaking water from my hands, I caught a glimpse of Geoffrey's back as he walked quickly down the corridor. He looked around, then unlocked what might have been a storage room—it definitely was not Mayor Rawlings' office—and stepped inside. Shortly afterward, he was joined by another man, who looked like a million other white blue-collar workers in a dark shirt, sport jacket and pants. He was carrying a bulging leather briefcase. A tryst? Not from the apprehension I'd seen on Geoffrey's face. And this man had a good twenty years on Geoffrey, a far cry from sleek young men like Marc and Joe.

The transformation of Geoffrey from suave politico to nervous sneak had piqued my curiosity, and I decided to wait around for further developments. I hauled a double crostic puzzle out of my bag and leaned against one of the post-earthquake reinforcements that make City Hall look like we're in the aftermath of a war. I'd filled in three of the clues, and was concluding that at least one must be wrong, given the sentence they were forming, when Geoffrey came out of the room and headed in my direction. I ducked behind a tarp hanging from the scaffolding.

Geoffrey and one or two others paused a few feet from where I was hiding. Some of Geoffrey's words were audible. I made out "morning" and "eight o'clock." Then he hissed something that sounded like "missed" or "fist"—or "list"? The others were less articulate, and I caught only fragments of words. When their footsteps receded, I stuck my head out in time to see Geoffrey limp to the anteroom to his office. He waved aside a message his secretary rose to give him, and slammed his office door behind him.

From my vantage point I could see only the ordinary-looking man who had followed Geoffrey into the locked room. He made a dismissing hand gesture in Geoffrey's direction and said good-bye to the third person, who remained just out of my vision.

When I could no longer hear shoes clicking on the marble floor, I came out of my hiding place. Dozens of people were in the vicinity. Any of these could have been the third person. I didn't even know whether it was a man or woman I was looking for. I looked over the balcony and saw the non-descript man walking down the stairs. I ran to catch up with him, then slowed to keep a cover of several people between us.

He walked quickly to a phone booth on Van Ness, where he made several short calls. I followed him onto a crowded bus, and off again only four blocks later on Market Street. He joined the crowd waiting to transfer to another bus. I took over a phone booth and checked my home answering machine (nothing) and office (Ricardo reporting that T.M. Neighbors would be available for my call at exactly six o'clock that day).

My man took the 8 Market bus, and I ran to board it at the last second. We both got off at Castro and 17th Streets, and I trailed him into A Different Light bookstore. He objected to checking his briefcase at the front counter, but gave in when the clerk insisted. He stopped still as he took in the merchandise. A sale table displaying half-price calendars blocked his path, and he recoiled from the glossy, full-color flesh displayed on their covers. Finally he appeared to become aware that his blatant discomfort was attracting attention and pulled himself together. His self-consciousness made it unlikely that he'd notice my interest in his activities. I stepped behind a bookcase and peered over the New Fiction section as he headed for the back of the store.

"Maggie!" I turned at the screech and found myself surrounded by Lynnette McSorley. "I'm so glad I ran into you. Now I won't have to call you," she said, beaming. "I need an update for tonight's Executive Committee meeting. Let's go get something to eat."

I whispered to Lynnette that this wasn't the best time, meantime trying to keep an eye on my quarry. He was moving toward the cashier with some piece of merchandise in his hand. This meant rotating Lynnette too, since she had a lock grip on my upper arm. I started to explain that I was following someone who might be connected with the case. However, she is so accustomed to being put off that she simply assumed I was lying to her, the way everyone else did. Having spent nearly two hours of billable surveillance time with nothing tangible to report, I concluded that my case for further pursuit was less than convincing, and caved in.

Lynnette was prepared to forgive my attempt to duck out on her, and bought me a huge cafe mocha and a buttered bagel at the Village Deli. Between bites and sips I recounted the little I had so far, including the anonymous notes and my attempt to visit Morris Drake at the SNEWS. As Miranda had asked, I omitted the part about the list, in spite of my reservations about it. Without the list, the case was a wild goose chase, following a bit of gossip dropped in the SNEWS by a writer who'd been fired for his efforts.

Lynnette shared her dissatisfaction with my progress, in detail and at length. What did she expect—news flashes on the hour, along the lines of the Channel 4 news team reporting on a fire?

"You know, it was not a unanimous vote to hire you," Lynnette informed me. "I have to be able to convince them to continue this. And the money to pay you is coming from Stephen and me, not club funds. If we hadn't offered to pay, it would never have passed in the first place. Couldn't you get something on Joe Leslie? Nobody but Geoffrey ever trusted him."

"If I got to pick who the bad guy was going to be, I'd go with somebody on the Joint Chiefs of Staff," I said. "Geoffrey's my favorite local boy, if we're going to go by plain old dislike rather than facts."

"But Geoffrey doesn't know anything about finances," she said, with puzzlement. "He was the best at schmoozing with major donors, but he never could tell you how much money was in our accounts. He always had somebody else deal with that."

"Somebody like Joe Leslie, for example. Do you honestly believe that Joe would be able to steal the club's money on his own?"

"Well, stealing is a very strong term. Lost, maybe, or mismanaged. Either of those I could easily believe." She took a big bite of her chocolate fudge cake.

"I'm late for an appointment. Gotta run. Let me know if you think of anything else," I said, and was out the door before she could chew, swallow and protest.

Chapter Eleven

I fetched my car from the garage at City Hall and drove it to the garage near my office. A space alien analyzing my day would likely conclude that I was a drone that lived only to transport my queen, the Toyota, from one large cement box to another.

It was time to call my maybe-client T.M. Neighbors, write up the day's notes and plan where to go next with the investigation.

My office building is only a block from the Powell Street Cable Car turnaround. Tourists wearing skimpy shorts were jogging in place to stay warm in the rapidly cooling end of the day. Sellers of sweatshirts emblazoned with ugly pictures of the Golden Gate Bridge were doing a brisk business, as was a takeout espresso place.

Near the end of the line two women tourists in "I Heart San Francisco" sweatshirts stood hand in hand, oblivious to how soon, or whether, they got on a cable car. This made me smile, then reminded me of my own tangled sex- and love-life. When was the last time I'd been starry-eyed? When had I become so cynical? I caught myself sliding into a reflective funk. This was the wrong time for cosmic introspection. I shook my head the way Loba shakes off rainwater and half-walked, half-jogged up the street and into my building.

Although it was only a few minutes before six o'clock, the hall was deserted. The marble-paneled hallways echoed the sound of my shoes on the marble-tiled floor as I narrowed the distance between the elevator and my office as quickly as possible.

Ricardo was gone for the day, and the office door was locked. A plain white envelope had been pushed through the mail slot in the door. There was no name on this one but I knew what it was. My name had only been on the outside when Ricardo might be the one to find it. This time, my correspondent must have known Ricardo would be gone.

The urge to leave it there, to wait until Ricardo and dozens of others were around me, was a powerful one. Instead I stretched latex gloves over my fingers and opened it. The print was hard to read, because my hand was shaking. "THIS IS YOUR LAST CHANCE. WE KNOW WHERE YOU LIVE. WE KNOW WHO YOUR FRIENDS ARE."

I dropped the paper. Although the office was warm and the window was closed, I shivered. My practice of leaving the door between Ricardo's cubicle and the outer hall unlocked whenever I was there had seemed like a normal business practice. Now it seemed childishly careless, and I put the lock on. I'd never felt unsafe in the office, certainly not during the day. I didn't even keep the .38 loaded, and it wasn't close at hand, anyway.

For a full minute I contemplated dumping the Pride Club investigation. It would be tempting to say that high-minded principles alone led me to stick it out, but in truth, economics played a strong supporting role. I'm always two or three clients away from returning to the temp agency.

There was my ego, too. I'm anything but a hard-boiled

type, but I wanted to vindicate myself to Betty, whom I respected, and Lynnette, whom I wanted to get out of my hair. I also wanted to justify the trust of Miranda, who saw me as a heroine. And, yes, the prospect of putting a spoke in Geoffrey's wheels was thoroughly appealing.

Sipping tepid coffee, I leafed through the messages Ricardo had taken. On top of the pink "While you were out" notes was Ricardo's daily summary, in his breathless style:

> Are you sure these are all from the same group? (Joke) None of these guys' records match up. It's like they started all over each time.
>
> Can you believe these printing bills? They paid three times what my Uncle Gustavo charges for flyers.
>
> They paid $10,000 to have everything translated into four languages, but I don't remember seeing anything in Spanish in the neighborhood last year.
>
> There was a door-to-door canvass for five months before the election. They paid for 12 people in the canvass with just one check every week to the Democratic Alternative Collective. They're big checks!

Huge expenses, but not surprising. More and more, elected office went to the holder of the largest campaign chest. Maybe the list Miranda had told me about did represent multi-digit sums of money. But so what? The only suspicious part was how worried Joe Leslie was about losing it!

When the phone rang, I jumped. It was T.M. Neighbors, my potential client, at last, calling me because he feared my impertinent office help wouldn't relay his message. Neighbors told me he was having problems with theft at his exclusive men's clothing store, and that the man accused by the store manager was in a "sensitive position." (Translation: He was sharing T.M.'s bed.)

Neighbors said my name had been given to him by a

business acquaintance, but I couldn't pin him down as to the person's identity. We made an appointment for the next afternoon. He had bristled with irritation about his difficulty in reaching me. Just my luck if that kept him from hiring me. His type of work probably didn't result in threats arriving through the mail slot.

Chapter Twelve

I dialed the machine on my home phone to check for messages. There was a short one from Kristin ("Well, I tried"), a wistful one from my mother (letting me know it had been two months since my last letter and reminding me to send her and my dad an anniversary card), an impassioned phone tree message about a Stop the Bashing meeting, and three demands from Jolie, growing in intensity and anger, that I call her immediately.

The number she'd given me was somewhere in my purse. In my wallet, maybe? Yikes, I thought, fishing around for it, this woman isn't even in my address book yet, and already we have relationship drama.

She answered on the first ring. "Maggie?"

"Hi. You're supposed to say hello, then I get to tell you who I am."

"When were you planning to call me?" She inhaled deeply on a cigarette to punctuate the question.

"Jolie, what's the matter?"

"You are the matter." Her voice was cold. The coldness of an old bad relationship. I knew this tone too well. "Answer my question!"

"I was going to call you tonight. Remember, I said I would

85

if you didn't call first. It's hard for me to make personal calls during the day."

"You ran out this morning, after you conveniently over-slept, and then you left it up in the air about when we would see each other again. Are you always so male-identified?"

"I'm confused," I said. "I'd have said that oversleeping was the least convenient thing I've done in months. Couldn't you tell how hard it was for me to leave you this morning?"

"It's all about you, isn't it?"

"Do you want to get together and talk about this?"

"I want you to be here with me, right now! I want to see if you were for real last night!" Her voice dropped to a whisper. "I want to make you scream again."

"I think it would be better to spend some time talking, Jolie. Maybe you're right, I haven't thought enough about you. How about if we meet for dinner?" Suddenly I didn't want to be alone with her. Things that don't sound strange when you're entwined at midnight can sound pretty weird over the phone in broad daylight at your workplace.

"I want you *here* with me," she repeated. Reluctantly I took down her address and agreed to go to her apartment as soon as I finished at the office.

By the time I'd recorded the day's conversations with Pride officers and my visit to the *SNEWS*, dropped off the three anonymous notes at Marcia's, almost two hours had passed. I parked near Jolie's building, an Art Deco beauty restored to its 1930s glory. Her apartment, number 34, had "J.S. Krawczyk" taped under the buzzer. At least now I knew her last name—and why she just went by Jolie!

Jolie buzzed me in, and as I stepped off the elevator into the hall, she opened the door of her apartment and watched me approach. She was wearing only a pair of sheer lace leggings. Heavy makeup had turned her features into a mask, and she had reddened her nipples, which contrasted with her white breasts.

Some of my apprehensions melted when she smiled and put her arms around my neck. I looked into her eyes, and saw only pleasure at my arrival. She drew me close, and I slid my arms around her back, caressing the curves she hadn't let me celebrate the night before. Our kiss was questioning, exploring, almost like that first kiss in front of The Raven. But that had been before her angry accusations. Now I was on guard.

"Jolie—" She put her hand over my mouth, and led me into the apartment. It felt like a sauna. I took off my jacket, and threw it onto a large couch, which must have been impressive before it acquired the stains and holes that marred its surface. I looked around the room and saw that most of the furnishings had been equally posh, although they now looked as if they had been thrown about regularly. The windows were heavily curtained. I turned to Jolie and started to speak again. She cut me off.

"Why aren't you taking your clothes off?" She turned away as she spoke, her face unreadable.

"Like I told you on the phone, I want to talk to you," I answered, determined to act natural. "I'm sorry about this morning, but I have to go to work every day. We need to know these things about each other."

"You still aren't taking your clothes off," she spoke tonelessly. Finally her eyes focused directly on me.

"Jolie, please come sit down with me and talk for awhile." My smile froze when I saw the snarl on her lips.

"What the fuck are you doing here after leaving me like that?" she screeched. "Never leave me!" She slapped my cheek savagely before I could block her, then danced backward like a boxer, watching me expectantly.

"Well, what are you going to do about that?" Her pupils looked dilated. Was she using again?

"What the hell are you doing?" I yelled. She started to swing at me again and I grabbed her wrists. I crossed her arms in front of her chest and stood close to her. Rouge from her nipples rubbed off on my hands. I noticed several deep scratches on her hands, scratches that hadn't been there the night before. My nonviolence training from years ago kicked in: You lower your voice to lower the level of confrontation. "Please tell me what's wrong, Jolie."

"Never leave me again—I'll make you need me!" She was shouting although I stood inches away. "I can do things for you that your cold lawyer bitch would never do." She lunged toward my neck, teeth bared.

"Jolie, I don't know what you thought I wanted, but it's not this," I panted, thrusting her away from me, but still keeping a grip on her wrists. "We should have spent some time talking about it last night."

"You can't tell me you didn't *want* it last night! You could feel me all the way to your spine, admit it!" Jolie tore away from me and stalked the once-polished parquet floor, which was marred with ugly gouges. I didn't want to think about how they got there.

"Last night was terrific, Jolie. You're a fantastic lover." My words rang false. She was if anything more beautiful than I remembered, but she no longer attracted me, and everything I thought I knew about her had been wrong.

Her apartment was strewn with canvases. None were finished, although some looked as if they had been near completion when they were tossed aside. All were executed with savage stabs and wide brush strokes. They were representational, some violent to the point of gore, and most of them seemed to be depictions of women. One canvas in a different style stood out. It was a cartoon-like puppeteer dressed in a pin-stripe suit, manipulating the strings of much smaller puppets. One of the puppets might have been Mavis, but facial details were not Jolie's strong suit.

"Last night I thought you liked me." Jolie's words jerked me back.

"I did like—do like you. That's why I'm here now. Why don't you put on some clothes and we'll go eat." My craven instinct was to run, but my conscience and socialization wouldn't let me. Maybe she'd go back to her 12-step groups and pull her life together. Maybe we'd become friends. On the other hand, maybe she'd attack me on the street.

Jolie stopped in front of a mirror with several cracks in it, talking more to her image than to me. "While I was waiting for Mavis last night I kept remembering how it used to be. I never knew if she was going to beat me or fall down and worship me, and I never felt so alive in my life."

She crumpled to the floor, covered her head with her arms and cried great sobs like a child. "One day she told me she was tired of me. I was the only one who stood up for her when the men in the club told lies about her, and then she kicked me out of her life."

"Jolie, come sit on the couch," I said. My mind raced. If Tate the wise therapist were here, what would she say? Surely there must be something helpful to say or do. Or maybe not. Jolie was mourning a sick relationship, and using drugs to cover the pain. There was nothing I could say, and Jolie wouldn't want the kind of support I was willing to give.

Jolie stood and stretched her arms toward me. "When I

saw you last night, I thought we were meant to be together, and I would do whatever it took to get you."

"Jolie, look at me. Not at your fantasy, at me," I said, stepping away from her. "I hate fighting, and drama, and I already have more pain in my life than I can stand. I just want to share my life with a partner that respects me, and that I respect." And what a *magnificent* job you're doing, chimed in my Greek chorus.

"You think I'm sick, don't you?" Anger replaced the misery on her face.

"I'm no expert on mental health! But if you're hurting yourself or someone else, or you're using again, then yes, I think that you should deal with it."

She came very close. "Maybe I *am* sick. But you're the one who's letting yourself be stomped on and thrown away by Kristin. Okay, you don't get bruises, but you've *got* to get off on pain to stick with her." She pinned my arms and gave me a long, fierce kiss that left my lips bleeding. I twisted out of her arms and picked up my jacket.

"Good-bye, Jolie." I brushed her hair from her eyes with a parting caress. "You've given me a lot to think about. I hope you find what you want."

I turned and walked quickly to the door. The elevator wasn't at her floor. I ran down the steps rather than wait for it. Jolie's voice echoed down the stairwell, but I couldn't make out the words. I had to sit behind the wheel for several minutes doing breathing exercises before I could drive. When I shut my eyes, the image of the lovers at the cable car turnaround came back, and a deep loneliness dropped down on me.

Chapter Thirteen

Monday night, the worst of the week for parking, because of Tuesday morning street cleaning. Everyone without a garage had nabbed the spaces on the legal side of the street. I found a spot a block and a half from my house and trudged homeward. The fog had rolled in, and it was a typically freezing June night. I wanted to immerse myself in hot water. It wouldn't wash away the past hour, but at least I wouldn't be carrying Jolie's perfume around on me. Walking double-time to stay warm, I debated whether to take a shower now or to walk Loba and then take a long bath.

My cottage was tucked behind the full-sized houses that face the street. As I passed through the walkway to the back, I saw someone moving in the bushes in the yard on the left. Probably Mrs. Lee staking out her pea pods to keep out raccoons. Craning my neck to watch for her, I called her name. No response. Her hearing was getting worse all the time, although she denied it.

I fumbled with the keys in the dark, finally getting the door open. The force of the silence inside struck me. Something was very wrong. I was acutely aware of noises from the street—a van door slammed shut with a chunk-sound; a vehicle accelerated too fast and burned rubber. Then I heard a whimper. I moved to the light switch and nearly fell over Loba, sprawled on the floor. There was a hideous gash on her head, and a pool of blood had formed around her. She whined softly, and her tail wagged a fraction of an inch, but she couldn't get up. As I gathered first aid supplies, I called out soothing reassurances to both of us. Loba made heartbreaking moans but she didn't stir, and her eyes never left mine while I wadded gauze into the wound to stop the bleeding.

First I called Jessie to come get us and then the emergency line at Mission Pet Hospital to tell them we were coming. I phoned Liam to ask him to come over. Last, I called the police.

While we waited, I looked around the house. As I went through the rooms it occurred to me that I'd broken all the rules about what to do when you arrive home and find a break-in. If the intruders had still been there, I would have been defenseless, crouched over Loba on the floor.

A window in the bedroom had been taped and then tapped to break the glass. They must have worked silently to be able to surprise Loba and give her such a massive blow. My TV and stereo were still there, and except for the bedroom, where Loba must have put up a struggle, nothing was out of place, nothing had been disturbed.

The cats! I called, and a forlorn mew came from the top shelf of the pantry. Pod shrank away when I tried to touch him. When his environment went wrong, as it had in the last big earthquake, he lost faith in human beings. I had to climb onto a ladder and haul all seventeen pounds of him down to examine him. He seemed to be unhurt, but he was stiff with fear, the pupils of his eyes enormous. Fearless was nowhere in sight.

Jessie and Tate arrived right before the police, yet another testament to the Old Dykes' Network. They bundled Loba onto the bed of Tate's pickup, cushioned with pillows and blankets. Jessie held Loba while Tate drove them off.

I was left to show the police what had happened. The cops, a very tall middle-aged white woman and an impossibly young-looking Latino man of average height who looked short next to his partner, were polite but harassed. My minimal damage was not in a league with the steady stream of calls coming over their radio. Between domestic altercations and drug-related shootings, it looked as if that evening was going to break records.

"Full moon tonight?" I suggested.

"Not even close," the woman cop replied with a resigned shrug. "Some nights there's no accounting for it. People are just going off on their nearest and dearest all over the City."

"Plus," her partner said, through gritted teeth, "the Mayor's having a big campaign fundraiser tonight, and he's pulled patrols off their beats to make sure his rich friends feel comfy-safe on the way to their limos." The woman cop gave him a quelling look. He smacked his fist into his other hand and walked out.

"Don't mind Martínez. We're all on overload, and he's still pretty new."

She told me the fingerprint team would be by later, and asked me to go to the station next day to finish the paperwork.

Liam came in and made himself useful brewing and serving coffee to the fingerprint team and acting as host to Mrs. Lee from next door, who had been questioned briefly by Martínez and was now terrified to go to bed. Liam escorted her home and then boarded up the broken window. Jessie and Tate came back briefly to report on Loba. The vet had stitched her up, but was worried about the force of the blow she had received. They would keep her overnight for observation.

Jessie and Tate urged me to go home with them for the night, but I withstood their nudging. I wanted to stay put, partly from a territorial desire to reclaim my house, partly hoping my lost feline would return. I stood in the doorway calling for her and loudly opening several cans of cat food. No Fearless. Pod wouldn't eat and kept leaping onto my shoulder, his faith in humanity apparently restored.

After a muffled conversation with Jessie, Liam announced his intention of staying over. We attempted to make a joke of it, but I noticed that Liam kept the softball bat he had brought with him close at hand when he bedded down on the couch.

I went to bed too, but lay listening with tensed muscles to every sound. Pod positioned himself next to my pillow. Neither sleeping nor purring, he did not make a restful companion.

Chapter Fourteen

My alarm went off at 5:45 a.m., then 5:55 and 6:05. By that time, Pod was agitated by the racket and roused me by patting an anxious paw at my nose. This was a tactic Fearless ordinarily used, which reminded me of her disappearance, Loba in the hospital, anonymous threatening letters and Jolie watching me run down her stairwell.

No, it wasn't a bad dream. Although I was tempted to go back to sleep and pretend otherwise, I got up. Yesterday the idea of staking out Geoffrey's place and tailing him to his 8:00 a.m. rendezvous on some unspecified day had made sense. Now I was faced with the prospect of spending the early morning hours of potentially endless days in front of Geoffrey's house because of something I thought I heard. Ridiculous. Still, I got up.

We Californians are expected to do some morning affirmation thing, like naming your favorite facial feature, and repeating what a strong and proud woman you are, and visualizing what treat you expect the day to bring. I struck out. The best I could manage was that I didn't hate my nose; I hadn't exactly run away from Mimi, the ninety-pound Associate Publisher at the SNEWS, but I didn't feel lionlike; and the prospect of going to bed at the end of whatever the day brought didn't count as a visualization.

I covered my telltale red hair with a babushka scarf, and put on heavy sweats and an old pea coat. Dawn in June is not summer-like in San Francisco. I heated up some of last night's coffee to take along, and lurched zombie-like to the car. It only took ten minutes to reach the garage downtown where I keep the surveillance van, and another ten to get to Geoffrey's townhouse on Diamond Heights. It was dark inside. I parked a few doors away and set up the video camera in case there was any action worth recording.

At 7:15 the lights went on in one room. While I waited I made up a song about misappropriation of funds. Ricardo would be proud of me—it was a rap song. I was about to write down the lyrics for him when Geoffrey emerged to retrieve the morning paper from the sidewalk in front of his house. He had recovered his poise, and the limp had disappeared from his walk. At 7:58 his garage door opened and he drove out. He was alone.

If this was the day he was scheduled to be somewhere at eight o'clock, he was late, but he didn't drive like a man in a hurry. At the first stop sign I nearly overtook him and got too close as he checked his reflection at length in the vanity mirror. Sloppy work, Maggie, I could almost hear the caustic voice Jack Windsor used when he was both irritated and hung over. How many years you been doin' this kind of work now?

The rest of the way to the Civic Center Garage, I kept a safe distance behind Geoffrey. For a couple of minutes hope survived that he was meeting someone there, but he sprinted up the stairs without looking around. I trailed him on foot to City Hall. It was now after 8:30, so I packed it in. Maybe tomorrow. If I kept the van at home overnight, I could sleep an extra fifteen minutes the next morning.

When I arrived at my house, the homey smell of buttered toast cheered me. Liam was heaping masses of scrambled eggs onto two plates.

"Hi! I didn't think you were even up. I was about to wake you. Don't listen to that fat cat of yours—I already fed him. Want some juice?"

"Good morning. How many times have I told you Pod is not fat, he's part Maine Coon cat, and they run big. I've been freezing my butt and drinking reheated swill for two hours. I need fresh coffee. Besides, I don't keep juice around."

"Yes, Sunshine, I noticed. I walked around the neighborhood this morning looking for Fearless, and bought some at the corner store."

This simple kindness put me over the edge, and I started to cry.

"Hey, you don't *have* to drink juice. Probably half the world's population manages to live happy, productive lives without ever touching orange juice."

The phone rang. I blew my nose to compose myself for answering, but Liam was faster. "If it's Kristin, I'll tell her you've seen the light, and I'm your new, ultra-butch woman."

It was Ricardo calling from the office. Liam talked for a couple of minutes, then turned to me.

"You better take this." Covering the receiver, he whispered, "It's bad. Somebody broke into your office. The kid sounds like he's been crying." He handed me the phone.

"Ricardo, are you all right?"

"Oh, Maggie, they trashed the place, they spilled papers all over the floor. Maggie, they smashed up the computer!"

"It's all just stuff, honey. We have backups of everything important." He would hate being called honey, but probably didn't notice. "I've got insurance, and we can get the computer upgrade you've been talking about. How long ago did you find all this?"

"Five minutes ago. I called the cops. Was that right?"

"Yes. That was exactly what you should have done. Do you mind staying put 'til I get there?"

"Nah, I'm all right now."

"Did they break the coffee maker?"

"No. I'll make some."

"Extra strong, okay?"

"Okay."

After a few bites of the eggs Liam insisted I eat, I showered and put on a t-shirt and slacks, and added a blazer in case I got to pursue my profession that day. Liam dropped me off in the van, since I had left the car at the garage earlier.

Two uniformed officers were wrapping up their questions to Ricardo when I got there. One of the cops, a harried-looking Asian man, told me the lock had been professionally removed, and the alarm system disconnected. He and his partner sounded skeptical that such expertise would be used on a mere P.I.'s office. From the questions they asked, their suspicions centered on drug dealing, with me cast as the likely drug dealer and Ricardo in a supporting role as my accomplice.

Ricardo was bristling at their tone, and it seemed wise to get him out of the office for his own good. I asked him to get my car out of the garage, make up some "lost cat" flyers and post them in my neighborhood. Delighted to be getting outside and driving even my nonprestigious car, he moved out fast.

A third, non-uniformed, cop arrived. Ignoring my existence, he spoke briefly with the other two officers. They left to talk to other tenants on the floor. Finally, Detective Desmond turned to me and introduced himself. He was an ex-football-player type, whose muscles were sinking into flab. His worn tweed jacket strained over his shoulders, and the button would never meet the buttonhole again.

"Hmmm, I understand you also had a break-in at your home last night, Ms. Garrett," he said, leafing through his notebook, then peering at me over half-glasses perched on his nose.

"There was a break-in last night, but I don't think they got very far. They nearly killed my dog, but I think I must have interrupted them, because nothing inside was disturbed."

"Did you get a look at them?"

"No, just some movement around the side of the house as I was arriving. I also remember hearing a van door slide shut and then somebody driving off in a rush."

"Can you think of anyone who might want to harm you?"

"No one in particular, but in my line of work, sometimes I stir things up that people want left alone." I didn't tell him about the threats since I wasn't certain that the Pride investigation was the source of the break-ins. There are one or two out there who would celebrate news of my coming to a bad end.

"Do you keep valuables here? A safe? Any particularly hot cases you got going?"

"No valuables, no safe. I keep my gun here, but it doesn't look like they found it." We checked the hiding space and found the undisturbed .38. Then I produced my gun permit.

"How about your clients?"

"You know that's confidential. I can tell you that none of my recent cases has been hot enough for a break-in at my house and my office nearly being destroyed."

"Uh-huh. What about that kid you got working for you?

How long's he been with you? Any known gang involvements?"

As I answered his questions in an even voice, I mentally counted to fifty and warned myself not to ask whether he'd ask that question about a white teenager.

Once the police had gone I was able to assess the level of damage. The computer was demolished. Most of the disks were missing, and the ones that remained were strewn all over the room. Why beat up on a computer?

The file cabinet had been rifled, but its contents wouldn't have rewarded the intruders. My fear of an occasion like this has led me to keep archives of important and/or confidential papers and computer disks in a security storage facility that mostly serves law firms.

Ricardo keeps our current files on computer backups at home, under his bed. This is much more secure than it sounds. Since he lives with four working adults, all on different shifts, two retired matriarchs, two other teenagers and five small children, someone is always home. Their apartment is unpopulated only on Christmas Eve when the entire *familia* Galvéz goes to Midnight Mass.

If I wasn't the drug dealer the cops suspected me to be, why was my office trashed? I ticked off my recent cases. It couldn't have been a client, because I tell them everything I find out. That's what they pay me to do. But maybe someone that I'd exposed through my investigation?

The week before, I'd finished an investigation for a wealthy gay man who had been on the brink of changing his will in favor of his much younger lover. I had amassed photos, names and addresses to document Robert's unprotected, drug-influenced activities. Could my home and office have been targets in revenge for my telling young Robert's rich lover that he was in the running for Mr. Unsafe Sex of the year?

Then there was the child-support scofflaw I had tracked down two weeks ago, at the behest of the ex-wife's furious mother. Grandmama could have just given her daughter the piles of money she was spending on me, and would continue to spend on attorneys' fees. But it hadn't been about logic. Revenge cases left a bad aftertaste. True, I had discovered along the way that the ex-husband was gay, but then his wife had also come out after their break-up, so they were even in the social stigma department if they ever went to court over custody.

Get real, Maggie, it's the damn Pride Club case. The anonymous notes were about Pride, and so was this. Did my affairette with Jolie fit into the scenario? How very convenient that I had been at her place on Monday evening. Had she lied about cutting her ties to the club? She'd admitted that she still was obsessed with Mavis. Maybe it was Mavis who had broken into both places. Would a background check on this successful realtor reveal a past history of expert breaking and entering? I'd put Ricardo on it.

I arranged with the building management to have a cleaning team come in right away. Then I called Miranda Post and told her about the threats and break-ins.

"I think you might be a target, too," I said. "The only reason I can think of for the break-in is to find out how much I know about the Pride Club finances. I've been wanting to talk to you about that car that almost ran you down Sunday. Have you had any threatening phone calls or letters?"

"Now that you mention it, there was a strange message on my machine several days ago, but I didn't think anything of it. The guy who had my phone number before me must've had every credit agency in the country on his tail, and some-times they still call." She didn't respond to my remark about the near-hit and run.

"Do you still have that message?"

"Gee, I'm sorry, it's been recorded over several times with new messages."

"Be careful, Miranda. I don't know how far they'd go. They nearly killed my dog."

"I promise, I'll keep an eye out." Her voice lacked con-viction. I doubted that violence had ever touched her life.

"My office is a mess, and it's not going to be fit for sitting in today. Would you feel all right about meeting me some-place?"

"Sure. How about 8:00 at Zorya's, the new bar on Collingwood? I know one of the owners. I've been wanting to check it out, but I'm too chicken to go by myself. It's al-ways easier to walk into a bar with someone else the first time."

"That sounds perfect. I could use a change of scenery."

"I can't wait to talk it all through with you. Having this list feels like holding on to dynamite. If it's what I think it is, the club was being used for money-laundering. When it all comes out, politics in the City is never going to be the same, and I don't know how happy the other Pride leadership are going to be about that."

"Miranda, who else knows about the list?"

"Let's see—Joe Leslie, of course. He's the one who lost it, and I'm pretty sure he'd tell Geoffrey. I told Larry Gross all about it, you know, the guy who was treasurer at Pride for years? He's so bored, I thought some political gossip might take his mind off his treatments. But he'd never tell anyone else. And Lynnette, I told her a little today. You know how she keeps at you and keeps at you until you'll do whatever she wants to get away from her? I played it down with her. She has such a big mouth that I didn't want to make a big deal of it 'til we get a chance to talk about it. And, uh, I didn't tell her, but Mavis Baker knows about it—"

"What makes you think Mavis knows?"

"She came over to me after the meeting Sunday night and did a real number on me about where were my loyalties, and I should think twice before I do anything I might regret. She didn't mention the list specifically, but she said I'd know what she was talking about. She's so big, and she can be pretty intimidating without saying a word."

Feeling like a smothering Victorian parent, I repeated my cautions to Miranda and said good-bye. Her choice of Zorya's for our meeting was reassuring. Transportation was good and we'd be surrounded by hundreds of people in the heart of the Castro District.

Chapter Fifteen

Marc Romano had agreed to meet me for lunch at a cafe near the Community AIDS Project, where he worked as the fundraising coordinator. He was pacing the sidewalk near the door when I got there. I recognized him from photo spreads on his organization in the gay press. Marc was a slender man with a babyish face, spiky blue-black hair and a mustache/goatee combination that he might believe made him look more grown-up. As in the pictures I'd seen of him, he didn't smile. He wore the standard activist's black leather jacket with a STOP THE BASHING sticker peeling on his sleeve.

Of the former Pride treasurers, Marc particularly interested me because he had been appointed, and then pressured to leave, by Geoffrey. Bounteous possibilities for intrigue, drama and resentment—and juicy revelations about the cause of those emotions.

We sat down at a table and I tried some warming-up small talk. Several topics went down in flames, and I concluded that it was a language Marc didn't know or care to learn. How did he schmooze major donors? His frown began to look more like a sneer. He held his Coke glass in a death-grip. His jaw was clenched. In fact every muscle in his body seemed to be rigid. Was our meeting responsible for his stress level or was he always like this?

Enough chat. I got down to business, elaborating on the lesbian/gay history book story, which repetition had made so familiar that it rolled off my tongue. I emphasized my special interest in the role of the Pride Club.

"What role are you talking about?"

"That's what I want to understand from you and the other people who shaped it."

"But, see, the club has never had a permanent shape. It's like that Silly Putty stuff that you can push in any direction." He watched his hands twist imaginary putty, as if they belonged to someone else. "Every time there's a new leadership, there's a turnover in membership. The old people leave, and new people who like the agenda of the new leadership come in."

"Can you tell me how they were different from one another?"

"Well, Geoffrey ran Pride as the 'gravy train club.' He and a few other guys used it to get jobs for themselves. Now there's the 'purity' club. They always have to be on the absolutely correct side of every issue. Before Geoffrey there was the 'assimilation' club. They thought if they acted like straight people, then straight people would tolerate them. Even before that, before AIDS, there was the 'get naked and do it in the streets' club. They built *fabulous* floats for Gay Pride. . . ." He practically spat out the last words.

"You certainly know plenty about the club. Are you still involved with it?"

"No, these days, I'm lucky if I get my laundry done. I don't have time for outside activities with a job like this."

"Oh. So when you took the position at the Community

AIDS Project, you left the Pride Club?"

"Well, no, um, actually I took on being the treasurer maybe a month after I got hired here at CAP. I guess I just used to have more energy." He didn't look like a burnt-out case. It was hard to imagine anyone with more energy.

"You were appointed by Geoffrey Lawrence after Mavis Baker quit?"

"Yeah. It was always meant to be temporary, to get things straightened out."

"Do you know why she quit as treasurer?"

"No, you'd have to ask her that."

"It must have been difficult for you, picking up the books someone else abandoned."

"That's not what I said! I didn't say she abandoned the job." Now his busy fingers were turning a piece of nine-grain bread into little tan bullets. "Mavis was having problems with her business, and it was always her first priority. Also, she was in the middle of breaking up with that crazy artist—what was her name?—Jolie."

"You said you had to straighten out the treasurer's records?"

"The books were a godawful mess. Mavis may know real estate, but her records were full of holes. She was only in the job for a few months, and there was one month that showed no money in and none out! She's computer-phobic, won't deal with any kind of computer. Everything she did was on little pieces of paper. She probably just lost the Post-It that had April on it!"

"And you were treasurer right around the time of the election last year, too. That must have been super-hectic."

"It was pretty crazy. We lived and breathed that election. If our friends weren't involved in politics we never saw them.

I didn't sleep for about two months." His eyes closed for a moment, and his voice had taken on a dreamy quality.

"Did you have anyone to help you?"

"No, nobody wants to do that kind of work. The thing about political groups—hell, any nonprofit—is nobody wants to deal with finances. They want somebody else to take care of it, and they don't want to hear anything except 'everything's fine, folks!'" His face assumed its accustomed frown.

"Pride had a high profile in that election. Even I went to one of the neighborhood forums. And you had a full-time canvass and distributed hundreds of thousands of pieces of literature, in four languages! Keeping up with the bills alone must have been overwhelming."

"Uh, yeah, it was. Who—um, who told you about the canvass?" Marc looked downright scared now. His eyes darted around the room, avoiding contact. I must be close to something.

"Oh, it was Geoffrey Lawrence, of course. He's definitely not shy about his accomplishments, is he?"

"No, Geoff's his own biggest fan," he said evenly. He would have come across as calm if he'd remembered to breathe. Time to move in for the kill.

"I know this is a very personal question, but were you and Geoffrey lovers?"

"I don't know what that has to do with anything!"

"Oh, I'm sorry, how stupid of me! I forgot to tell you that the title of our book is *An Army of Lovers*—you know, from that old saying that an army of lovers can't be defeated? One of the themes of the book is the interconnections between people's intimate lives and their political activities." Marc's mouth twisted in distaste at the word "intimate," but his shoulders lowered a bit in relaxation after I dropped the topic of election expenses.

"An army of lovers . . . Yeah, well with Geoffrey, you're going to have to go to extra small print to fit everybody in!" He sighed and played with the straw from his Coke. "Yeah, Geoff and I got together right before I took over as treasurer."

"How was it, being lovers and running a dynamic political organization together?"

"It was the best, the kind of life you dream about as an activist. You do work that means something all day, together, and then you go home together. Geoff and I were a red-hot item for about six months, and then he dropped me. That's longer than most of his lovers lasted, so maybe I should get an extra mention in your book. I was useful to him for longer than most."

"Useful? How?"

"Uh, look, I've already said way more than I should, and what I said about Geoff and me isn't for publication." I'd lost him. His expression was closed up and his posture defensive. "I won't sign a release for it and I'll deny it if you print it." He stood, ready for flight.

"Marc, I'm sorry I dredged up things that are painful for you. Of course I wouldn't think of using anything that wasn't comfortable for you, or Geoffrey, for that matter. Please sit down and finish your lunch. It's on my publisher."

"I don't think that would be a good idea," he mumbled. All my interviews were ending abruptly, I reflected, munching Marc's home-style potato chips. I found myself liking him. Other than being congenitally humorless, he was a decent sort. If he hadn't been involved in siphoning funds, why did he get so nervous when I talked about the canvass? There was no question that he'd been in love with Geoffrey, so he must be able to find qualities in the man that were so far invisible to me. He had revealed a great deal about their relationship before catching himself. What had stopped him, painful memories, or fear?

Chapter Sixteen

The Pride Club case was making me eager to meet T.M. Neighbors, even if he was as much of a jerk as I expected him to be. Taking on somebody else's problem would make a nice counterbalance to the Byzantine workings of the Pride Club. And, of course, there was the money.

I entered an ugly gray box of a building on Fremont Street and took the elevator to the thirty-fifth floor. An ostentatious brass plate listed the suite numbers of a half-dozen companies, including "Neige Verte—Distinctive Men's Clothing."

Neige Verte occupied a small but elegant space. The walls were covered in eggshell-colored watered silk and hung at intervals with Japanese prints. Low-slung leather couches and chairs in a deep apricot shade were placed in conversational groupings. When would anyone ever converse in them? A decorative young man in the reception area nodded me into a chair, with no interruption to his own phone conversation. Two Filipinas came in, probably from a coffee break, and waved at the receptionist on their way to a side door. When they walked through it, I caught a glimpse of clerical workers bent over computer terminals in a room of gray metal desks and scuffed yellow walls. The receptionist ended his call and spoke briefly on the phone with Mr. Neighbors, then showed me to his employer's office.

T.M. Neighbors was dressed in a sage-green silk and leather suit with slashed sleeves, à la eighteenth-century courtier, the sort of haute couture that Neige Verte probably carried. The suit did not become him, to put it kindly. He was short and stocky, and the suit was designed for tall and willowy. The receptionist could have carried it off.

Neighbors waved toward the interior of his office. "Please come in, Ms. Garrett."

His office was impressive, if nonfunctional, the walls covered in what looked like dark suede, the centerpiece a huge oval marble pedestal table. Neighbors returned to his side of the desk and nearly disappeared into the depths of a monumental leather chair. He gestured to one of two lesser chairs opposite his desk.

After some throat clearing and a false start, he began. "I'm being made to look like a fool, and I need to know what's going on at my main store in the San Francisco Centre." There was a sheen of perspiration on his upper lip, which he dabbed at with a handkerchief. He was strangely ill-at-ease for a man sitting in his own office talking to the hired help.

"You said your manager has accused one of your employees of theft?"

"Yes, and what's more, he's told several other employees about it."

"Have you reported the losses to the police? You'll need to do that if you plan to collect from your insurance company."

"It's not that cut and dried, and I don't want the police involved. I'm going to go public with stock in the company next year, and I can't afford so much as a whiff of scandal." Now his whole face was shining with sweat, although the room was downright chilly.

"What did you have in mind, an undercover investigation?"

"No, that wouldn't be possible. I don't have any female employees in the store. I want you to be there openly as my representative every day, for as long as it takes. Plan on at least two weeks. Get the employees' confidence. Go out for coffee with them, and get them to tell you what's going on."

"As I understand it, what you want me to do is stop the thefts and avoid any further talk about them. Do you think my being there openly would accomplish this?" My conscience nudged me to point out that this was the most harebrained scenario I could imagine to net anything useful, but then this was a man who spent thousands covering his round body with leather ruffles. I wouldn't cost him much more than his suit had, and considerably less than his executive desk.

"I've got to do something," he said. "Like I told you, you come highly recommended. You'll start today. I have a letter of introduction for you to take to Lance Crowther, the manager." As he spoke, he rummaged through a tray on the table top, the only desk accessory, aside from his phone and a marble pen stand.

"Carter," he flipped on the speaker phone and barked into the air. "Where's that letter of introduction I told you to prepare for Ms. Garrett?" Something that sounded like a muffled curse responded from the speaker. Neighbors grimaced.

"Mr. Neighbors," I said, "I'm sorry if I gave you the wrong impression, but I couldn't possibly go full-time on your investigation before next Monday."

"And why not?" He looked stricken. Not a response I would have expected.

"I'm already on one investigation, and my office was broken into last night. Between the two, I'll be too busy to give your case the attention it deserves before next week."

"I couldn't possibly wait that long." He clambered to the front of his huge chair and sat upright to stare earnestly into my eyes. "This is an urgent matter, and I'm prepared to double your usual fee for your urgent attention. That should help with the expenses for your office. Surely your other clients can wait a couple of weeks. It's now or forget it, Ms. Garrett."

"Then I'm afraid we can't do business. I could give you the names of a couple of my colleagues, if you like." Images from childhood cartoons—dollar bills with wings—flashed through my mind.

"Ms. Garrett, I have to tell you that your business judgment leaves a lot to be desired!" He looked apoplectic. What if he had a heart attack? I hoped Mr. Willow outside knew CPR. Mine was pretty rusty. "I'm offering you an opportunity that could net you lucrative contacts for the future, and at double your usual fee, and all you can say is 'Take a number, I'm tracking down a bunch of wild rumors'?"

"Excuse me—what did you say?" Was he talking about the Pride Club? How could he know about it?

"Never mind. Just forget it!" He climbed out of his chair and for a moment I thought he might hit me before he slammed his palm on his desk. Crossing the room to the door, Neighbors held it open for me. "Good-bye, Ms. Garrett."

The receptionist didn't bother to hide his curiosity about my abrupt departure. We regarded each other in mutual puzzlement until my elevator arrived.

Chapter Seventeen

Time to check my messages. I found a quiet pay phone out-side the garage entrance of Neighbors' building and fished dimes out of my billfold. On the office machine, the building maintenance manager had left a message that their crew had cleaned up the worst of the mess from the break-in. Marcia, my ex-cop friend, said there were no prints at all on the notes I'd left with her. Ricardo informed me that my car was back in the parking garage, and that he needed me to call pronto, because they had a "situation" (NYPD Blue lingo for problem) at his house. I dialed my home number. On that machine, Jessie had left a dramatic reading of an Enquirer exposé of aliens posing as lawyers. The vet left a message that I could pick up Loba anytime. Actually, it was more of a plea, since Loba takes up as much space as several average-sized dogs. Liam's mes-sage announced that he was inviting himself to "enjoy the ambiance of Chez Garrett once again" this evening, adding that he preferred his pillows to be stuffed with down, not cat hair, so he was bringing his own. No message from anyone about my missing feline.

I called Ricardo's house. He picked it up on the first ring. "Boss, this weird guy came by my house. Everybody was out but the grandmothers and my cousin Antonio—he's sick and stayed home from school—and the babies. The man said he was INS. He showed them some kind of badge, and he was waving a gun around. He told them everybody in the house had to stay in the kitchen so he could search the place for illegals and drugs. But Tía Dolores, she's the one who's about a hundred years old, she told him to go on and shoot her, she wasn't going to let some strange man go through her drawers without her keeping an eye on him, and Great Grandma— you know, she can't hear anything and can't see very much— she just stood there and said her rosary real loud."

"Ricardo, for God's sake, are they all right?" If he were in the same room with me I might have shaken him to move the narrative along. I was already imagining the conversation I'd be having with Ricardo's mother about how this had happened.

"Yeah, when Antonio heard it start to get loud, he called my mom. But by the time she got there, the guy had taken off. Tía Dolores told him we all had AIDS, and that she didn't care whether he shot her or not. Then she cut her hand with a vegetable knife and held the blood out at him. Great Grandma just kept goin' with the rosary. Tía said the man cursed them a lot on the way out. She told my mom she didn't understand the words, but if she didn't understand, how did she know it was cussing?"

"I guess your great grandma wouldn't be able to tell us much, but did Tía Dolores tell your mom what the man looked like?"

"She said he looked like a guy who plays a doctor on one of the soaps she watches. Anglo, *rico, suave*. You know, rich and smooth-looking?"

"Young, old?"

"Come on, Maggie, everybody looks young to Tía

Dolores!"

"Did they call the cops?"

"My mom tried to talk them into it, but you know they don't like to have anything to do with police. Besides, they think they did just fine all by themselves."

"So do I!" we whooped simultaneously, through relieved laughter.

"Seriously, though," I said, pulling myself together, "maybe we need to stop using your house as storage for our sensitive materials. See what your mom says about it. Your family's safety is what matters the most here. The Pride Club archives are still at my house, and I'm going to pull out some pictures to show the grandmothers. I think we may know this phony INS man."

"They'll love it. Just like *Cops!* See you later."

Not until I hung up did I notice that my hands were shaking. I'm a slow reactor, and rage that Ricardo's family had been endangered was now stiffening my body. I wanted to howl and kick something. Could it have been Geoffrey, Joe, Marc? Or would they hire someone? What to do now? Stay busy, catch the perp, and let justice prevail. Yeah, right.

There was time to do some checking on the club's main vendors before my meeting with Betty Hastings, the current Pride president. Any invoices or files on the printers and other contractors of the Pride Club had burned in the fire at Joe Leslie's, but Ricardo had traced the names of recipients of large-denomination checks. The biggest bills had been for printing, mostly from ValuMark Printers. The company wasn't listed in either the current phone book or the one for the past three years. The checks from Pride had been deposited to an account in the name of Kyle Winter, who was also the person on record with the Clerk's Office at City Hall as "doing business as ValuMark." His records listed an address on Mission Street. The phone number he had given the City was disconnected. There was time to try his address. I made a lucky connection on the BART train, and was in the Mission District in ten minutes.

The address turned out to belong to "Salón de Belleza," a one-chair beauty parlor wedged between a shop full of frothy first-communion dresses and a *panadería*, a bakery. A small girl with a chocolate smear on her nose stood in front of the shop handing out flyers in English and Spanish about the Salón's Grand Opening. She pressed one into my hand with a grin. The flyer had a chocolate smudge, too. I stepped inside and was appraised critically by the proprietor, a heavily corseted matron with improbably black hair, and her elderly client, who was getting pincurls of the kind my Grandma Faith in Iowa had favored.

"*Buenas tardes,*" I began.

"I speak English. May I help you?" she asked with extreme skepticism. I hadn't thought I looked that hopeless.

"I'm looking for a man named Kyle Winter. He used to have this address. Do you know what business was here before you opened your shop?"

She consulted her customer in rapid, whispered Spanish about the appropriate title. "It was a—*cómo se dice*—post office."

"A post office?"

"People paid *la señora* to get their mail here."

"Oh, a commercial mail service." They both nodded.

"Did you know the owner?"

"No."

"*Muchas gracias.*" I fled next door to the *panadería* before they had a chance to turn their attention to my haircut and makeup.

I picked up one of the aluminum trays stacked near the door and a pair of tongs, and made my selections while I waited for the owner to finish his phone conversation. He talked for several minutes, by which time I'd loaded my tray with macaroons, squares of dense bread pudding, cookies with lemon and pineapple fillings, a small dough alligator for Ricardo to take home to my godchild Cristabel and *pan dulce* shaped like croissants and rolled in sugar.

Counting out bills to pay for my purchases, I complimented the owner on their quality. We agreed on how imaginatively the baker had portrayed the alligator. I asked if he knew the former proprietor of the shop next door. He told me that the owner of the mail service had died during the last winter. Her daughters had come from out of state for the funeral, and while they were here, they had put the store up for sale. No, he didn't know their names, they were married and had their husbands' names now.

Oh, well, not a complete loss. Licking sugar remains from the *pan dulce* off my fingers, I thought how much Cristabel would love her alligator, and pressed on.

I suspected I would meet a similar dead end with the canvass. The contact person for the Democratic Alternative Collective had been a man named Mario García. It's a common surname in San Francisco. The Pacific Bell directory listed no Marios, but there were almost twenty M. Garcías. Calling them and trying to trace Kyle Winter would give Ricardo a workout on the phones.

From friends who used to work in the CISPES Red Star Collective canvass, I knew that canvass team leaders met periodically to divide up the good "turf" in the Bay Area, to avoid having two groups knocking on doors in the same neighborhood at the same time. I decided to consult my friend Oberon, who has connections with several canvass teams. She occasionally switches to door-to-door work when she can't stand being in an office all day.

I took BART back to the Financial District and dropped in on Oberon at one of her sit-down jobs, minding the front office of an engineering firm. The state of Oberon's hair is always a good indicator of her state of mind. Today she had put up her light brown hair in at least a dozen braids, each embellished with a different-colored ribbon. She must be bored enough to leave this job, if not this continent, at any moment.

Delighted with the diversion of sleuthing, she popped one of the cookies I'd brought into her mouth, pointed me to a chair in the corner and started dialing her contacts. It being midafternoon, canvasses hadn't gone out yet, and she reached three coordinators. One remembered the group, pronouncing it "Dack." He was still angry that the DAC canvass rep had claimed enough turf for twelve people, but neither worked the turf nor informed the other canvasses that it was available. Oberon's friend couldn't remember the DAC rep's name, but did recall that he'd been a "pushy college kid type." Oberon blamed squandering turf on amateurism, but I suspected there had never been any intent to run a canvass. Nor had there ever been twelve canvass members, for that matter.

I thanked Oberon and wrote her a fifty-dollar check as a consultant's fee for her escape fund. Of course I would get Pride to reimburse me for expenses. I cursed myself for not getting a receipt from the bakery for the same purpose. Another illustration of why I'll never be wealthy.

I walked the seven blocks from her office to the parking garage where I rent monthly parking spaces for my van and car, paying about the going price for a four-bedroom ranch house in Iowa. But then, of course, you would be in Iowa. Walking presented an opportunity to mull over what I'd learned so far.

Many thousands of dollars had gone to individuals for whom no record now existed, for services that were never intended to be performed. Who gave the money, who ended up with it, and how did they get away with it? The editorial about finance-phobia in the newspaper kept coming back to me. Almost no one in Pride had been willing to get involved with the details of tracking income and expenses. People join volunteer groups like Pride to change society, or find friends, or make careers for themselves, not to scrutinize financial statements or screen potential printers for cost-effectiveness. Members would want, at most, a bank balance from the treasurer.

This almost universal lack of interest in balance sheets offered the perfect opportunity for theft. A cynical leader (okay, I admit it, I meant Geoffrey) could appoint and drive out treasurers and keep them from talking to each other by manipulating their personal jealousies and political differences. Finally, I thought, I understand what I'm looking for here.

On the stairway to the tier where my Toyota hangs out, an adrenaline surge hit. My car and van were the only areas of my life that hadn't been attacked or, in the case of Kristin, eroded. I looked at the underside of the car and scanned surrounding vehicles for potential assailants.

No one attempted to grab me. The car started instantly and did not explode. My natural optimism soared. Even though it was a cool day, I drove with the window open, breathing deeply, enjoying the sensation of the breeze on my hair. I was taking on more and more qualities of my dog boarder. Too bad Loba wasn't here. We could both bark at passing vehicles.

I resumed my analysis of groups and money, and by the time I entered the fog of the Sunset District, where Betty Hastings had an in-home desktop publishing business, I could envision Geoffrey Lawrence convicted of financial trickery and decked out in an unflattering orange prison jumpsuit.

Chapter Eighteen

Betty Hastings lived on a treeless street that looked exactly like the others on either side. There's something eery about driving through row upon row of pastel stucco houses, with the light filtering through the constant overcast. No shadows, and no pedestrians on the sidewalks, no cars on the streets. It always reminds me of those Cold War classic movies about "After they drop the Bomb."

Betty met me at the door wearing an old, rumpled sweatsuit large enough to have belonged to her son. Earlier in the week, speaking at the demonstration and chairing a difficult meeting, she had performed exacting roles with poise and grace. On those occasions she had been carefully dressed, her hair and makeup perfect.

Today she looked as if she hadn't slept in days, her hair was matted and when she took my hand in a perfunctory shake, I felt a tremor in her grip. She gestured toward a chrome chair at her kitchen table and slumped onto one herself.

"Every night this week I've been getting calls," she said without formalities. "I've got kids going to school out of state, my dad has a heart condition. So whenever the phone rings, I answer it. Sometimes they call two or three times an hour. Usually they hang up. But last night a voice—I think it was a man—said 'Call off the investigator. Think about your kids.' Then this morning my daughter calls and says, 'Thanks for the cookies, Ma. When did you learn to bake?' I asked what she was talking about, and she said she'd got a Federal Express package of cookies from me." Betty angrily dashed a tear from the corner of her eye. "I yelled at her to flush them down the toilet. She must've thought I was nuts, told me she and her roommates already ate them. I lost it and told her never to eat anything that came in the mail again." She compressed her lips tightly and shot me an accusing glance.

"Did your daughter keep the wrappings?"

Betty shook her head. "Down the garbage chute and onto a truck with tons of other campus garbage. The girls don't seem to have any effects from eating the cookies, anyway. I guess it was just a subtle hint."

"Betty, I'm so sorry. What about contacting the phone company? They can put a trace on calls coming through to your phone."

She looked at me with disbelief. "Volunteer to put a tap on my own phone? Get real! How many politicos do you think would be willing to talk to me if, right after I said hello, I also had to say, 'Oh, by the way, everything we say is being recorded, so don't tell me about your plan for civil disobedience for the demonstration next week'?"

"I see your point." Mortified by her scorn, I tried to regroup. "Still, you can't go on like this. What do you want to do?"

"What do I want? I want to stop this thing right here. Let the good ol' boys win this one." She pushed a strand of hair out of her eyes and leaned toward me. "I'll come right to the point. Even before this mess about hurting my kids, I voted against hiring you. Lynnette and a few others think they're going to save the club this way, but nothing good is going to come from digging up old skeletons. You know as well as I do that the ones who always benefit from scandals on the left are the right wing."

"What about the effects of the rumors on the club itself? Somebody even brought it up at the meeting on Sunday."

"As soon as something juicier comes along, they'll forget ninety percent of it. Besides, for anything that happened last year, the blame lands exclusively on Geoffrey and his people."

"I guess this means you won't tell me what you know about past club finances?"

"It means that I've gone out of my way not to know anything about what they did, so I don't have anything to tell you. We started a whole new club when the Diversity Slate got elected, and as far as I'm concerned the past can stay in the past. I can't afford the luxury of involving myself in what happened two years ago."

"But—"

"I'm not finished—hear me out! I am a single, African-American, lesbian mother. Talk about three strikes! Nobody is watching my back for me. The second I take a wrong step, I'm history. I'm trying to do what nobody else is doing—put together a multiracial, multicultural gay organization, and I'm dogging the pastors of the churches my sisters and brothers give their money to every week to admit that AIDS is killing our people. That's all I care about—that and my kids."

"Betty, I believe that someone on the Executive Committee is helping keep the past covered up, and may also be involved in the dirty tricks—like the break-ins at my house and office, and the cookies that your daughter received. Someone who is acting as if he or she wants to build a new club is really fighting like hell to keep the good ol' boys safe from prosecution and rich off funds that could have helped make a difference!"

"Fiery words—maybe you should run for office! Do you have any evidence to back up what you're saying?"

"Nothing that I'm authorized to tell you by the person who revealed it to me. . . ."

"Pardon me if I don't find that a compelling argument! I'm going to try to get the Executive Committee to call this off tomorrow night. This is not the battle we should be worrying about, Maggie. Don't worry, Lynnette and Stephen will pay you for your expenses."

"In the last two days my house has been broken into and my office is trashed. Money isn't my only concern here. Besides, it may be too late to call this off."

"They're coming through loud and clear to me that when we end this, so will they. And to tell you the truth, I don't want to find out what they'll do if we continue."

She gestured to the door, either too angry or too tired to see me out.

As I drove back into the sunshine of the Mission District, I tried to fight the depression that had settled over me in Betty's apartment. She certainly was persuasive. If I'd been a member of the Executive Committee, I might have voted against the investigation myself. But I didn't see any way of turning back now. War had been declared. Too bad I didn't know who was an enemy and who was a friend. Nor for that matter, did the members of the Executive Committee—most of them, anyway.

Whoever those enemies were, they had known I was on their trail from the beginning. Lynnette talked to me on Saturday. That same day, before I even went to a Pride meeting, I got the first anonymous note. By Sunday Betty started receiving calls, and Miranda was nearly run down on her way to the Pride meeting. By Monday night my house and office were their targets.

Somebody on the inside, somebody who was claiming to want the truth to come out, was deploying a whole arsenal of tactics to stop me from digging any further to find it.

Chapter Nineteen

A solicitous receptionist at the Humane Society had suggested that I come there myself to look for Fearless, then leave a description. I resolved not to hope for too much and walked through the "found" cats section, peering into cages at the incarcerated animals. Some paced their tiny spaces while others slept, curled into oblivious balls. An engaging young black and white tom strained his paws through the wires trying to snag my sleeve. No Fearless. Steeling myself against the urge to bring home at least one of the unclaimed cats and refusing even to look in the direction of the kittens, I wrote up a description of her, stapled a photo to it, and drove to the Mission Pet Hospital.

After I negotiated the many installments that would be required to pay her bill, Loba was brought out to me and we headed for the car. She cavorted about, ecstatic to be outside, away from the terrors of the hospital, and with one of her humans. A group of nursery school children passing by shrieked in terror at the spectacle. Loba did look more like a demented sea monster than a dog that had narrowly escaped death. I coaxed her into the car and, stopping only at a convenience store to pick up some milk and a bottle of wine, drove home.

Pod met me at the door, crying piteously. He ignored Loba's eager snuffling and wrapped his paws around my ankle. "I know, big guy, I miss her too." I picked him up and let him drape over my shoulder like a fat fur stole as I walked around the cottage. He refused to eat the first can I opened but consented to the second flavor. I diagnosed moderate feline depression.

The message light was blinking on my answering machine, and I approached it with dread. Unless it was Liam or Jessie, all potential callers had only bad news to offer. Well, maybe T.M. Neighbors, if he'd come to his senses about my starting date. Or, more realistically, if his conscience had gotten the best of him and he was calling to explain why he'd wasted my afternoon.

It was Tom Ng from the Pride Executive Committee. He, Miguel Alvarez and Warren Coleman wanted to come see me as soon as possible. He insisted that they could not wait to come to my office the next day. He said they would arrive within fifteen minutes.

An hour later they were seating themselves cautiously on my couch, all showing varying degrees of distaste as they sought places free of cat and dog hair to put their suited bottoms. Tough. Neither the meeting nor the location had been my idea, and I was fresh out of hostessy graciousness.

"Thank you for seeing us on such short notice, Maggie," Warren said, with a conciliatory smile.

"No problem," I said, forcing a smile. I'd been doing that so much lately that my teeth were beginning to hurt. "What can I do for you?"

"Well, it's about your meeting with Betty this afternoon," Tom said, then ran out of steam. He looked to the other two men.

"We know you have progressive politics, Maggie," Miguel said. "Even though you may not have much faith in elections or in our kind of organization, you must have seen that we do good work."

"Yes, I'm impressed by your history. That's why it's so important to clear the name of your organization. I'm glad you've come to agree with that—"

"Maggie, we want to appeal to your consciousness on racism and sexism in the gay movement," Warren said. My face must have registered something along the lines of "Thanks for sharing, white boy," because he blushed. "Betty is concerned that any further efforts on your part may profoundly damage the most important political organization in the Bay Area."

"Did Betty ask the three of you to come here?" Even in extremis, I couldn't believe Betty would sic these guys on me.

"Not exactly," Miguel applied, looking very uncomfortable.

"Does she even know you're here?"

"Well, no, but—"

"So when she talked to you, it wasn't to persuade you to act like shining knights for her and take care of things, so she wouldn't have to worry her pretty little head?" Oh dear, I was yelling at clients again.

"Look, we obviously haven't gone about this the right way," Warren said. He was absently fingering the frayed cuff of his shirt. Our eyes met, and he casually placed his palm over the spot. "We'd all do anything for Betty. Tom called me right after he talked to her, and then I called Miguel. We're all concerned. Your visit got her terribly upset today."

"I got her upset? Hold on a minute, did she tell you about

the phone calls, about the cookies her daughter got?" They gave me—and each other—uniformly blank looks. Marvelous. All they knew was that Betty was stressed out, presumably because of being terrorized by me. Why hadn't she told them what was really going on? Unless she was an Oscar-level actress, she was genuinely worried about her kids. Why was she hiding it from her fellow Executive Committee members?

Miguel continued, "Tom and Warren thought maybe we could make this go away by having a talk with you."

"So what do you want me to do, call up Lynnette and tell her I quit?"

"In a word, yes," Tom said, not meeting my eyes. "If this remains a point of contention in the club, nothing else will get done. And we have to get back to business. The City administration's planning to close several anonymous HIV test sites and counseling services."

"And the investigation doesn't reflect well on the party organization in the City," Warren said. "That may not mean much to you, but the progressive wing of the Democratic Party is the only hope we have for change."

"I appreciate your concern. However, my contract is with the Pride Club, not you. I've accepted a retainer, I've done a substantial amount of work—"

"We can take care of that," Warren said. "Just send your final bill to Tom, and we'll take care of it. Tom, have you got one of those impressive business cards on you?" Tom handed me an embossed card from his law firm, listing him as an associate.

"Let me think about it. But for now, fellas, I am still on the case, and I have work to do." I bustled them out.

Damn, it was hard to stay on this job.

Ricardo arrived with printouts of what he had on the Pride Club treasurers' records, and a pizza. We pored over the accounts as we chewed the pizza. Wednesday I'd turn them over to an accountant, who would spot things we couldn't, but I wanted a chance to look for gross discrepancies first. It didn't take professional training to see that there was no continuity from one set of records to the next. The matter of ethics aside, a reasonably intelligent leadership would know that tough campaign financing laws made the disarray of the past several years downright suicidal. A hostile city district attorney could demolish Pride with an investigation of its books.

"Maggie, are these people stupid?" Ricardo asked, reaching for the last slice of pizza.

"It's hard to believe they could be so naive about skimming. Maybe they didn't care."

"Like suicidal?"

"No, more like they knew they wouldn't be around to be prosecuted when the inevitable exposé comes along."

"I don't get it."

"Maybe the plan was to use the Pride Club to launder money for all it was worth, and then split—in this case lose the election—and leave the new leadership holding the bag."

"You're thinking it's all this guy Geoffrey Lawrence?"

"He couldn't do it by himself, but I think he was in charge of it. None of the treasurers could have carried this off without his help."

"So is he the one who tried to waste your dog and trashed the office?"

"I can't prove it yet, but I'm sure he's involved in that, too."

Chapter Twenty

I took Ricardo home and stayed long enough to present Cristabel with her dough alligator, admire the new kitchen stove, and hear the latest saga of my friend Alicia's cold war with her boss. Even so, I was a few minutes early for my meeting with Miranda at Zorya's.

Zorya's had taken over the site formerly occupied by a male leather bar. It didn't look like the new owners had touched the decor. Only the clientele and the music on the jukebox would give a clue that it was a lesbian bar.

When I got my "lite" draft from the bartender, I was duly checked out, but everyone ignored me after I settled in at a table in the corner.

Two large women in flannel and denim played a companionable game of pool as if they'd been at it for years. Maybe, like some TV series, they had gone into hiatus during the years when there was not a single lesbian bar in the City. The place was about half-full, a fantastic turnout for a Tuesday night. Looked like the brave women who'd put their life savings on the line to open the place were right: There was a demand for a lesbian establishment that wasn't a "club" for hot young bodies and hot young wardrobes.

For half an hour I was entertained and inclined to be indulgent about Miranda's lateness, remembering what she'd said about not going into a new bar alone. This way I was guaranteed to be waiting for her. After that I became irritated, then worried. This wasn't an appointment she would forget or blow off.

I checked my home and office answering machines. Nothing. I called Miranda's apartment twice and left messages on her machine. I tried Lynnette's house and got yet another machine. After another hour, half the tunes on the jukebox and two bottles of mineral water, I admitted to myself that Miranda wasn't coming, and went home.

Greeted by Loba's pleading eyes when I opened the door, I caved in and said the magic words, "Let's go for a walk!" I scooped up some "Lost Cat" flyers in case any had been taken down and snapped Loba's lead on her collar. Because she was still convalescing, I kept us at a sedate stroll out the door and onto the street.

Two blocks from home we arrived at a full-scale crime scene: three squad cars parked at haphazard angles blocking the street, their radios squawking, uniformed and plainclothes officers all over. Neighborhood people stood in clusters talking in clumps, filling in details for new arrivals. An ambulance was pulling away slowly, no lights or sirens. I looked around for the wrecked car or busted dealer, and instead saw a chalk outline of a body on the sidewalk, and a pool of blood.

A uniformed cop was keeping the onlookers at a distance from the scene. He looked quite young, but exhaustion was weighing on him—his broad shoulders sagged. He turned toward us at the sound of Loba's soft inquiring whine.

"This is a crime scene, miss. Please keep your dog out of the way." He was edgy, flexing the fingers of his hands.

"Of course, sorry. Sit, Loba!" Miraculously, she sat. "I live near here. What happened?"

"A woman was beaten to death about half an hour ago." His expression was one of dazed disbelief. Surely even a young cop would have seen plenty of murders. A domestic dispute that got out of hand, perhaps? Noe Valley wasn't the kind of neighborhood where drugs and prostitution resulted in violence. A chill passed through my body as I imagined a lone woman set upon in the dark.

"Did you catch the one who did it?"

"No, ma'am. By the time the neighbors responded to the noise of the attack and called 911, the victim was down, probably dead, and the perpetrators got away."

"Look, I was expecting to meet a friend tonight who didn't show up, and I'm worried about her. Can you tell me the name of the victim?"

"I'm sorry, we can't do that. We have to notify next-of-kin first." He wouldn't meet my eyes now.

"Could you just tell me—" My mouth couldn't form the words. "Was it a short blond woman, young-looking, with curly hair?"

He hesitated, then said, "I'm sorry, ma'am, like I said, I can't give out any information," but his eyes gave him away. A plainclothes cop motioned him back to the scene. He took a few steps in that direction and then turned to me. "Be careful, okay?"

I'd known it was Miranda as soon as we arrived. Thousands of women had been on the City's streets that night, there was no reason for Miranda to be in my neighborhood, and there were dozens of plausible reasons why she hadn't shown up to meet me. Still, I knew viscerally that she was dead.

The plainclothes man took the uniformed cop aside, then

gestured toward a tall, well-dressed woman who stood observing the forensics crew. They spoke briefly, then she walked purposefully toward me. She had a grave smile and a firm handshake. Her appearance was unremarkable except for her large, deep blue eyes. Her evening suit was cut like a tuxedo, but in a soft fabric in midnight blue, even darker than her eyes. She had long dark brown hair that waved around her face, and she impatiently brushed back a stray lock behind her shoulders.

"I'm Sergeant Hoffman." She handed me her card. "That officer said you told him that the deceased might be a friend of yours."

"If it's Miranda Post, yes I do—did—know her."

"I'm sorry for your loss." She probably had to say that kind of thing regularly, but she sounded as if she meant it. "I'll be in charge of this investigation, and I'd like to talk to you. I have to stay here at the scene for awhile. Could I come by later?"

I gave her my address and took Loba home. While I heated up some leftover soup, I switched on the TV. The top item in the news was the murder. "Tonight a young woman on a quiet Noe Valley street became the first fatality in a recent series of violent attacks on gay men and lesbians in San Francisco," the anchor man intoned. "Twenty-seven-year-old Miranda Post was already dead when police arrived on the scene. Shocked residents of neighboring houses reported hearing the victim cry out for help as her attackers beat her to death. We will have more on this senseless act of violence, including interviews with several of the neighborhood residents who dialed 911, after these announcements."

On another channel a Live-On-The-Scene broadcaster was shown pointing at the spot where Miranda was killed. Then the report switched to City Hall, where Mayor Rawlings was holding an emergency press conference. The Mayor appeared to be brushing a tear from his craggy cheek as he deplored the violence against young Miranda Post. He repeated the details of his offensive on crime and announced an all-out effort to catch the murderers, including police decoys in gay and lesbian neighborhoods.

I hit the Mute button to avoid the "happy talk" delivery of the weather report, and sat in silence thinking about the Mayor's announcement. Finally, there would be action on the bashings. All it took was a murder. I noticed that I was still clutching the untouched mug of soup and took it to the kitchen. I washed the dishes mostly for the sensation of hot water on my hands. I didn't seem to be able to feel anything else.

Chapter Twenty-One

The phone rang, forcing me back to activity. It was Lynnette. "Maggie, I'm so glad you're home!" Her call-waiting tone sounded. "I've got to talk to you, but let me see who's on the other line." A minute later she was back. "Let me call you back—don't go anywhere."

As soon as I put down the phone, it rang again. Jessie told me that she and Tate had just watched the news report of Miranda's murder, and they were concerned about me. Did I need them to come over? Would I like to bring the whole menagerie over? (This was no small offer. Tate is allergic to cats.) I told her that I was waiting for Sergeant Hoffman to arrive, but that I did need to talk. Tate got on the extension phone, and I poured out the events of the evening. Sharing the horror allowed me to let go of some of it. They insisted that there was no way I could have prevented Miranda's death. I only partially believed them, but it was good to hear the words.

Immediately after I hung up, Lynnette was back, swearing. "I wish you'd get call waiting. I'm arranging for a press conference tomorrow, and talking to you on the phone now isn't going to work. Betty and Miguel have both called me. They say they've got a majority now who want to fire you and pretend all this never happened. Miranda's gone, and now David is caving in, too. But I said—" Her other line rang again, and she put me on hold. "That's Mavis. I've got to talk to her." We agreed to meet the following afternoon at my office.

Sergeant Hoffman came to the door at about ten-thirty. She accepted a cup of coffee with such gratitude that I was glad I'd made it. There was a big greasy streak on the sleeve of her beautiful suit. She noticed it at the same time I did, and groaned.

"I almost made it through the first act of the Strindberg play at ACT tonight," she sighed, then returned to her police persona. She had a slight down-home drawl that softened her voice. Part of my mind tried to place what part of the South she was from.

We exchanged information. She took down what I told her about my investigation and why I was meeting Miranda, but I got the impression that she considered it a tangential thread: fill in the blank of the victim's destination. She didn't react to my insistence that Miranda was supposed to meet me at a bar a dozen blocks away from where she was killed.

Sergeant Hoffman told me that, because of particular characteristics Miranda's murder shared with the gay bashings, it was being treated as a "hate crime." Miranda had become the first fatality of the men who had been terrorizing the Castro and neighboring areas.

"One thing still doesn't make sense to me," I said. "This isn't known as a gay neighborhood, and the people that the bashers attacked before either were in the Castro, looked gay, or were obviously in a couple. Why would they attack Miranda?"

Hoffman gave me an odd look and said, "Her appearance did fit the profile."

"Oh." Miranda hadn't struck me as the type for outrageously "out" clothing, but then I hadn't known her well. Maybe she'd been dressed to make an impression at Zorya's.

Sergeant Hoffman left, after thanking me again for the "background information" and the coffee, to interview the inhabitants of houses near the scene of the crime. She shook my hand again and our eyes met for a second longer than necessary.

Alone again, I went over each part of the evening. I was responsible for Miranda's being out alone. What could I have done differently, what might have kept Miranda from being killed? Maybe she'd been confused about when we were meeting? Could we have missed each other at Zorya's? I should have sat next to the door and watched the whole time. And I had gone to the restroom once.

Then, remembering Hoffman's certainty about the murderers being the gay bashers, I told myself I was being self-centered, inventing a conspiracy as a response to my own guilt. Miranda had simply been at the wrong place at the wrong time, the unlucky recipient of the bashers' vicious hatred, like the other victims.

The phone rang again. I almost didn't answer, then picked up the receiver and heard a raspy, staccato noise. A crank call or another threat? Then words began to emerge. It was Larry Gross, the Pride treasurer who was hospitalized with pneumocystis.

"Sorry. Hard to talk. Need to tell you . . . I saw on TV. Miranda. . . friend of mine. She called tonight. Told me—" His voice broke into long racking coughs.

"Larry, maybe it would it be easier to talk face to face. Do you want me to come see you?"

"Sure. I'm always here. Come tomorrow. They killed her."

"They—you mean the gay bashers?"

"No. They . . . knew her. See you tomorrow."

Liam arrived, exhausted from a board/staff fracas at his non-profit agency that had dragged on for hours. He was solicitous when I gave him a rundown of what had happened, and I knew he'd stay up with me if I asked, but even during my brief recap, his body had slowly listed toward the pillows at the foot of the couch. I pretended to go to bed so that he could.

Although I turned out the lights in my bedroom, my brain refused to follow suit. When sleep finally came, so did the dreams: the frightened faces of Marc, Betty and T.M. Neighbors were superimposed on splatters of blood, which formed a thick pool, only it was in my office. I kept shouting at everyone to stand still, so we could sort through everything that had happened, but no one would listen to me. I could hear Fearless crying, but I couldn't find her.

I awoke at 2:10 a.m. with my heart pounding. For a few seconds I thought there must have been an earthquake. Then I remembered the swirling, bloody scenes of my dreams. I turned on a lamp, and the images receded. That's what I got for drinking coffee late at night. I was putting on the kettle for tea when I heard the plaintive cry again, and ran to the door.

Fearless streaked inside. I picked her up and she climbed purring onto my shoulder. My lost cat had come back on her own, unscathed except perhaps a little thinner. I hugged her, and realized that there was a familiar scent on her fur. It took me a few minutes to remember that it was the distinctive perfume that Jolie had worn, and that had permeated her apartment. Why would my cat smell like Jolie? Had Jolie taken her? And, if so, why simply return her now?

Fearless objected to being hugged and jumped down to check out the food supply and exchange sniffing inspections with Pod. In celebration I opened three cans of Sheba (lobster au gratin or something like), and let each cat and Loba have one, warning them not to get used to it. I finished up a pint of Ben and Jerry's I'd been pretending wasn't in the freezer. I looked at Liam, dead to the world on the couch. "Help, help, Liam, aliens have come to steal our uvulas," I said in a normal tone of voice. He mumbled an affable response and slumbered on. Some protection.

As I tossed in my bed, the anger, sadness and frustration of my dream returned. I'd hardly known Miranda, and death at a young age had become unbearably common, almost normal, in the time of AIDS. But sudden, violent death was not part of my experience.

Miranda's friend Larry believed she'd been killed by someone who knew her. If her murder hadn't been another gay bashing, but had been set up to look that way, her killers must have been following her. But why was she alone on a quiet, dark residential street in Noe Valley when she should have been with the crowds in the Castro District?

From what officials were saying in TV interviews, I doubted that the police would investigate the murder independently of the gay bashings. Sergeant Hoffman was convinced that the "particular characteristics" of the crime linked it to the other attacks. I wondered who else had access to information about those characteristics. I wondered again what Geoffrey could have been doing that would take precedence over the chance to appear on TV with the Mayor. I wondered how long it was going to be before I had a normal night's sleep.

Chapter Twenty-Two

Getting up before dawn was even worse on Wednesday than it had been the day before. My throat was sore, and the glands under my ears were swollen and painful. The alarm must have rung for some time before I woke, since my dreams had featured bells and whistles. Pod, now accustomed to this early activity, wrapped his fluff of a tail over his eyes and slept. It was a first for Fearless, and she leaped from the bed to a nearby dresser and assumed an outraged stance.

"You're absolutely right, it's way too early," I said. My voice sounded an octave lower than usual, with a Tom Waits quality that could have made me a star in my rocker days. In an effort to placate her, I scratched the itchy spot on her chin. "It won't be much longer, I promise." She looked skeptical.

I tossed back some vitamins and aspirin and wrapped a scarf around my neck as well as my hair. Now I looked conspicuously incognito. All I needed was a pair of Rayban Wayfarers. Greta Garbo does surveillance.

The heater in the van kicked in as I neared Geoffrey's neighborhood. I parked a few doors down from Geoffrey's place and settled in, expecting another long, uneventful hour before there was any activity. At least I'd remembered to bring something to eat with my reheated coffee.

As I unwrapped the banana bread Liam had brought over the night before, I nearly missed seeing Geoffrey at the door. I switched on the camcorder and recorded the brief kiss he gave Marc Romano. Marc stumbled down the steps and walked blindly by my van toward his car. Geoffrey's expression was unreadable, shadowed by the doorway. He shut the door after a few seconds.

Marc looked back toward the house at the sound of the closing door and nearly tripped over an uneven spot on the sidewalk. I could see the gleam of tears on his cheeks, and when he got to his car he sat for several minutes, shoulders heaving, his head down and arms crossed over the steering wheel. His windshield wipers were on, wiping off the heavy accumulation of dew. He must have been parked there for some hours. An attempted reconciliation? If so, it had been a failure. My heart went out to Marc, regardless of my dislike and distrust of Geoffrey.

Marc finally drove away, and for another half hour nothing happened. Then Joe Leslie's van pulled up.

Again I turned on the camcorder, and ended up with footage of Joe leaving again a few minutes later, looking grim as he screeched off. I hesitated too long about whether to follow Joe or wait for Geoffrey, and got Geoffrey by default.

We repeated the previous day's journey. I bailed when we reached City Hall and went home to take an indulgent shower. Medicinal purposes, I told my conservationist conscience—everybody knows steam is good for a cold. While I lathered with my favorite bath gel, I mulled over how long to keep up the surveillance of Geoffrey. That eight o'clock appointment could be for sometime next month. Or he might have made a phone call and rescheduled. I decided it was worth one more morning.

All my probable activities for the day called for casual clothes, so I put on my favorite outfit: black jeans I've had so long that they've molded to my body, a turquoise and magenta cotton sweater, suede boots and turquoise earrings that my first girlfriend gave me. Wearing these clothes, I feel powerful and sexy. I'd wrap up this damned case and meet a woman who'd do me right, and then it would be time for lunch.

Since I was meeting Mavis Baker for breakfast at nine-thirty, there was no point in going to the office first. I rifled through the Pride Club materials Lynnette had brought me for pictures of the Pride leadership. Maybe Ricardo's great grandmother or Tía Dolores would recognize one of them.

A check of my messages yielded one potential new client, one check-is-in-the-mail call from the former client who'd promised me payment the prior Saturday, and Ricardo, saying he had to take one of his cousins to the doctor and would be late getting in.

My appointment with Mavis was at an outdoor cafe in the Castro District better known for the hunkiness of its waiters than for the quality of its food—Mavis' choice. As I waited for her to arrive, I tried to guess what made her pick this place. When she came in, ten minutes late, I got my answer. This was her hangout. Nearly everyone in the place knew her. She greeted waiters and customers by name, and paused to talk at several of the tables.

Today she was wearing a shapeless brown pantsuit with a green blouse and an ugly man's necktie. As I watched her work the room, I decided that her frumpy style of dress must serve as a kind of camouflage, to make unwary property buyers underestimate her.

By the time she heaved herself into a chair at the table where I was sitting, I was working on my second cup of watery coffee and an unripe cantaloupe. Without a word to me, she ordered from the waiter who had materialized at her elbow. When he left, she gave me a steely look over the rim of her cup and said, "I know what you're up to."

With the investigation? With Jolie? With thinking Miranda's death wasn't a random bashing? I tried to look innocent and bland.

"What do you mean?" My sangfroid was somewhat undermined by my voice's sudden dips into Lauren Bacall-after-a-pack-of-Camel unfiltereds.

"I know you're not a writer, you're an investigator. I know you're taking money that the Pride Club hasn't got to waste on this kind of nonsense." Her breakfast arrived and she stabbed a sausage. "Lynnette and her gang are paying you to spread dirt on Geoffrey Lawrence and me and everybody else who worked with him. That's some of the things I know." There was tremendous venom in her voice, and she held her fork like a weapon.

"Where'd you hear all this?" I used every bit of coolness Jack Windsor had taught me to keep my breathing even and easy, my hands steady as I brought my coffee cup to my mouth.

"From blabbermouth Lynnette herself, of course," she answered with a smile. Mavis was thoroughly enjoying this. "That woman can't keep her mouth shut about anything. She told me you had stuff on Geoffrey that was gonna blow him right out of a job. So, let's hear what you've got." Thanks again, Lynnette.

"I have to maintain the confidentiality of my sources. I can't tell you anything one way or the other, Mavis. But if you think I'm not getting at the truth, maybe you'd like to tell me how things have gone down at the Pride Club. I'm pretty open minded."

"Not open minded enough for our Jolie, I guess." She leered at me as she brought a forkful of eggs into her mouth. "She came by to get some comfort the other night. Told me you couldn't take the heat."

Watching Mavis stuff masses of food into her mouth at the same time she spewed innuendo was just too much. I was close to rising to her bait.

"Mavis, my private life is very private. I will not talk to you about Jolie. If you want to give me your side of the Pride Club, I'm waiting. Otherwise, I'm out of here." Then I gave her that hard-boiled look that Jack had made me practice in the mirror.

"All right, Ms. Private Eye, what do you want to know?"

"What is it that Geoffrey Lawrence has over everybody? Did he loot the Pride Club and lose the election on purpose? And, if he did, who helped him?"

"That all?"

"It would do for a start," I said, and gulped some more coffee.

"Don't want much, do you?"

"Being forced to sit here and watch you eat should be worth something."

She guffawed and choked on her toast. "And to think, Jolie said you were a wimp! But then she never was much of a judge of character. Screwed-up wench." She drank deeply of her orange juice, then set the glass down sharply. "Seems like you're fixated on Geoffrey. Why is that?"

"He was the president of Pride, and he stood to gain from all the double-dealing I've discovered so far. He got out of the club and into a cushy job one step ahead of the auditors. Nothing I've heard makes me believe he'd draw the line at arson, phone threats, break-ins, maybe not even murder."

"Being a slime-ball doesn't make a man a crook, though it does help his political career."

"If Geoffrey isn't behind all this, who is?"

She stared at me hard and spoke slowly, as if to a small child, "Well, Maggie, for reasons I can't explain, I like you. So here goes. There are people whose business has included dealings with Pride, but Pride is nothing to them. If there was a chance that Pride might cause them even a little trouble, Pride might have to stop existing. Is that clear enough for you?"

"What are you, the Oracle of Delphi? That didn't tell me anything."

"I'm trying to tell you that there is no point in your pursuing this, that more people will get hurt. You're letting your personal likes and dislikes steer you in the wrong direction. But you're better off just fucking up and wasting the club's money than if you were on the right track. Take it from me, sometimes it's better to be incompetent, if you know what I mean. Take the check Lynnette gave you and move on to one of your nice surveillance gigs."

"End of story? You're saying there's nothing anyone can do about this?"

"What one can do is turn one's attention to other things," she mimicked me with an accuracy I would have admired in someone else. "I was around before the Pride Club and all the other play-at-politics gay groups. And the reason they all have to deal with me is that I take the long view. I live in the real world and I would have expected somebody in your line of work to have the same philosophy. There are some things we just can't afford to see, even if they're there."

"A woman died last night, and I think it's because she got too close to something very real. I find myself wondering how much you might know about it. Are you taking the long view about that, too?"

"You honestly don't know how much trouble you're courting, do you? Suppose you go on smearing the Pride leadership, embarrass the Mayor by stirring up shit about his liaison to the gay community, and make the club members look like a bunch of dupes. Imagine what the papers would do with that! Do you think you'll come out of it looking good? Any future you have depends on the good will of the community. You think about that, Ms. Thing. Of course, if you drop this digging around, it's possible that the community might be grateful to you." She gave me that reptile smile and put a whole slice of toast in her mouth.

I waited while she chewed, carefully maintaining eye contact.

"So, what's your answer?" She was losing her temper. A small victory for my team.

"I'm waiting to hear more about what you, or whoever it is that you represent, would do for me if I bag this whole thing?"

"I'm not stupid." She threw down her napkin. "For all I know you're recording this whole conversation. Let's leave it like this—we'll be watching what you do and we'll act accordingly. I'll give your regards to Jolie." She smirked evilly and was gone, leaving me with the check.

As I finished my coffee I replayed the conversation in my mind. Mavis had implied that I was letting my loathing of Geoffrey get in the way. She'd said I was on the wrong track pursuing Geoffrey, but that it was safer for me that way. If she was messing with my mind on Geoffrey's behalf, I could ignore her observation. But why would she shield Geoffrey? From everything I'd heard, he hadn't stood up for her in the past—quite the contrary. The rumor about Mavis being removed as treasurer for ineptitude and/or theft must have originated with him. If Jolie knew about the "lies spread by the men in Pride" about Mavis, surely Mavis would know about it, too.

But what if Mavis was as independent as she said she was? That would give her warning a very different twist. Who were these people "whose business had included dealings with Pride," but wouldn't hesitate to destroy it, if not Geoffrey, Joe Leslie and Mavis herself?

Jolie could have told me much of what I needed to know about Mavis. The first night we were together I thought that there was all the time in the world, that I could resume being a P.I. at a tactful time. Then came the baffling scene at her apartment Monday night. Unless she approached me, it was doubtful that there would ever be a right time to talk to Jolie again.

Chapter Twenty-Three

I called the hospital to see if Larry Gross was up to seeing me. He was eager to talk and asked me to bring him a coffee milkshake from Double Rainbow. Several other visitors were with Larry when I arrived, and I waited in the hallway while they said their good-byes. Near the door was a dresser covered with boxes of candy, flowers and cards. Propped among them was a teddy bear dressed in a tutu holding a picture of Larry, handsome and buffed, as a Gay Games silver medalist in swimming. Larry called my name and I approached the wraith-like man on the bed.

"Somebody finally came through with an honest to God milkshake! You guys—lose the daisies and bring me mocha fudge next time," he called as a parting shot at the last two visitors, with a shadow of the dazzling smile in his Gay Games photo. He turned to me. "Hi Maggie. Thanks. They try to fool you into drinking the petroleum byproducts they serve here by calling them milkshakes. Somebody oughta sue! Nobody can beat Double Rainbow. Have a seat."

"Larry, I don't want to wear you out. Let me know if you get too tired—"

"Don't worry about it—I don't. Besides, I'm on a roll today. It's always the worst at night."

"I need to know what you meant about Miranda knowing the people who killed her."

"Like I told you, Miranda called me last night. I was pretty out of it, so I only remember she was scared. She said somebody had called and told her your meeting place had changed to a street corner. While she was on her way there, she saw somebody following her and she freaked. I told her to try calling you at the bar. I guess she never reached you?"

"No" was all I could manage. I willed myself not to cry. The feeling that somehow I could have prevented her murder came back, even stronger than the night before. "Who called to tell her that the meeting place had changed?"

"I don't know. When she couldn't get to the place where she'd been told you'd meet her, she called me."

"How much do you know about all this?"

"She came to see me a couple of days ago. Said she found something that belonged to the old treasurer. . . ." Frustration crossed his face as he struggled to remember the name.

"Joe Leslie?"

"Yeah. Leslie was sloppy. He must not have seen the writing on the wall before the election, 'cause he was totally unprepared to turn everything over to Miranda. Poor guy had to torch his own place to cover it up!" He took a deep breath that turned into a coughing fit. I handed him a plastic cup/straw combo with tepid water in it.

"Thanks. She told me . . . found something Leslie left in his records. Did she tell you about it?"

"Yes. Can you tell me what you know about it?"

He reached under his pillow, his gritted teeth revealing the pain that every movement cost him. He brought out a letter-sized envelope.

"This has the list, plus her notes inside. It's people that

Geoffrey and his crowd gave money to and got money from, and for what." Even whispering had become a visible effort. Larry's thin chest heaved.

"Did Miranda tell you it was about Geoffrey?"

"Didn't have to. Nobody else could know that much. Or if they did, Geoffrey'd know it, too."

"Sounds as if you like Geoffrey about as much as I do. But I still don't get it. Why would anyone put that kind of thing in writing?"

"Probably Geoffrey . . . just made notes to jog his memory. But Joe ended up with it. You ever meet Joe Leslie?" I nodded. "So you know—he's no rocket scientist. Thinks Geoffrey is Jesus Christ come again, too. Probably figured if it was Geoff's, he ought to keep it. Losing the election surprised 'em. Didn't have time to clean everything up."

The stress of talking about this couldn't be good for Larry. I was torn between wanting to let him rest and knowing that he was the only one I could talk to about the list now that Miranda was dead.

"Would you like to rest a bit before we talk any more? I could come back." He shook his head vehemently and I continued.

"Even if some officials' initials are on the list, so what? It doesn't prove anything."

"If different people's initials together make . . . pattern, give leads to other deals."

"Did Miranda tell you any of the names or what the payments were for?"

"She said she thought . . . slate card endorsements of candidates, proposition campaigns."

"She told me it was in code. Do you know how she managed to work it out?"

"No. Wait! . . . Said—once she found out, the main guy was totally obvious. She didn't say who, but I figure—had to be Geoffrey."

"When Miranda talked to you last night, did she say who was following her?"

Larry's contorted features showed his anguish. "I don't think so, but like I said, I was pretty out of it last night. I thought my lover Ben came to see me, and he's been dead for two years."

"Larry, does anyone else know about her coming here and giving you the list?"

"No, she was really paranoid about it."

"Good. Because if you're right and they killed Miranda over this list, they could come after you too."

"I'm petrified! Like when . . . say smoking's gonna give me lung cancer! Good luck, you're the one who needs to look out. Once those people taste power . . . like vampires. Always gotta have more. Keep in touch, all right? Thanks for . . . milkshake." He shut his eyes.

Chapter Twenty-Four

Back in the office with twenty minutes before Lynnette was due, I examined the day's mail. Only bills today. No prizes, but no threats either. Maybe my anonymous correspondents were no longer nervous about what I might discover, since they had no way of knowing that I had the list.

I called Sergeant Hoffman of the azure eyes and Detective Desmond. Neither was in, so I left messages on their respective voicemail numbers about Miranda's list. Maybe one of them would be interested in Larry's revelations about what had happened the night before.

My voice was changing again, from Lauren Bacall to Froggie the Gremlin. If I called my doctor's office they'd tell me to come in, and then they'd prescribe bed rest and no talking. None of this was possible. I took another vitamin C, this time with echinacea, Jessie's miracle herb of the month. Its main advantage is that it doesn't taste as bad as her second-favorite, goldenseal.

Ricardo came in reeking of cigarette smoke, a sign that he'd spent his lunch hour riding around in his friend Ludo's car, smoking and playing the stereo at maximum volume.

"Boss, I got zip out of those phone calls, and I must've talked to every García in San Francisco. None of them even knew what a canvass was. And nobody's ever heard of your printer guy, Kyle Winter, either."

"I'm not surprised, but we had to check. How about your, uh— other work?"

"Ludo and me—Ludo and I got into that guy Geoffrey's accounts. He doesn't have much in his checking accounts, and he really tears through it. End of the pay period, there's nothing left. He's got a savings account, and every month there's one deposit, some kind of trust fund. He takes money out of it sometimes, but he never puts anything in. There wasn't any pattern of cash deposits like you said to look for."

"Great work, kid. Do you have a printout of this, or did you just get access to read it?"

"We didn't get, you know, an official approval to look at it," he said proudly. "But if you need me to look for something special, I can always get into it again."

"I'll let you know." I hadn't seriously expected to find records of Geoffrey socking wads of cash into the bank. Still, as Jack always insisted, people often thought they were too brilliant to be caught, and took stupid risks. Besides, breaking into Geoffrey's accounts had given Ricardo so much enjoyment.

I pulled out the envelope Larry had given me. Inside were the list that I believed led to Miranda's death and two pages of her notes interpreting its contents. The dates on the list were easily identifiable, but everything else was open to speculation. The letters were probably initials, as Miranda thought, and the corresponding columns could be amounts of money, but some contained four- and five-digit figures, unrealistically high to be funds given or received by a local gay political organization. They could as easily be winning Lottery combinations, for all I could tell.

I didn't see the evidence making Geoffrey the arch-villain that Larry had talked about. I suspected that his case of anti-Geoffrey Lawrence bias was even worse than mine.

The two pages that contained Miranda's notes were plainly intended for her use only. There were totaled columns of figures interspersed with brief notes ("KPH for 11/94? BWA says only 500—really 10K").

I showed the list and Miranda's notes to Ricardo and asked him to have a go at them. His face lit up at the prospect of doing "real detective work" for a change. I also gave him the pictures from Pride archives to show his family. He went down the hall to the dentist's office to make copies. The blond hygienist must not have been on duty, because he returned immediately.

After warning Ricardo not to tell anyone about the list and to keep the original safe, I sent him off to Judy Willis' Tenderloin apartment with all the financial information we had gathered. Judy is an ex-con ex-CPA I use whenever an unofficial expert is good enough for a job. She mostly gets work doing data entry these days, so I like being able to give her a project where she can use her skills. She had promised to get back to me with her findings the next day.

Lynnette stormed into the office and threw herself into a chair across from my desk. While she was making a critical commentary on my office decor, I slipped Miranda's notes into a drawer. Lynnette's personal decor was mesmerizing. Her entire ensemble, except for yellow Birkenstocks and African textile bag, was or had been black: old San Francisco Mime Troupe t-shirt, leggings, motorcycle jacket. Was this her interpretation of a "mourning" look? She had been talking for awhile before I dragged my attention from her outfit.

"You've got to give me something to tell the Executive

Committee tonight. Betty, Miguel, Warren and Tom have been talking and they're going to put stopping the investigation to a vote. And I can tell they've been working on David, the wuss. They've got him afraid that it'll be the current leadership (in other words, him) that will end up in trouble if this all breaks open. I know that Betty's pushing hard to drop it. She says it's because we need to focus on fighting the cuts in AIDS services, but I think it's because she's scared, too. She just won't admit it. So what can you give me?"

There were a few choice words I had to say before I could act like Lynnette's contracted employee. "This morning Mavis informed me that she knew about Miranda finding something that incriminates Geoffrey, and that the Executive Committee had hired me—because you told her! One of the people you said couldn't be trusted! Who else have you talked to, Geoffrey, Joe Leslie?"

She drew up herself up and clenched her jaw. "It's my business who I talk to about this. Remember, we are employing you, not the other way around." Having put me in my place, she subsided and looked rather embarrassed.

"Anyway, Mavis makes me so mad! She always acts like she knows everything, and usually she does know more than anybody else. She buddies up to people and they tell her things they shouldn't. Sometimes I forget what I've told her, and she's been around in leadership so long, that well, I told her about why we hired you. Then, of course, to make me look bad, Mavis had to show you that she knows. She called up Betty, too! Betty ragged on me for half an hour about talking to Mavis."

"You do understand that both Betty and I might be upset at you blabbing to someone who may be part of the lying, stealing and God knows what else, don't you?"

"Don't patronize me, Maggie! You and Betty don't know Mavis the way I do. She'll always end up on the winning side. She was a conservative closet case until it got profitable to be out and progressive. If the old Pride officers are shot down in flames, she won't go near them."

"Lynnette, you are still running around gossiping, treating this like the club's endorsement for school board! Miranda was murdered last night! My house was broken into, and my office was trashed. They're all connected. Whoever is behind it has already killed once. For all we know, they may be planning to kill someone else! When are you going to understand it's not a game?" I was yelling by the time I finished. Since I couldn't strangle her, maybe I could shake her out of her complacency.

Ricardo, back from his errand and alarmed by the uproar, peeked around the door and retreated quickly when he saw that no blood was being shed.

"I know it's not a game. That's why you have to tell me what you've got for tonight's meeting. If we can't give them something solid, they're going to chicken out."

"From what I've been able to trace, it looks like the Pride canvass only existed on paper, and Pride's printer operated out of a commercial mail box. Both have disappeared now. So far it looks like flat-out embezzlement. Miranda had found a coded list in Joe Leslie's treasurer papers. She told me she'd worked out part of the code, and it involved some big names. She was going to meet me at Zorya's last night, but somehow she got diverted to another place. Then she was murdered a few blocks from my house."

"Is that all? I knew most of that already. You know, I went to bat for you with David and Betty and Warren—"

"Do you think you could convince them to keep me on

the case through Friday? At that point I'll give you a full report on everything I've managed to find out. Establishing an ending point for the investigation might satisfy some of their objections. If it'll help, I'll even come meet with the Committee tonight."

"That's a good idea. Maybe you can persuade them."

"Fine, I'll be there. Now tell me anything else you already know that would help me get there faster than finding it out on my own."

"Like what?"

"Let's start with Mavis. Why did she resign as treasurer? She's got to be competent to survive in real estate in a recession. But she let Geoffrey put it out that poor, dumb, overwhelmed Mavis couldn't keep up with the demands of being the treasurer."

"Well, there's a lot of stories," Lynnette began, almost purring with pleasure. Mean-spirited gossip was her favorite hobby. "Somebody told Stephen Leong that when Mavis found out there were accounts she didn't even know about, she quit. Geoffrey told me (this was in confidence, so don't tell him I told you) he had to set up the major donations to bypass Mavis completely, because she was skimming off the top to save her real estate business. He said he'd had to open new accounts, with new authorized signers, because he didn't want to confront her about the thefts."

"Lynnette! Why the hell didn't you tell me this before?"

"It's all gossip! I thought you only wanted facts." She took a sip of her coffee, prolonging her triumph.

"What else?"

"Your very good friend Jolie, before she broke up with Mavis, was telling anybody who'd listen that Mavis had been getting death threats telling her to quit as treasurer and keep her mouth shut. I don't think anybody believed her. Consider the source. There's always lots of rumors about Mavis. I think she starts half of 'em herself."

"Do you believe any of these stories?"

"My dear, I believe all of them!" She did a poor drag queen pose. "But why all the sudden interest in Mavis?"

"I've begun to think that Mavis might be as important in this investigation as my original prime suspects, Geoffrey and Joe."

"Not because she used to be an item with Jolie?"

"No, but while we're on the subject, what about Jolie?"

"Mmmm, I'd think you would know more about Jolie than I would. Mavis told me you'd been her latest. I didn't think you went in for weird scenes. Does Kristin know? Did you get any of that primo coke I hear Jolie's started to do again?" This was Lynnette's chance at payback for my yelling at her earlier, and she was savoring it.

"You'll just have to rely on your imagination about what we did together, Lynnette. Does Jolie still have any links to Geoffrey—or anybody in the current Pride leadership?"

"Nobody in their right mind would count on Jolie doing what they want her to. She's rich, she's an addict and she's nuts!"

"How about Marc? When I interviewed him, he practically ran away from me when I started talking about club finances. Why would he be so scared if he got out?"

"Maybe he's afraid of going to jail, or having his name smeared in the papers. He's got a good job now. Even after he left the club, if there was scamming with the money while he was treasurer, he'd still be in trouble up to his ears."

"Let's try a different angle. Of the current active membership in Pride, who besides Mavis, Geoffrey and you are leftovers from the old days?"

"Ugh, what a way with words! But I guess I see what you mean. David Lindley, Mr. Touchy-feely, has been around for-years. Tom Ng was a founder of the club. His parents are long-time Democratic Party regulars. His mother is Mary Ng, you know, the head of the County Central Committee? Warren Coleman's been around forever, too. Somehow, when the Diversity Slate got put together, all three of those guys managed to cross over from Geoffrey to Betty."

"How about David?"

"God, I wish you could get something on him! He's got lots of money, and he uses it to get influence. He's a sponsor for every event, too, so he'll automatically get invited to things and people will have to be nice to him. Then he drives everybody crazy. He's been in therapy since he was two, and he has feelings about everything that he absolutely has to share with everyone for the sake of his recovery."

"Recovery from what?"

"Who knows—Pissant Personality Disorder? Why are you asking me all these questions about this Executive Committee? What difference does it make? We want to know about the past leadership!"

"Someone from the current Executive Committee has been leaking your decisions to people who'd be exposed in an investigation. The threats to me started before I'd so much as opened a folder on the case! Whoever killed Miranda knew when she and I were going to meet. She told Larry that someone she knew called and told her I was changing the meeting place. How else could you explain all this other than a leak?"

Lynnette poked at a hole in her sock, fiddled with a stray lock of hair and chewed off a hangnail before speaking. "So what do you want to know?"

"I want to know who the leak might be."

"Nobody if they like living! Betty wants to stop the investigation, but if she found out anyone on the Committee was breaking confidentiality, they'd be better off dead. She's not somebody you cross."

"But all the same, someone *is* breaking confidentiality, Lynnette."

"Honestly, Maggie, I thought that was what we hired you for. I don't want to have to sit in every Executive Committee meeting looking at people and thinking, 'Is it you?' Come meet them yourself! Speaking of confidentiality, I heard Morris Drake got fired for printing rumors about us and not telling his boss who his sources were."

"Right, Lynnette, I'm the one who told you, remember?"

"Oh! Yeah, I guess that's right. Well, the new dish is, he's disappeared! Packed up all his stuff and left without saying good-bye to anybody. I guess he must have been too embarrassed to stick around."

"Or too scared."

"Scared? What would he be scared of?"

"Never mind." Why had I expected anything to come from this discussion? "Thanks for coming over, Lynnette. What time should I show up at the meeting?"

"You're not that far away from my place. I'll call you when we're ready for you. It might be late—we once had a seven-hour meeting. And that wasn't nearly as important as this."

Chapter Twenty-Five

With the tromp of Lynnette's departing sandals down the hall still audible (she is the only one I know who can make a racket in Birkenstocks), I leaned against the door and reminded myself to breathe. I hadn't told Lynnette I had the list that Miranda left with Larry Gross, let alone shown it to her. Lynnette represented Pride as my employer, but loyalty to Miranda and Larry kept me from turning it over to her. I had no faith in her judgment or discretion, and I was certain that at least one member of the Executive Committee was implicated in some way in Miranda's death.

All right, we've heard from the left-wing conscience. Equal time for the wannabe hard-headed businesswoman: Where did I get off, withholding information about the list to the people who were paying me? Miranda was dead and Larry was no longer an officer of the Pride Club. This was highly unprofessional. I was acting as if I were the client, and the old saw, "a man who represents himself in court has a fool for a lawyer," goes double for private investigators.

The phone interrupted my soul searching. Ricardo was on the other line, so I picked up. It was Larry. "Just got a call from Miranda's neighbor. Somebody broke into her place . . . turned it upside down. Be careful." I started to thank him, but he'd hung up.

Ricardo's knock made me jump. "Maggie, it's the pig—cop," he said in a stage-whisper. He probably hadn't bothered to cover the receiver, either, the macho turkey. First Lynnette, now Detective Desmond. Who next? I took a deep breath and picked up the phone.

"Tell me why you think there's a connection between your break-ins and the Post girl getting killed." He managed to convey boredom and condescension as well over the phone as he had in the flesh in my office.

I gave him the bare bones of the case, ending with the list Miranda had found, her interpretation of it, her appointment with me Tuesday night, her murder in my neighborhood, Larry giving me the list and my interview with Sergeant Hoffman.

"So now you've got this list, but you don't actually know what it means—if it's anything other than somebody's shopping list."

"Not yet. But Miranda told her friend Larry—"

"And her friend told you, right? And you want the Homicide Unit not to look for the guys that've been beating up homosexuals for months now, no, they should find these special guys who only go after you and your friends. This is not the kind of material we can do much with, Ms. Garrett. I can understand that you're wrapped up in this case. But it looks to me like the Post girl got attacked by your basic homophobe types."

"How can you be so sure it was the same men?"

"Look, I'm not supposed to let this out, but there's a pattern here. We've got witnesses that heard what the perpetrators hollered while they were beating the victim. These perps yell out the same things every time they wail on some fag—excuse me, no offense. We got a psychiatrist consultant on the case, and he says it's like a ritual with them. That's how we're sure it's the same guys. The Mayor himself said it was part of all the 'gay bashing' your people have been complaining about."

"Right before you called, I heard that someone broke into Miranda's apartment. Doesn't that bear out what I'm saying, that she had something important enough for someone to kill her and then tear her place apart?"

"Or maybe that some junkie reads the newspapers and sees a chance to clean out her place, knowing the girl isn't gonna come home and interrupt him." An angry noise forced itself from the back of my throat. In response, he sighed wearily. "All right. We'll look into it, Ms. Garrett, I'm not saying we won't. Just don't expect everything to fit together as tidy as you might like. Good-bye." He clicked off.

Finally I was able to settle in with Miranda's notes. Some of the initials matched those on the list, but many did not. The initials LRT, PCI and HHM appeared frequently, sometimes followed by exclamation marks or framed by doodles, as if Miranda had been especially interested in them. Geoffrey's initials were not on the list, but in her notes Miranda had drawn lines connecting many of the items with his name. None of the initials of current Executive Committee members were on the list. After an hour I decided to give it a rest.

On the way home I stopped at the 24th Street Spinelli's for coffee. There was a queue as usual. The people around me were talking about normal, wonderfully mundane issues: new relationships, broken plumbing, whether the latest Almodóvar movie was worse than the one before. The stress of the past twenty-four hours, combined with accelerating flu symptoms, made me feel like a member of the Undead, shroud wrappings clinging to me.

I ordered my usual Viennese blend, beans for home and ground for the office, and a corn muffin, and watched my triple-strength free cup being poured by the sulky, multiply-pierced baby butch behind the counter. She addressed me as "Ma'am" when she asked if I wanted a bag for the muffin, which made me feel old as well as morbid. Nobody except cops and the child laborers at McDonald's had ever called me Ma'am. Was it my clothes? Was it an early sign of aging? I resisted the urge to ask her what exactly had put me in the "Ma'am" category, and ate my muffin, tossing back another vitamin C for good measure.

The coffee and complex carbohydrates made a good dent on my funk. However, a quick check of the week's local lesbian/gay press brought it back. All the papers had made last-minute front page changes to carry headlines about Miranda's death, and two featured a black-bordered photo of Miranda. The most conservative of the rags supported Mayor Rawlings, while the rest attacked him for doing too little, too late. There were only two references to last week's gossip about Pride Club funds: the first was an editorial by Morris Drake's replacement at the *SNEWS*, which made critical mention of Drake's piece on the Pride Club in its near beatification of Miranda as a model activist in a fine club; another paper's "think-piece" used Pride to illustrate the need to focus our energy on legislation and political pressure to attain justice. The writer encouraged readers to support the club regardless of mistakes made in the past.

What to do now? I couldn't just keep batting away at this by myself, but the people who could be most helpful were the ones who also had reason to avoid the issue. Marc Romano knew something, maybe everything. He had refused to help, but that was before Miranda's murder. Maybe I could appeal to his conscience? Lynnette was unwilling to get any closer than financing my involvement, and her only activity consisted of badgering me for results. Anyway, I didn't think she knew anything more than she had told me. Whatever Betty might know, I was unlikely to hear about it.

There were the three musketeers who had barged into my house and demanded I stop the investigation: Tom Ng, Warren Coleman and Miguel Alvarez. Their interactions had the stiffness of members of a temporary alliance. I doubted that they would normally find common cause. Could I drive a wedge in there?

Mavis said she was steering me away from looking in Geoffrey's direction—for that matter, away from the investigation altogether—for my own good. Mavis was still active in Pride, in spite of her contemptuous attitude toward the current leadership, and she must have maintained allies among those who remained from Geoffrey's regime.

Then there was Jolie. I believed that she had taken Fearless, but why? And why return her unharmed? It hadn't served any purpose except to work my nerves. Of course, Jolie's world didn't exactly turn on a rational axis. Could her demand that I come to her on Monday night have been part of a plan to keep me away from my house while it was searched? If she'd wanted me to stay, she could have seduced me instead of slapping me—again assuming that her actions were thought through. Jolie had gone directly to Mavis after our exchange at her apartment. Was it to report to Mavis on what she had asked Jolie to do, or to try to re-establish their bizarre relationship?

The police weren't interested. The immediate question was whether the bad guys still were. Whoever tossed Miranda's apartment must have been looking for the list. Maybe they'd assume that if they couldn't find it, it couldn't be found, and drop their guard. Maybe they didn't care, now that Miranda was dead.

Sometimes when I'm completely stuck I have conversations in my head with my late mentor Jack. It gives me a perspective on what a real P.I. should do. I knew that Jack's reaction to my recent activities would be scathing criticism of my subjective over-involvement in the case. "Leave it to the cops. If you want to change society, change your occupation. It ain't gonna happen in this job." Oh well, listening to what I imagine he would advise doesn't mean I follow that advice. It never had, why change now?

But it was clear to me now that I had to show the list to the Executive Committee. Not the original, and not even Miranda's notes, but enough to make them see that there were genuine grounds for fighting back, and even winning. It was time to tell all, or close to all.

Chapter Twenty-Six

At nine o'clock Lynnette called. The Executive Committee members were taking a break until 9:30, and they wanted me to be there when they reconvened. Lynnette's apartment was only seven blocks away, although the route was almost vertically uphill. It made more sense to walk, since trying to park in her neighborhood was pointless, and I persuaded her to let me bring Loba for protection.

We set off at 9:10. Loba was recovering quickly from her injuries, and we'd have plenty of time for a long walk. She pulled me along at a brisk trot. The fog had socked in, and it was cold. Pedestrians wouldn't be tempted to stray out. Traffic was sparse here, too. The streets in Lynnette's neighborhood form a confusing maze, intersecting at strange angles, sometimes simply ending in a cul-de-sac, to accommodate the hilly terrain. This means no through-traffic. It seemed like miles between street lights.

I dragged myself out of the semi-oblivion that comes over me when I'm trying to tie together apparently unrelated strands of an investigation. The Pride Club Executive Committee was sure to provide enough new strands to keep me up all night. Why bother with the ones flapping about now, when so many more were on the way?

We were in the cross-walk of a street with a burnt-out light when I heard the roar of a powerful engine. A car was hurtling toward us. Loba and I leaped as one and landed in a tangle on the sidewalk. I hauled myself up quickly and shook myself. Nothing broken, and Loba was moving without a limp. Halfway up the street the car, a big old American model, was turning around in a driveway.

They were getting ready to come at us again. I tried to scream for help. Only a squeak came out.

"Hey, Loba," I whispered, "come on." She growled, the hair on her back rising. I could feel my own neck hairs standing on end. I yanked on her lead, but she resisted. She wanted to go after them! I had to throw my full weight into moving her. Then she changed her mind and bolted, pulling me along the sidewalk.

I looked over my shoulder. The car was following us, its headlights off. I slowed our pace slightly, and let the car get closer. Then I spun around and hissed "Let's go!" We tore past the car in the opposite direction. It would take our pursuers a couple of minutes to follow suit.

When we reached the next corner, I stopped to look back. They were nowhere in sight. We were only three blocks from Lynnette's, but it might as well have been miles. I wished for a phone booth, for a passing cop car, for the .38 stashed in my office. Our best chance was heading toward the closest busy street. That meant running up one of the steepest hills in the City, and in the opposite direction from Lynnette's. We took off, Loba still tugging at the leash. I turned at the sound of an engine. It was the same car, a hefty Nova, and it was aimed at us. We tumbled off the sidewalk and rolled behind an ornamental rock formation in front of a high stone wall.

The car careened onto the sidewalk, brakes squealing. Two

figures in jumpsuits and ski masks climbed out. The absence of features made them even more menacing. From the way they walked I guessed both were men. One carried a wrecking bar. The other reached for something bulging at his belt. His partner gave him a swat and gestured toward the back of the car. The second man cursed but reached into the car for a baseball bat.

You're supposed to yell "fire." I tried, but only a soft, anguished cry came out. Who was around to hear me, anyway?

They advanced toward us cautiously, about ten feet apart. Loba growled louder and strained toward them, nearly pulling me off balance.

Half a block away I could see a wooden stairway that zigzagged its way to the top of the hill. I gave a sharp tug on Loba's leash, and we raced past the men toward the stairs. I caught a glancing blow to my shoulder from the bat as we dashed by. The force of the hit threw me off balance, and I staggered. They were almost on us. Loba barked and the taut leash helped me stay upright.

We reached the wooden stairs and started scrambling upward, the two men still close behind. The steps ascended sharply to the top of the cliff, with a landing every twenty steps or so. The pounding of our followers' feet on the wooden steps echoed in my ears. Overhanging branches caught at my clothes and hair. My whole existence became the stairway, Loba's panting breath, the feet approaching from below.

Then the pounding ceased. I paused at a landing, with Loba a few steps above me, to look back. Had the men gone back down or were they just waiting for a moment, listening like us? If they were coming up, it was with super-stealth. Loba snorted in confusion, then gave an impatient jerk to the leash. We took off again, up the last few dozen steps to the top. I looked down into the darkness. No movement, no footsteps. They must have gone back to get the car.

The stairway gave out onto cement walk. I leaned on its railing and got my breath. The street in front of us curved along the ridge of the hill, with houses and apartment buildings on one side, and a steep drop on the side we had just climbed. Few windows were lighted in the houses. Had everybody gone out tonight? I thought of Miranda dying alone in the dark, then pushed it from my mind.

A few houses down was an apartment building with a spacious entryway. I pushed every buzzer. No response. I tried them all again. Nothing. Maybe if I made a racket, threw bricks, or a rock. But there was nothing to throw. This was a pristinely maintained neighborhood. The concrete planter weighed more than I did.

A station wagon with a bunch of kids in it traveled slowly around the curve of the street. I dashed into the street waving at the driver, who gave me a terrified glance and hit the gas pedal. What driver would stop these days, given the fear bred by car-jackings? Maybe he'd call the cops.

The next building over had a buzzer/intercom. Maybe tenants would be more likely to answer a buzzer if they didn't have to leave the safety of their apartments or risk letting in robbers. I pulled Loba to it and we moved behind a column, where we would be partially hidden. To get to the intercom I had to move into the brightly lit area in plain sight of the sidewalk and the street. With the passing of every minute it became harder to step out, to leave the relative safety of staying semi-concealed. Every noise was threatening. Loba's anxious eyes followed my every move. We were both shaking uncontrollably. But I was afraid that the men from the car might be going house to house on foot. If we stayed here and did nothing, they'd eventually find us.

I sprinted the twenty feet to the building lobby and pushed all the buzzers. Nothing happened. I buzzed again. A squawk came out of the intercom. I put my mouth to the microphone and rasped, "Please, help. Call . . . police!"

"What?" a man's voice came over the microphone. "It's nobody. Just those damn kids again." He was talking to someone else in his flat. I didn't know which flat had answered, so I rang all the buzzers again. Silence.

I withdrew into the shadows. Still no sign of the car. Where were they? There was no doubt in my mind that the men in the car would keep looking until they found us.

The other houses on the block were all single-family residences, each with multiple steps leading to its entrance. I tied Loba's leash to a metal fixture on the building, where she would be out of sight. "Stay!" I hissed, using all the authority I could muster. She gave a short bark of protest. Maybe she'd make enough racket to bring the people in the building down to investigate, instead of leading the men in the car to her.

After two long flights of stairs to two empty houses, I was thoroughly winded. I'd reached the doorstep of the third house when I heard that now-familiar rumble. I looked down and saw the Nova tearing around the sharp curve of the street. Loba stood in the street, baying, her teeth drawn back. I grabbed a large rock from the border of a flower bed and ran back down the steps in their direction. I heard two gunshots and prayed that they missed.

As I rounded a curve, a tree obstructed my view. There was a piercing screech of tires and a crunch of metal against rock. I scrambled to get an unobstructed view, and saw the Nova teetering on the fulcrum formed by a stone wall that bordered the street. One of the men from the car, pistol grasped clumsily in both hands, was trying to get a bead on Loba. She was barking furiously, and looked about to spring.

As I arrived on the street, three women armed with what looked like large sticks came running toward us.

"What the hell's going on?" demanded a huge woman in pink flower-sprigged pajamas and a headwrap. She was brandishing what I now recognized as a golf club.

"They're trying to kill us," I gasped, and pointed at the man.

He spun in our direction, then back toward Loba. She moved several feet closer to him while he was distracted. The man must have injured his right hand in the crash, because his grip on the gun was wavering. He looked about wildly for somewhere to run, then dived over the side of the cliff. Loba crouched at its rim, baying into the darkness.

A thin white-haired woman in a fluffy yellow bathrobe, also carrying a golf club, moved in my direction. "We've called 911. Did you say there was more than that one, dear?"

I nodded and whispered, "The other one may have a gun, too. Be careful!"

Now the third woman, who wore a satin smoking jacket over something long and slinky, spoke. "I think we can handle that eventuality." What she was carrying was definitely not a golf club.

"Cover us, Mary, while we take a look in the car," said the fluffy bathrobe woman. Mary pointed her shotgun in the direction of the car.

We climbed over the stone wall and got as close to the cliff edge as we could. The empty car was balanced so precariously that a touch might tip it over the side. I noticed Loba's paw prints on the windshield—she had charged them.

"There are houses down there," my companion said. "I hope the tow truck gets here before this thing crashes down on top of them." Loba was still barking ferociously. Maybe she could see her attacker, but we couldn't see a thing. We returned to the other women.

It took a few minutes for the first police to arrive. By that time I had become acquainted with Ora, Patrice and Mary, all retired nurses in their seventies. It was like being rescued by Great Aunt Lobelia, my "spinster lady" ancestor who was always spoken of in hushed tones as being "that way."

The cops were able to prevent the car from plunging over the side of the hill. I sipped the cocoa that Mary (of the smoking jacket and shotgun) had put into my hand while I answered dozens of police questions. Loba had attached herself to my side. She was still shaking. To tell the truth, so was I.

Police searching the area at the base of the hill found a pistol. They were unable to find either of the men. Later that night they would identify the car as one stolen earlier in the day. The gun, the car and the tire iron found inside the car were all free of fingerprints.

When the initial round of questions was finished, the cops let me go, on the promise that I'd come by the Mission Station and sign my statement the next day. Patrice let me phone Lynnette's house to tell her what had happened. Most of the Executive Committee members were still out picking up ice cream or burritos, but Stephen Leong was there, and offered to pick up Loba and me. I invited Ora, Patrice and Mary to my house for dinner the following week, and Stephen arrived to take Loba and me to Lynnette's.

Chapter Twenty-Seven

Stephen acted almost as unnerved by the attack as I was. He apologized several times for involving me in something that had almost cost my life.

"Thanks," I whispered, "but taking risks is part of the gig. Do you mind if I ask what you think has been going on?"

"I don't mind, but I don't have much to tell you. I joined Pride as part of the Diversity Slate. Before that, I never was involved in electoral stuff, and it's all pretty new to me. Maybe that's why I have the attitude that we should come clean, find out the truth, no matter how bad it is. I don't have anything to lose by it."

I leaned toward him as much as my seat belt allowed to make myself heard. "How about the other members of the Executive Committee?"

"All of us except David and Miguel have been clear about where we stand on the investigation from the beginning. Betty, Warren and Tom opposed it from the start—for different reasons, though they all say it's for the good of the club. Miguel supported hiring you at first, but he's been persuaded to change his mind for the 'higher good,' since the investigation might take energy away from the areas he's interested in."

"Persuaded by whom?"

"Beg pardon?"

My heart sank. I was unintelligible. A critical presentation was waiting for me at Lynnette's, and someone sitting a foot away couldn't understand me!

"Who talked Miguel into it?" I tried for maximum enunciation.

"Oh, I don't know. Betty, probably. She's been making a lot of calls. Or maybe Warren. He can be pretty persuasive, too."

"I hardly know some of the other Executive Committee members. Can you give me a little background?"

"Sure, what did you want to know?"

"Start with Tom Ng. I was surprised to find out he's an attorney—he's so low-key."

"That's a charitable way of putting it. His nickname is 'The Slug.' I don't know how he ever passed the bar exam. But he's pretty good at looking very busy while doing nothing. My guess is, Tom is only in Pride because he wants to make his parents happy. Which, if you ever met his parents, you would know is ridiculous, because they're never going to accept the fact that he's gay. Being in a gay club just rubs their noses in it."

"But he's on the Executive Committee. He must do something."

"He makes plenty of promises, but nothing much ever comes of them. Now, Warren is a different matter. Last year he did an amazing amount of work on the election, behind the scenes—precinct kits, literature distribution, the kind of stuff nobody wants to do. That surprised me. I always assume that guys like him and Geoffrey and David are only in it to network and suck up, but Warren worked on things that had to be done but that nobody was going to notice. Not the usual pattern for getting yourself nominated to an office. And Warren's like Geoffrey. He really, really wants to get elected."

"I think one of my problems with this investigation is that I don't see why anyone would want to be in office in a city that's going broke."

"Tell me about it! You know I'm new to all this stuff, too. Probably it's another genetic thing, or maybe in political families they get fed it with their oatmeal."

"Did Warren come from a nest of Democratic Party players, too?"

"I don't know. He's from the East Coast, and I don't know anything about his family. He spends a lot of time with mainstream Democrat types. Every fundraising event, Warren is a sponsor, or he buys a table, so he's got major money."

"What does Warren do?"

"He's some kind of a computer consultant."

"That doesn't sound like big bucks unless he's super-technical or super-creative."

"Maybe his family has money, like Geoff's."

"What about David?"

"When I was a baby commie, I'd have called him a bourgeois parasite. Now I'd just say he's trying to buy friends, but he's so obnoxious that even money doesn't work. Still, he's harmless."

"Miguel?"

Stephen weighed his words for a few moments. "I knew him before he changed his name from Mike to Miguel. He's the kind of activist I've met a dozen times. A good man to have on your side—but pay attention to whether that side changes."

"What do you mean?"

"A few years ago, we were both working with a solidarity organization that sponsored a tour of insurgent leaders. One of them raped the North American volunteer who was putting him up at her house. Miguel was in charge of damage control. He got one of the women in leadership of our group to convince the victim not to tell anyone else about it, even her friends, and to pretend it never happened—for the sake of the revolution."

"My God!" Our eyes met, and we both looked away. "It's going to be hard to sit in the same room with him."

"It made me sick, too," Stephen said. "I didn't find out about it until we were both on the Pride Diversity Slate. Now I try to put it out of my mind so I can still work with him. He's very dedicated. I don't want to talk about it any more." We were both silent for a minute.

"One last question," I said. "When I called Lynnette's, who was there besides you?"

"Nobody! This group is so individualistic! We always get food during our breaks, but we can never agree on getting one thing. Tonight everybody insisted on driving their own cars. They all took off to get their own food. Except Betty said she had to drive over to Townsend Street to check on a printer's blueline for one of her freelance jobs, so David said he'd pick up some chicken for her, and I think Warren said he had to get gas before it got too late to find an open station."

Great. Everyone on the Executive Committee knew I was walking over and almost all of them had been in their cars at the time I was attacked. There wasn't time for any more questions. Stephen had managed to get a spot right in front of Lynnette's.

"Cheer up Maggie," Lynnette bellowed from the doorway. "You're safe now!"

Chapter Twenty-Eight

It took a while to settle Loba on Lynnette's back porch. She didn't want to be parted from me, and growled at everyone. When I entered the living room, I wished I'd kept her with me. The Pride Executive Committee, even Stephen, watched me take a seat with the kind of attention my cats give to an unfortunate moth that makes its way into my house. It was not a reassuring comparison.

"Hi Maggie, sit down," Lynnette said. "Do you want some tea?" I turned down the tea and sat on a straight-backed wooden chair within the circle of Pride leadership, who were comfortably seated in the upholstered couches.

Betty brought the meeting to order again, and turned to me. "We're grateful you could come after your horrible experience, Maggie. We'll try to make this brief. Do you want to make a presentation or shall we ask you questions?"

I lip-synched "neither" and started writing on a notepad Lynnette had produced for me.

"Oh, terrific, only in San Francisco would we have a mime investigator!" Betty laughed, for the first time I could remember. The other members gave dutiful chuckles. I smiled and threw up my hands. "Well, that's okay," Betty said, "we'll probably do most of the talking anyway."

First I wrote: "Can anyone here read shorthand?" I'd learned it in a rip-off business course ("Shorthand is your passport to exciting career opportunities").

"Put myself through college with it," Stephen said, with just a touch of defensiveness. I scribbled symbols madly, while Stephen read it aloud: "I want to tell you about the list Miranda found in the treasurer materials she got from Joe Leslie. Together with a make-believe canvass and printers' bills from a nonexistent printer, it's an indictment of the old Pride leadership. Miranda believed it also linked some big names in City politics to money-laundering through the club. The list is your inheritance from Miranda, and I don't have any right to keep it from you."

The faces of the Pride leaders, caught off-guard, revealed surprise, anger, worry. Betty's mouth pursed tightly, and the stress lines around her eyes deepened. Stephen's expression was thoughtful, but I noticed his chin stuck out a bit more.

"You told us what Miranda believed. What about you, Maggie, what do you think?" Miguel was watching me closely. The partially eaten burger he held was being squeezed out of its bun by the tightness of his grip.

"I'm still investigating, and I don't have all the details. That's why I need your help," I wrote, and Stephen read.

"May we see this list?" Warren asked mildly. He didn't look stricken by my announcement. He had rolled up the sleeves of his shirt and taken off his tie. His dark blond hair was rumpled, but otherwise he was ready to pose for an election flyer as "the hardworking candidate."

"The original is in a safe place," I wrote. "I had no intention of carrying it around, because I was afraid something might happen. I'm sure the men who attacked me tonight were after the list, and—"

"Too bad the guys who tried to run you down didn't know that," Lynnette said, cutting off Stephen's reading of my narrative.

"Excuse me, but this conspiracy theory stuff is a little more than I can take," Miguel scoffed. "Maybe you didn't know there was a group of maniacs going after queer people, Maggie?"

"Yeah," David Lindley was quick to agree. "Why should any of us think the attack was anything except another bashing?"

I interrupted, risking long-term damage to my vocal chords. "Just forget the attack for now. You should also know that Miranda kept the list from you because there was at least one Executive Committee member that she didn't trust." This was met with a collective gasp.

"How could she say that? I feel personally attacked." David drew his knees up to his chin and wrapped his arms around his legs.

"Trust me, David, you'll know when you've been attacked!" snapped Betty.

"How do we know that's what Miranda told you?" Tom Ng's face gave nothing away, and in contrast to his words, his delivery was soft and uninflected. "You say we should stop talking about why you were attacked, but it goes to the heart of what's going on here. Why would Miranda talk to a stranger instead of to one of the members that she *did* trust?"

"Larry Gross is the one she talked to," I whispered, abandoning the pen and paper. "You could ask him. But the important point is not what she told me—or Larry. It's what she *didn't* tell all of you that's at issue here."

"I still don't understand," said Miguel. "It's one thing for Miranda to withhold the list, although it was irresponsible.

But you're working for us. How can you justify waiting until now to tell us about it?"

"He's got a point, Maggie," said Betty. "First you withhold it, and now, when you know we're about to scrap the investigation, you trot it out with a story that can't be verified because Miranda is dead."

"This could destroy the club. You should turn the list over to us as the elected club leadership." Tom's voice was losing its careful modulation.

Stephen stopped translating and raised his hand pointedly. Betty called on him as the others paused for breath. "If we didn't do anything wrong, we don't have anything to worry about. I think we need to take a look at this list. Maggie was right to respect Miranda's concerns about its safety. Maybe we could see a copy and keep the original in a safe place."

Betty exchanged a meaningful glance with Miguel, Warren and Tom. Then she nodded slightly to Stephen and turned to me. "You said you brought a copy with you?"

I smiled and wrote: "Yes, just one. It seemed best not to circulate it widely." I pulled a single copy of the list out of my bag and passed it around. I had not included Miranda's notes.

There was an intense quiet as they huddled over the list. While they tried to make sense of it (or covered up their reactions), I wrote out my pitch: "There are already rumors about this. You read the article in the SNEWS. There will be more of the same, and worse. If you don't help me establish who the guilty parties were, everyone will assume that it was you. Fill in any of the initials you can, and be prepared for some heavy press when all the connections get made."

Stephen read it aloud. I looked at the tense faces around me, some thoughtful, some in full panic. So far so good.

"Give me until Friday," I resorted to raspy vocalizing again.

"After that, if you want to drop the whole thing, I won't object."

"If there are Democratic Party regulars in this list, it could damage the Party in this city for years," Tom said. Beads of perspiration had formed on his high forehead.

"If there are Democratic Party regulars that have been pimping off this club and undoing everything we're trying to do, they better worry about the damage I will personally do them," Betty retorted, fire in her eyes.

"I think you're both making valid points," Warren said, looking around the room. "But we should consider the long-term impact of any hasty actions. Our responsibility extends beyond the reputation of the club or any particular leadership of the club—"

"I joined Pride instead of the Gay Asian club because of the Diversity Slate's integrity," Stephen said, interrupting Warren. "Now I want to see some, or I'm out of here!"

"Be careful what you threaten," Miguel said, his lip curling slightly. "Someone may take you literally."

"Come on, boys! This is absolutely the kind of pissing contest we don't need," said Lynnette. "All Maggie is asking for is that we give her two more days on this."

Betty intervened. "Maybe this would be a good time for you to leave, Maggie, and let us chew on this in executive session. Looks like it's going to be a long night. When I don't know how I'm gonna vote, I know we're in trouble. We'll let you know what we decide. David, could you give Maggie a ride home?"

David sulked like a four-year-old, but complied. I wasn't surprised to see that he owned a new Jaguar. He worried that Loba would damage his leather upholstery, fretted over a speck I couldn't see on the windshield, and predicted that he'd never find a parking place as good as the one he was leaving to drive me home.

I ignored the fussing and seized the chance to talk to him alone. I had to lean very close, and blow out what was left of my vocal chords. Luckily, the car barely hummed.

"David, it seems to me that your contributions to Pride don't get as much credit as they should."

"I'm glad *someone* else has noticed that! Nobody asks me for anything except more money—"

"For example, in this investigation. You've worked with all the principals for years. I'm sure you could help settle this quickly, and the club could move on to other things, like that honors dinner you were talking about at the membership meeting Sunday."

"That dinner! If we don't move on it soon, we'll lose our deposit, and—"

"Exactly! I'd really like to hear your evaluation of the treasurers." David made a gratified noise and I moved in fast. "For example, Mavis Baker. What was her story?"

"Well, Mavis was only treasurer for a few months. There were wild stories floating around about why she left. I heard that Geoffrey fired her when he found out that club money was going up her trashy girlfriend's nose. But several other people thought that Mavis was framed."

"Do you remember the names of any of those people?"

"No. They've all left the club now, anyway. We've always had a big turnover. One time I overheard Betty telling Miranda that when Geoffrey realized Mavis wasn't as dumb as he'd thought she was, he got nervous and kicked her out of the leadership before she could take it over herself."

"But what's *your* take, David?"

"I don't like her. She causes chaos wherever she goes.

She's just evil." That was a new angle. Satanic possession.

"What about Joe Leslie?"

"U.S. Grade A beef. He doesn't have the brains to do anything on his own, though he'd be good for muscle. Making him treasurer was Geoffrey's biggest mistake as club president. We compared him to Dan Quayle during the club election campaign. Joe worshipped Geoffrey, though, and anything Geoff wanted, Joe would try to come through—"

"What about Marc? I don't understand why Geoffrey made Marc quit as treasurer. Marc must have worshipped Geoffrey as much as Joe, and he was bright and competent, too."

"Marc's got a conscience, and he's smart enough to know that he'd be in trouble if he put his name on books that had been cooked. Joe wouldn't have problems with that kind of thing. What was strange about Marc getting dumped is, he never said much about it. Usually a faggot scorned is one hellfire furious faggot, but Marc went off and licked his wounds in private."

We had reached my house, and David wouldn't linger long enough to watch Loba and me get inside, let alone let me pump him for more information. He drove off, in as close to a roar as his well-mannered Jaguar could be said to approximate.

It was almost midnight. My answering machine was full of calls. Liam's message announced that he had a semi-hot date, but would check in to see if I needed him. Jessie demanded to hear that I was alive and well on a regular basis. Kristin left an annoyed "Hope you're not doing anything stupid." None of them required a late-night response (one of the few consolations of getting home late). I poured myself a glass of Bardolino and settled in for an hour of junk TV.

When the phone rang, I jerked and spilled my wine all over myself. This was what people meant when they said something was working their very last nerve. Mine had been worked big-time. It was Liam, calling from the restaurant where he was having a candlelight dinner with the new man, Mr. "semi-hot."

"Maggie, ye bonnie lass!"

"Liam, you're never dating a Scot! Whatever would your da say to that?"

"I don't think the fact that Bruce is Scottish would be the main point of contention, wee Maggie, though it might run a close second. But, to get back to why I called you . . . . You remember, don't you, that I have to go to Chicago in the morning for that fundraising workshop?"

"Is that tomorrow? Damn."

"I can come over tonight, and we'll just round up some other sucker, I mean friend, to keep you company and help fend off the bad guys while I'm gone."

It was very tempting to wail about the attack on Loba and me. But I lied, the same way he'd have lied to me.

"Nah, I'm fine, give the new guy a test-drive."

"You're lying."

"No, really. I've got your Loch Ness monster dog here, and I'm going to lock everything down and go to sleep. I wouldn't even know you were here. So, do you think young Bruce is a keeper?"

"Too early to tell. I keep thinking he's got a fiery nature hidden in there behind the dourness."

"Does he have any conversational abilities, or is he another one of those sweet, doglike ones? Does he read?"

"My judgment is clouded by lust."

"What else is new? I have no doubts that he's unworthy

of you, but you might as well have a good time before you start seeing all those fatal flaws. Call me from Chicago, okay?" I hung up, feeling alternately lonely, angry and more than a little scared.

While I fed the cats I tried to remember when I'd last eaten an actual meal, gave up, and fixed a grilled cheese to go with my new glass of wine. The appeal of a sitcom had vanished. I paced for awhile, Loba dutifully at my heels. She needed extra space to turn around so she kept having to catch up with me mid-room. Pod spread himself luxuriantly over the back of the couch and looked on, his tail twitching in disapproval of so much activity.

The lesbian and gay press had accepted Miranda's death as another attack by the bashers. The police had added another "hate crime" to their statistics. The frame-up would work. Only die-hard homophobes would have any sympathy for the bashers when they were caught, and no one would be surprised that after all their attempts at murder, they had succeeded with Miranda. Meantime, her real killers would get away with it.

In the past week I'd been nearly run down, my house had been broken into and my office violated, my dog nearly killed and my cat kidnapped. The case had become very personal to me, and regardless of what the cops thought about who killed Miranda, and whether or not the Pride leadership wanted it, I promised myself I would find out the truth about Miranda, and about the Pride Club, even if it did mean having a fool for a client.

Chapter Twenty-Nine

I'm not sure how long I slept—it felt like five minutes—before the alarm went off at 6:00. The cats slept through. My early risings had become just another one of those bizarre human rituals that happily did not involve them. "At least you could get up and make me breakfast before my last dawn patrol," I complained. They didn't stir. My voice still sounded like something dredged from the swamps, but I had more volume than the day before.

The only parking spot was over half a block away from Geoffrey's place, but I had a good view of his front door through the back curtains on the van. I propped my binoculars so I could watch through them without developing "surveillance neck." While I waited for someone to arrive, or for 8:30 to come, I replayed the Executive Committee meeting, trying to remember the range of emotions each member had shown. Who was sincerely concerned about the attack, who was concealing anger that I'd lived to get to the meeting?

The lights were on in the house, but there was no activity. No one arrived. No one left. The *Chronicle* remained on the front steps. At 8:15 I began to speculate that Geoffrey might be sick—or had skipped town. By 8:30 I knew something was up.

At 8:45 a tired-looking Latina wearing an over-large house dress and carrying a string bag labored her way up the hill past me. It would be a long trek from the nearest public transportation. She used her own key to enter Geoffrey's place. A minute later she ran back outside and looked up and down the street. Her eyes were wild. Her mouth opened and closed, but no words came out.

I leaped out of the van, clutching my trusty heavyweight flashlight and wishing again that I had my gun. The woman stepped backward when I approached, looking as if she might run from me.

"*Señora, qué pasa?*" I asked, as softly and calmly as my croaking voice allowed.

"*Matanza—una matanza.*" She spoke in a low, urgent whisper and glanced fearfully about, as if the killers might hear and come after her, too.

She gestured me inside, pointing into the back of the house. Either she was incoherent from shock or she was speaking a dialect I couldn't comprehend. The only word I could grasp was *matanza*, a slaughter.

I walked slowly through an airy reception hall, past a kitchen and two closed doors, toward the light-filled living room in the back of the house. Uncurtained floor-to-ceiling windows gave a sweeping view of the City, and morning sunlight streamed over two lifeless forms.

Joe Leslie had been flung to the end of a long couch, head and arms thrown back, by the force of what must have been a gunshot at close range. Blood from the gaping hole in his chest had turned his shirt dark red. Only a bit of white at the neckline of his t-shirt showed. The couch and thick plush carpet were stained in a rough circle around him. Nearby, a .45 revolver lay on the floor.

I've seen maybe a dozen dead people in my life, and all but three had been strangers. The ones I'd known had died of cancer or AIDS, in their beds. None of that experience prepared me for this. My knees buckled, and there was a strange buzzing in my ears. You will *not* faint, I told myself. Get over to Geoffrey. He might still be alive. Gradually the room stopped spinning and took back its regular proportions, and I was able to move again. I ran to where Geoffrey lay.

He had fallen from a chair at a desk near the windows. A smudge that looked like gun powder extended up the right sleeve of his shirt. I couldn't see any wounds or marks on him. He was wearing a dress shirt and tie, and except for the fact that his eyes were open, he looked as if he might have curled up on the floor to take a nap. I lay my fingers on his throat for a pulse. Nothing.

The cleaning woman hadn't followed me to the back of the house. I returned to the entrance, calling "*Señora*," and looked for her outside. She was gone. I didn't blame her. She was almost certainly an immigrant, possibly undocumented, and she wouldn't want to be involved in this.

I returned to the living room to look for a phone. It was on Geoffrey's desk. I was reaching for it when I snapped back to why I was there in the first place. My initial panic had passed, and this was the only chance I'd have to look around. Past experience told me that my delayed reaction would be devastating, but wouldn't hit until the crisis was over. I'd develop chills and tremors and want to hide under my quilt in bed, but now while the adrenalin was rushing I might as well take advantage of it.

It was 8:50. I could look around for a few minutes and fudge the time when I called the cops. Even if the cleaning woman reappeared, a ten-minute gap in our time estimates wouldn't surprise them.

Geoffrey's Macintosh was next to the phone. The screen saver showed an ever-changing aquarium of deep-sea fish. The burbling sound effect that accompanied it was jarringly loud in the utter silence of the room. I pulled my latex gloves out of my pocket, and put them on. When I hit ENTER on the keyboard, the screen lit up. It showed a confession/suicide message. There was a date, yesterday's, but no salutation. It went on for about twenty lines, semi-coherent and rambling in the style of someone on drugs or very drunk. Geoffrey confessed to stealing money from the Pride Club through falsified records and sham operations (including the canvass), aided by Joe Leslie. He said that he could no longer live with the stress of potential exposure. He absolved all other individuals and organizations of blame, and asked his parents and Mayor Rawlings, "who treated me like your own son," to forgive him for taking his own life and that of Joe Leslie.

He hadn't printed the message. The printer wasn't even turned on. Whatever substances Geoffrey had ingested must have killed him before he got to that stage. I thought about trying to print out a copy for myself, but concluded that it would be too risky. I'd have to discover the print commands, and it would take time to warm up the printer. Besides, the police might notice that the printer had just been used. Resorting to the old-fashioned way, I pulled a small notepad out of my pocket and copied the text off the screen.

There was still time for a quick look around. So far, the undisturbed state of the townhouse supported Geoffrey's confession. He had caught Joe off-guard, shot him, and then written his note and finished himself off. Two pillows made of the same fabric as the couch had been tossed to the floor near Joe's body. Otherwise nothing in the room made it look like the scene of a struggle. It certainly didn't look as if armed intruders had staged a hit.

On an enormous low oak table next to the couch, cocaine paraphernalia, a nearly empty bottle of Scotch, an ice bucket half full of water and two glasses showed what the main activity of the evening had been. A corner torchiere lamp was lit, and recessed lighting highlighted the lithographs on the wall.

The first door off the hall opened onto Geoffrey's bedroom. It was sparsely but elegantly furnished, and the open door of his walk-in closet displayed his extensive wardrobe, arranged by colors. A cleverly designed rack held ties, belts and braces ready for accessorizing. All his clothing was put away, and only a large vase of flowers and a pair of antique brushes were arranged on the walnut dresser that took up most of one wall.

The kitchen was all white and sterile as an operating room. Except for several ice cube trays stacked in a puddle next to the sink, this room looked as if no one had set foot in it since the cleaning woman's last visit.

The remaining room had to be the bathroom. I opened the door, flicked on the light, and nearly dropped my flashlight when my own image leaped at me on all sides. The walls were mirrored, floor to ceiling. On the counter next to the washbasin, a 500-count-sized bottle of Seconal lay open on its side. There were maybe a dozen capsules left, and several of those had spilled into the sink. I opened the medicine cabinet and found several other kinds of downers on its shelves.

Could it all have been as simple, sordid and tragic as the computer message spelled out? It vindicated all my suspicions about Geoffrey, everything I'd set out to prove. Then why didn't I believe it?

Time to find out what the police would make of it. I dialed 911, then went out to the van to wait, wishing I hadn't given up smoking.

The first car arrived within four minutes, with two more close behind. I showed the cops my P.I. license and told them about why I had been parked in front of the house, the arrival and departure of the cleaning woman and my check on whether the deceased were in fact dead. The officer in charge asked me, in the no-uncertain-terms manner of a command, if I could please stick around. I returned to the van, sank into the reclining leather chair that had been Jack's favorite possession, and watched the convergence of dozens of police and criminal justice civilians into the house. The press was arriving too. This was a dream story: sex, drugs, a gory murder and a suicide note/confession left on a computer screen.

After about half an hour, Sergeant Hoffman was dropped off in front of the townhouse by a City black and white. I got out of the van and watched her progress. She was dressed for work this morning, in well-cut gray slacks, with a darker gray houndstooth blazer over a white open-necked blouse. A uniformed cop approached her and pointed in my direction. Her composure might have been slightly ruffled when she glanced over and caught me watching her, but she quickly regained her usual demeanor. Giving me a mock salute, she called across the thirty feet separating us that she wanted to talk to me and she'd like for me to stay put. She turned and walked toward the house.

The scene-of-the-crime team arrived and took over. I returned to the van and waited. Another half hour went by.

Diana Hoffman knocked on the window and then opened the van door, head tilted as she gave me that cryptic smile. A shiver that had nothing to do with fear of police or mortality passed through me. She was wearing her hair tied back today. I liked it better soft around her face. Maybe she only wore it down when she was going out with her lover. Maybe I should think about the subject at hand.

"How long had you been staking him out?" She dispensed with formalities, but then the smile had taken care of that.

"This is the third morning." My voice had taken on more definably human qualities, but I would have been hard put to carry on a conversation that didn't heavily feature hand gestures. I told her about my suspicions of Geoffrey, his clandestine meeting at City Hall and my observations since Tuesday morning. I "forgot" to tell her about the videotapes I'd made of Marc and Joe the day before. Finding out about Geoffrey would be hard enough for Marc. Why make it even harder?

"Did you read the message on his computer monitor?"

For a split second I considered lying, but truth might get me more in return. "Yes, I did. Do you buy his confession?"

"From your question, I take it you don't believe it. Why not?" She was brisk, almost hostile, but maybe that was what a murder scene did to her.

"I'm not sure. If it were true, it would wrap up my investigation perfectly. I've had my eye on Geoffrey Lawrence from the beginning, and I even suspected that he had a role in Miranda Post's death. But this morning I've had time to think. This suicide-murder scenario is too damned tidy."

"On the other hand, maybe you were right from the beginning. As you know, the obvious suspect usually is the guilty party."

"If you'd met Geoff, you'd know he wasn't the type of person to do this. His type spends millions on a defense—if he's ever caught—and persuades a jury to let him off because he's too charming to send to jail! It's so handy for Geoffrey and Joe Leslie to die this way, with Geoff's confession convicting them. Just the two of them cooked up phony projects and lied to donors, and then Geoffrey killed himself and Joe. End of story, all around."

"Suppose, for the sake of argument, it was a double homicide dressed up like a murder/suicide," Hoffman said. "What's the angle? Who killed them, angry club members? Businessmen involved in illegal campaign donations who were afraid they'd be exposed? An ex-lover?"

She was watching me closely. I called on Jack Windsor's poker training: No tell-tale expressions. I was holding some wild cards. There was one ex-lover I wanted to see as soon as possible. Maybe I could break the news about Geoffrey to Marc before the police arrived to interview him. His prints would be in the apartment.

"The only thing I feel certain about," I said, "is that this is related to my investigation of the Pride Club. I also believe it's related to Miranda Post's murder." She raised an eyebrow. "Who killed Geoff and Joe? Maybe it was their accomplices in looting the Pride Club. Or other club members. Or outsiders not even related to the club—I don't know yet. But I do know that if the murder/suicide story is accepted, then that would sew up the Pride Club's investigation. With Geoff and Joe dead and most of the club's records destroyed, how likely is it that the people who laundered money through the club accounts will be pursued?"

"I need more than theory, and that's all you've given me about either of these cases. Do you have anything more I could go on?"

"On Monday, I was meeting with Geoffrey at his office at City Hall when he got a call that turned him into an anxious wreck. He slipped into what looked like a store room near his office, and two people, I think both men, went in after him. They roughed him up. I heard him set up a meeting at 8:00 some morning. Maybe he couldn't or wouldn't get them what they wanted, so they killed him and Joe. I only saw one of them, but I could definitely I.D. him. I tailed him for over an hour, though I have to confess, the only memorable thing he did was go into A Different Light Bookstore."

"Ms. Garrett, the people you saw may have nothing to do with your investigation, or this crime. They could be drug dealers or people who'd loaned Mr. Lawrence money. They might even have been legitimate. Nothing you've told me contradicts the suicide scenario."

"He had rich parents, a trust fund, a cushy job. I can't believe he'd kill himself or Joe."

She gave me a long look. "We don't know what we may uncover when we look into his situation. I have to go by what's put in front of me. The forensics team will be busy for hours on this. Maybe they'll find something that supports your theory. Keep me posted on any other ideas you have. I do respect your opinions, you know."

I was dismissed. Whatever she was thinking about this case, Sergeant Hoffman was not going to give anything away.

Chapter Thirty

I drove home to take Loba for a walk, shower and change. But first a couple of phone calls. I hated the thought of Marc finding out about Geoffrey from the police or a newspaper. There was no answer at Marc's apartment, and no answering machine. I called his office and croaked out an urgent request on his voicemail for him to call me. I checked in with Ricardo and told him I'd be in shortly, but, with the exceptions of Marc Romano and my friends, to tell callers that he didn't know when I'd be in. He loves to do that kind of stuff.

While we were talking I noticed that the message light on my answering machine was blinking. It turned out to be Detective Desmond, saying that anything relating to Miranda's death was Sergeant Hoffman's responsibility, and that he would leave me in her capable hands. The snigger that accompanied this last remark led me to believe I had guessed correctly, and Diana Hoffman was a lesbian.

I'd allowed for an hour of reacting time, to let myself feel the horror of the morning—and the night before. I couldn't do it, not yet. My Grandmother Faith died at a time when circumstances kept me from being able give in to my loss. Only when I could let myself fall apart completely did I grieve for the most important person of my childhood. This felt strangely like that time. The crisis wasn't over yet, and it looked as if I'd have to wait a while longer before I could feel the emotions surrounding the murders of three people I knew, and nearly getting killed myself.

Back to work. Ricardo met me at the door with a cup of coffee. He tossed aside any pretense of staying cool, and pressed for details about the murder scene. It helped to talk it through, so I complied, until my patience wore out.

"Did you throw up?"

"No, I was too busy to think about throwing up, though I am feeling a little queasy now. . . ." I leaned in his direction. He moved back to give me lots of room, and I changed the subject.

"Did you have any luck showing the pictures to the grand-mothers?"

"Yeah. They picked every one of them."

"What!"

"Every picture I showed 'em, they'd say 'Ah, sí, that is the one.' All the men, and Tía even picked the big woman—what's her name—Mavis."

"Well, we had to try." I handed him my scribbled notes. "Here's where each member of the Pride Executive Commit-tee claimed to be during their break on Wednesday night. I want you to verify their alibis. Talk to people in the neighbor-hood, at local takeout places, access their credit card records. Use your imagination! I also want background checks on the people I circled in green. This is important, and I wouldn't trust anyone else with it."

"Cool." He was not very excited. "Maggie, who are all these other people you could ask to do this stuff, but that you don't trust?" We made horrible faces at each other. I do not have proper command and control over my work force.

I called Larry Gross in his hospital room and asked him to convene a meeting of current and former Pride Club officers. "I think they may be more open to it, now that Geoffrey is dead."

"Sure, I can do that, but why not just call them yourself?"

"Because Pride has to do this for itself, and as the only former treasurer who doesn't have a cloud over his head, you have the moral advantage."

"Not to mention that I can use the old 'last request of a dying man' routine," he answered, with a laugh. "Yes, I'll be glad to, but we'll have to meet here. Maybe I can get us the sun room."

Judy Willis brought back the treasurers' materials I'd given her. By this time I wasn't surprised to learn that over a hundred thousand dollars was unaccounted for. The discrepancies showed up at the times of transition between treasurers. Judy had used some of her old contacts to trace bank accounts. A total of sixteen accounts at nine banks had been identified so far, and there probably were more. Until he lost the election in the spring, Geoffrey always had been one of the authorized signers of these accounts. The other signers changed every time a new treasurer was installed, and occasionally, as with Mavis, they had changed while that person was still in office.

All of this damning information fit in with Geoffrey's confession. Had I heard it the day before, I'd have welcomed it with a crow of triumph. All my class-based bias was vindicated. The spoiled rich kid I despised was the guilty one, just as he should be. But it wasn't that simple. The picture kept getting cloudier all the time. I hated when that happened.

It was lunchtime. I wasn't hungry but Ricardo was, so I volunteered to walk to a small Vietnamese takeout place near the office. I also bought an afternoon *Examiner*. Its headline read, "Aide to Mayor, Companion Found Dead: Suspect Murder/Suicide." The article included the complete text of Geoffrey's confession. I was grateful to see that the paper identified me only as an "unnamed visitor" who had discovered the bodies. The other major story was an announcement by an assistant D.A. that an arrest was imminent in the outbreak of attacks on gay men and lesbians, because of the Mayor's dedication to the safety of the homosexual community.

On the inside was a small story about how neighbors had come to the rescue of a woman jogger and her dog in Noe Valley. Both of the assailants had escaped. The car used in an attempt to run down the jogger had been stolen only hours earlier, and had been supplied with stolen plates from another vehicle. Police investigation was continuing. Featured anonymously in two news stories on the same day. That had to be some kind of record.

I left another message on Marc's office voicemail. There was no answer at his house, and his machine was turned off. I hoped the police were being sensitive in their dealings with him. Hard as it was to understand why, he had loved Geoffrey, and he should be allowed to grieve in peace.

Tom Ng called. "Congratulations on your work. You were right to hang in there. Guess you can take a break now."

"What do you mean?"

"You were right, Geoffrey was stealing from the club. The investigation is over."

"If I stop now, are you comfortable living with the fact that someone from the Executive Committee was helping Geoffrey sabotage the investigation?"

"Well, Joe Leslie—"

"Joe wasn't on the Executive Committee, either. The corruption at Pride couldn't have been limited to the two of them. How could Geoffrey and Joe know to send me a bribe an hour after Lynnette hired me? And who broke into my house and office Monday night, when both Geoff and Joe had iron-clad alibis?"

"How do you know that?"

"I checked, of course, because I wanted them to be guilty! It was a terrible disappointment when I found out they'd been with six other men at a surprise birthday party for Geoff. But I recognize facts when they hit me on the head hard enough. Now I'm trying to do the same for you folks."

"The Committee members consider your work finished now—"

"Well, I don't. Not by a long shot!"

"We hoped you wouldn't make this so difficult. . . ."

I hung up on him, and kicked the wastebasket. Then I kicked the file cabinet. After I kicked the wastebasket against the file cabinet, I had a good rhythm going, but the high-strung Hungarian accountant in the next office started pounding on the walls, and I stopped.

Ricardo came in, grinning ear to ear, to tell me that our neighbor was threatening to complain to the building management if I didn't cease the construction work during office hours. Then his smile disappeared and he told me that his mother had just called with an ultimatum. "She says next week we've got to find a new place to keep stuff. She can't sleep, thinking that guy might come back."

"I don't blame her. Tell her I'll give her a call. By the way, where are you keeping the original copy of the list?"

"In with Grandmama's receipts. Anything she buys, even a Coke, if they give her a receipt, she saves it. They go way back to when she lived in Mexico. I put the list in with 1983.

Nobody's ever gonna find it there."

I turned reluctantly to my final report to the Pride Club leadership. Ricardo stuck his head through the door again to say that I had a call. I gave him an inquiring look. He shrugged. Either he hadn't asked or had forgotten who it was. "You mind if I leave now?" I shooed him out the door. It was so hard to get good help.

The caller was Jolie. "I was afraid if I said who it was, you wouldn't talk to me," she said softly.

"How are you?"

"You mean am I stoned? No, I've been clean and sober for oh, forty-eight hours now." She gave a short bitter laugh. "Maybe I should go to a meeting and get a chip before I fuck up again. Sorry. I called because I thought maybe we could see each other, just to talk."

"All right. Let's meet at The Raven."

"I was wondering if I could come by your place in a couple of hours. It'll just be for a little while."

"Sure, that's fine. At six." Of course I had to see her. She had important connections to the case. She kissed like a demon. She had kept me away from home while my place was broken into and most likely she had nabbed my cat. She could provide invaluable details about Mavis. She had found erogenous spots that were new to me . . . .

After another hour on the Pride Club report, I read over what I'd written. It didn't make any sense. Oh well, I could take it home and try again, after talking to Jolie. I dumped the Pride folders and a stack of bills that needed paying into a large leather tote, and locked up the office.

Precisely at 6:00 the doorbell rang. When Fearless saw Jolie at the door she hissed and sprang to the highest spot in the room. Her tail was puffed up and she managed to look twice her size, ready to take on a pack of dogs. Pod watched this, saucer-eyed. He slunk behind the couch where he stayed, uttering sorrowful cries.

"Your cat remembers me," Jolie said. She sidled into the room, keeping a good distance between us. I made a gesture toward the couch. She shook her head, and walked over to a window. There was a purpling bruise under her left eye. From Mavis? Jolie had made no attempt to conceal it. Her hair was tied back and she wasn't wearing any makeup.

"I'd already figured out it was you who took her. Was that why you wanted to see me?"

"Part of it. I also wanted to tell you that some of what happened was for me, not because anyone told me to do it. What happened with us Sunday night—that was real. Wasn't it?" She kept her eyes averted.

"Sunday night was magic. I felt it, too." My anger had evaporated, replaced by a mixture of feelings too complicated to give a name. "But Jolie, what about Fearless? Why did you take her?"

"Mavis told me to do it. The plan was that on Sunday night I'd chat you up, maybe pick you up. The main thing was to get you to let me inside your place, so I could come back later and grab one of the cats. But when I met you, it all changed." She glanced at me quickly. "Like I said, that was real. But then, Monday morning, you left me. I was there by myself, and I got afraid, so . . . ." Her voice lowered to a whisper. "I got high, and I called Mavis. She said that I had to do what she'd told me before—take the cat and kill it." We both looked over at Fearless, who was now crouched on top of the refrigerator in the kitchen, ready to move again.

"Did Mavis tell you why you were supposed to kill my cat?"

"No, but I knew it was to scare you away from Pride. I saw the letters she wrote you about what would happen if you didn't stop."

"So that was Mavis, too. She's not in this by herself, is she?"

"No, she's working with somebody else. Actually, I think it's for somebody."

"Who?"

Jolie didn't answer right away. She was moving around the room, touching things: a picture of my Grandma Faith, an antique salt cellar in the shape of a top hat, a stone fish from Nicaragua. She picked up a small Russian doll, the kind that has smaller ones nested inside, and opened it. It was empty, the other pieces scattered in my childhood. Jolie carefully replaced the top, set the doll on the table top and looked at me.

"I thought it was Geoffrey, but it's somebody else."

"For money?"

"No, I don't think so, she's doing fine with her business. She told me she'd take me to Fiji next month if I wanted to go. I think that whoever she's working for has something on her."

"What made you think it was Geoffrey?"

"Even when he made her quit being treasurer, she seemed afraid of him. She'd talk about everybody else, but not him, even in the days when she and I knew everything about each other."

"Have you heard about Geoffrey and Joe?"

"Yeah, it was on the news. I know it's awful, but I can't feel anything for them."

"The media are saying that Geoffrey confessed to stealing from the Pride Club and that he killed Joe and then himself. Does that make sense to you? Would he do that?"

"Geoffrey didn't care about anybody but himself, so I can believe he could kill Joe, but why bother, if he's going to kill himself anyway? What I really can't see is Geoffrey killing himself. He honestly expected to be President someday. Talk about scary ideas!"

"Jolie, what was going on Monday night at your place?"

"I don't remember many details about that night. It's pretty much a wash. I was doing drugs that didn't go very well together. I remember kissing you." Our eyes met and we both quickly looked away. "Then I got mad and ruined it. I was supposed to keep you there with me, so somebody could break into your place—"

"Not Mavis?"

"I don't think so, but she didn't say one way or the other. Anyway, after you left I crashed, and woke up about three o'clock. I called Mavis, and she said to get over to her place immediately. She hit me a couple of times. And she yelled at me. That was even worse. She told me I was worthless, couldn't even keep someone in bed with me." Jolie's voice quavered and her glance was soft and unguarded. I resisted the urge to go to her. Then her eyes and voice hardened. "She kept asking me if I'd killed your cat, and I told her yes, just to get her to shut up. But when I got back to my place, I couldn't do it." She looked up at Fearless, whose tail started slashing back and forth again. "It took me a long time to get her into a box, but I brought her back here."

"Thank you, Jolie. Fearless means a lot to me. Was that the first time you ever went against what Mavis told you to do?"

"The first time I wasn't too smashed to remember afterwards."

"Someone on the current Pride Executive Committee has

to be leaking information to Mavis and whoever else she's working with. Do you know who it is?"

"No, she wouldn't tell me that kind of stuff."

"Any guesses?"

"Maybe Tom Ng, I've never seen anybody so afraid of scandal. Or Miguel. He reminds me of Geoffrey—he's got his own ideas of what's right and wrong, and if anyone was in the way of what he wanted, well—"

"Whoever it is may be involved in murder."

"Maybe the person inside the club didn't know that it would get so heavy. Maybe it started out as just 'dirty tricks,' you know, enough to scare you off."

"Thanks, I'll think about that." I smiled at her, and for the first time she smiled back.

"Maggie, if I get sober, is there a chance for us?"

Chapter Thirty-One

The phone rang. I silently blessed it for the moment's reprieve. It was Kristin. Holy Mother of God, it was Thursday and I had missed picking her up! Guilt washed over me. How to even begin to explain? Would she be furiously accusatory, or cold and indifferent?

"Maggie, where have you been? I've been trying to call you since this morning!" Ricardo must have stonewalled Kristin's calls along with the rest.

"I'm so sorry, Kristin. I don't even know where to start about what's happened in the last few days."

"Well, pick a place and start." Mystery solved. She was being the cold-blooded interrogator. She sounded far away. Could she still be at the airport? I gave her a ninety-second run-down of the past few days.

"That's awful! Are you all right? Are they after you?" There was old-fashioned human concern there. I was close to tears.

"I don't think I'm in danger at the moment. They wanted to get me before I took a key piece of evidence to a meeting with my clients, but they failed."

"Are you alone in the house?"

"Uh—Liam was here for two nights . . ." I started to ask about when she had arrived, but Kristin's attorney-warrior training kicked in and she sensed uncertainty.

"Maggie, what's going on? Have you been seeing someone? Is she there listening to this?"

"It's not that simple. Her name is Jolie." There was a refined snort on Kristin's end at the name. "We had an affair that turned out badly. We're processing, for lack of a better word. Damn. I wanted to talk about this in person." And without Jolie standing five feet away. I looked over at her. She was now sitting on the couch. Didn't look like she intended to leave.

"You didn't waste any time," Kristin said. She sounded rather pleased, the last response I'd have expected. "Maybe it's better to get the heavy things out in the open, so we can 'process' too, before we see each other again. I've changed my plans, and I'll be staying on here through the weekend. That's why I was trying to call you. Maggie, I've been seeing someone here, and it's given me so many things to think about."

"Who?" I was feeling cold and feverish at the same time. I had to hold onto the phone with both hands.

"Her name's Jennifer. We went to law school together. She's married to Jason, who also went to school with us. They both practice at firms in Palo Alto, and they have two kids."

"I don't understand where you fit in to all that." My brain felt fuzzy and slow. It was as if Kristin was talking at the end of a long tunnel, and only some of the words were coming through: married, two kids.

"Remember the girl in high school I told you about, the one that made me realize I was gay? It was Jennifer. Her parents knew about us, that she was a lesbian. But they wouldn't accept it. If you're a Sinclair you're straight, and you succeed. So she got her partnership, she married Jason and produced two children. And she inherited three-and-a-half-million dollars."

"But, what about her husband?"

"Maggie, Jason's gay, too, don't you get it? They stopped having sex after Jennifer got pregnant the second time."

"She told you that?"

"We're so close, Maggie. I'd forgotten what it's like to share so much with someone. Jennifer and I are from the same background. We laugh at the same jokes, have the same tastes. And we want the same things. I'd forgotten how that feels, Maggie. You always make me feel guilty for wanting to succeed."

"What you're telling me is that if you're rich enough, you can buy yourself such a splendid, luxurious closet that you don't mind living in it!" I was out of control, screaming at her. Part of me regretted the outburst already, part had been wanting to do this for months and was ready to pour more oil on the fire.

"Fine, you asked for it! I didn't ask to be born rich, or my parents' daughter, or gay! But I am, and I'm tired of apologizing to you! Yes, I like living well, and I work hard for it. And I like being treated like a beautiful straight girl, instead of a freak of nature."

"I'm going to hang up now—"

"You and I are wrong for each other, Maggie, and when you calm down, I'm sure you'll see my point. Even if I do come out at the firm—and it's not out of the question, you know—you're simply not the kind of person I could introduce to the senior partners." I finally got my hand coordinated with my willpower and hung up.

The phone rang a few times, but I didn't answer and after a while it didn't ring again. Jolie wrapped my Grandma Faith's quilt around me, and I sat on the couch and sobbed, feeling the way Jolie had said I would, "stomped on and thrown away."

"She's no good for you, you have to know that," Jolie now said softly. She was standing by the couch massaging my neck and shoulders.

"Yeah, I do. Somehow at the moment that doesn't help much."

"Would you let me help?" Jolie reached down and caressed my breast. I took her hand in mine.

"I think we're both too fragile right now. But thank you, Jolie. For everything."

Chapter Thirty-Two

The phone woke me at 7:00 the next morning. I croaked out something close to "hello." It was Marc Romano.

"Hi, Maggie. I was glad to hear that you got away from those guys Wednesday night."

"Thanks. I tried to call you yesterday, Marc. I know you must be having a hard time about Geoff."

"Yeah." His voice trailed off, overwhelmed by emotion. He caught a shaky breath, exhaled. "Geoff is the reason I called, Maggie. Could I come over and see you?"

"Of course. When did you want to come?"

"Um . . . Now?"

He sounded distraught and insisted that it couldn't wait until later, so I gave in. I put on coffee, hearing my mentor Jack's whiskey voice berating me for inviting into my house the very people I was investigating. Not very professional. Shut up, Jack.

There was only time to throw on a bathrobe and stick my head under a cold tap. Marc's call had been from a pay phone a block away, and he arrived almost immediately. He looked younger and smaller than I remembered, his pale features in sharp contrast with his black hair and beard. He'd picked up my newspaper off the front step and held it awkwardly.

I offered him some of the coffee that was in the mid-stage of brewing, and we stood waiting in silence for it to finish its cycle. Now that he was actually here, he seemed to be at a loss for words and stared at the toes of his Doc Martens. He declined my offer of food and threw himself into the middle of the couch. I dislodged Pod from a chair so I could sit down. He made a nest on my lap and fixed a mistrustful gaze on my visitor.

Finally Marc spoke. "The reason I wanted to see you is that I know you're an investigator, and I want to hire you myself."

Was there anyone who didn't know by now? Still, I asked. "Do you mind telling me how you found out about me?"

"Geoffrey told me Tuesday night. He called me in the middle of the night. He was drunk, crying. He told me he needed me, could I please come right over? So I did." He glanced at me, then returned his attention to his feet. "I know, I'm an idiot. Geoff had never told me he needed me before, and I thought he meant. . . Anyway, it turned out, what he wanted me for was an alibi for the night. He was sure you thought he killed Miranda, and he was afraid you'd convince the cops."

"He was right. At the time, Geoffrey was my prime suspect."

"He said he didn't kill her, and he knew who did. I believed him, because he did tell me about a lot of other ugly stuff. He said this guy gave him keys to Miranda's place so he could search for something. He didn't tell me what it was. The guy told Geoff it was safe, she wouldn't walk in on him. Of course she wouldn't! She was dead by then. Geoff didn't find that out until later, on the news. That's when he called me."

"And now Geoff's dead too. What do you plan to do about this?"

"That's why I want to hire you. I need somebody I can trust on this."

"I'm already working for the Pride Executive Committee—" Marc ignored me and plunged on.

"I called in sick Wednesday and just wandered around. I kept seeing Miranda, her smile." He put his hands over his eyes as if this could stop the vision. "She was like a goofy kid. Did you know she delivered meals for Open Hand? A guy in my building told me that when Miranda came by with his food it was the high point of his week." He withdrew his hands and looked at me. "Yesterday the cops came to my place. The landlady let them in when I didn't answer the door. That's how I found out about Geoff, and I lost it completely."

"I'm so sorry, Marc, I tried to call—"

"Then, today— Have you seen the newspaper?" He gestured to the *Chronicle* he'd brought in. "The cops have arrested the gay bashers. They're saying that clears up Miranda's murder. And they're saying Geoff killed himself and Joe. Maggie, they're trying to act like it's all over, and I know it's not!"

"I agree with you. The people who killed Miranda, and Geoffrey and Joe, are still out there. How can I help?"

"I was thinking maybe if I hired you, you could pass along what I know to the cops, or maybe to the media, since the cops think they've got it sewn up . . . ."

"I'll do whatever I can. Tell me."

"Geoff didn't make much sense when he was telling me about it. Like I told you, he was drunk. He said 'they' wanted something from him and he hadn't been able to get it. Two guys came to his office and beat him up this week. I said something about going to the cops, and he acted like I was crazy. He was at least as scared of the police as he was of these other people."

"Why was that?"

Marc stared at the empty cup in his hands. "I don't know. There are big gaps in what he told me. He thought he could make it through, like he'd always been able to do. He was scared Tuesday night, but by the time I left on Wednesday morning he'd convinced himself that he could take care of it."

"Did he describe the people he met at City Hall? I only got a look at one of them."

"One guy had been brought in from out of town. Geoff said he didn't know anything about him. It all sounded like a TV show about mafia hit men, but now I think that was the truth . . . ." He was close to tears again.

"What about the other person?"

"When I asked Geoff, he got evasive all of a sudden, so I guessed it was somebody I knew. I've thought a lot about who it could be, but I draw a blank."

"Are you certain that it was a man? Mavis Baker has been trying very hard to get me off this case. She might be involved in other things that have happened in the past week."

"I'm pretty sure he said it was a man. And I got the impression that the one he knew must have been the out-of-town guy's boss. Do you think they're the ones who tried to kill you?"

"Yes, and they must be the ones who broke into my house. That's why Loba hated them on sight Wednesday night. They nearly killed her."

"Well, there's other people involved, and they were the ones that Geoff was afraid of. He thought he could buy off the ones who beat him up. But the others—that was a different story."

"What do you know about those other people?"

"Just that Geoff didn't have any choice but to do whatever they said."

"Or what would happen?"

"I think you saw that at Geoff's house. He wasn't able to come through. Be careful, Maggie. Watch your back." He carefully placed his mug in the sink and let himself out.

I fed the cats and scanned the *Chronicle*. The front page was dominated by a New Jersey airliner crash. The second major story was the arrest of three men believed to be responsible for a series of attacks against lesbians and gays that had resulted in one death. The three had been caught in the act of attacking a man in Dolores Park. They were members of a right-wing organization devoted to purging society of "deviants." Police had found stacks of hate literature in the home of one of the bashers, who was also the group's leader. Much of the propaganda was based on twisted biblical references. Dear Jesus, they're at it again in your name.

The phone rang. This time it was Sergeant Diana Hoffman. She asked after my health, then got down to business.

"I'm trying to trace who leaked the message on Geoffrey Lawrence's computer screen to the media." She was so angry that her southern inflection was quite pronounced.

"You know I had doubts from the beginning that the message on that screen was from Geoffrey. Why would I contribute to making it look legitimate?"

"That's not why I called—I didn't think you leaked the story. I guess I was hoping you might have some ideas. We've always had a tight forensics crew, and we've always been known for our teamwork. But someone who was at the scene yesterday gave the text of Mr. Lawrence's suicide note to the press. This is going to send morale through the floor. Well, that's my problem. The other reason I called was to check on a statement you made yesterday, about the man you followed out of Geoffrey Lawrence's office into the Castro. Did you get a look at what he bought in the bookstore?"

"No, I'm sorry, I didn't. One of the people from Pride insisted on talking to me, and I didn't get to see what the guy bought, just that he was paying for something."

"That's too bad, but maybe one of the clerks will remember."

"They probably will. He seemed to go into a homosexual panic and forget that he was supposed to melt into the scenery. Sergeant, can you tell me what this is about?"

She told me that the police lab had run a chemical analysis of the stickers found on Miranda's clothing, and concluded that they had been in contact with the fabric for a very short time.

"What stickers on her clothing?" I interrupted.

"She had two of those Day-Glo STOP THE BASHING stickers on her jacket and one on her bag when police arrived at the scene of her murder. We assumed that the killers used the stickers to single her out as a target."

"You told me she was dressed like an activist!"

"Ms. Garrett—Maggie—you're right, of course. The stickers on her clothes fit what we expected to find. They made her look openly gay. Therefore, the logic went, it was the gay bashers who killed her. That and what—" She caught herself and changed course. "It was your telling me about seeing that man in the bookstore that made me go back over the details."

When I started to ask a question, she cut me off and suggested that we talk in person. We made an appointment to meet that afternoon. She asked me to get permission from the Pride Club leadership to turn over all my notes to her.

It was 7:45 and I'd had two major interactions on one cup of coffee and before my morning shower. I promised myself to let the answering machine take over for a while.

As I poured coffee and stirred in milk, the machine recorded Lynnette's threat to withhold my final pay for the investigation unless I called immediately. I put bread in my old-fashioned toaster and let it burn while I thought about Miranda's death.

When Diana Hoffman caught herself giving away details about the bashers she had stopped herself. Desmond had not. He blabbed to me about the bashers always yelling the same thing when they attacked people. But if Miranda's murder had been arranged to look like one of the bashings, how had the killers known about the common characteristics of the bashings? Maybe there were other cops as loose-mouthed as Desmond. Maybe they had run into Desmond himself at Happy Donuts and he'd confided in them as well as me, but I doubted it. The killers had access to police information. They might even have connections in the Police Department.

Leaving the situation in the hands of the police could be dangerous to my health—and that of my friends. The thought of the "INS" visit to Ricardo's family still made me shudder, especially after seeing the bodies of Geoff and Joe. Although I trusted Diana Hoffman, I didn't trust everyone who read her reports. Operating in secrecy would benefit the bad guys, not us. They might at this moment be preparing to shoot me or someone else I cared about. For a heart-pounding moment I relived that night: running terrified down the street, unable to call for help as the car bore down relentlessly.

Loba whined softly and jolted me back to the present. "Okay, you win." I dressed quickly in jeans and a sweatshirt and took her out for a short run. She snorted and bucked like a Brahma bull coming out of a rodeo chute when we got outside, nearly pulling her leash out of my hands. "Hey, Loba, relax, it hasn't been that long since you got all the exercise you could handle!" She put her nose to the ground and strained to explore the side of the house. I dragged her toward the street. Still sniffing the air and woofing, she finally let me take her for a few blocks.

Two hours and I hadn't thought about Kristin at all. Well, hardly at all. I was still angry and hurt by what she'd said. But Jolie was right. If I'd focused more on class analysis and less on the sexy associate professor in Political Economy 101, I'd have known all along that Kristin and I were a lost cause. It was time for a change. Even celibacy looked appealing compared to the wars we'd been waging. How in keeping with Kristin's new attitude that she would evaluate our relationship in terms of an unfortunate career move. I couldn't wait to share that one with Liam.

Back at the house, I checked the answering machine. Besides Lynnette's demand to call, there was a long message from Betty Hastings: "Where *are* you? This is urgent! An old friend of mine in the Force, someone that I trust completely, says the word's coming down the line from the top, *top* brass to lay off Miranda. The story is that she was killed by the bashers. Period. In other words, forget any doubt you might have about Miranda's case, 'cause we've busted the bashers. As for Geoff, the party line there is, Geoff blew away himself and Joe. Now that the Mayor has finally obliged us all by busting the gay bashers, the lesbian and gay cops are supposed to take their cues from Chief Cox. Some of them say it's a cover-up. My friend's going on personal leave for two weeks. That girl never could take the heat." She paused and exhaled deeply. "Where am I going with all this? I've changed my mind. Larry Gross called me last night, asking me to chair a meeting on Saturday, to get to the bottom of Pride's role in it all. I said yes. All the present Executive Committee members have committed to being there. Larry said you were coming, and I want you to get Marc Romano to come, too. 'Bye. Be careful, girlfriend."

Larry hadn't wasted any time.

Betty's conspiracy theory, which fit nicely with the one I was developing myself, hadn't helped my recurring case of the willies. I decided some music would help and turned on the radio for the "Morning Concert." It was a thoroughly silly operetta, and I hummed along while I washed my breakfast dishes. When it ended, the program host announced its title, HMS Pinafore, and I dropped the mug I'd been soaping.

Why hadn't it occurred to me that Miranda's three-letter combinations could be something besides a person's initials? HMS stood for Her Majesty's Ship. HHM would be His Honor the Mayor. Of course. "That's it!" I announced to the animals, who were watching me with concern. I felt elated and remarkably dim-witted at the same time. That must be what Miranda had called the "obvious once you saw it" aspect of the list.

No wonder City Hall wanted this investigation over and done, and the cops were being told to put on blinders about Miranda and Geoff and Joe's murders.

I dialed Diana Hoffman's office. It was only fair to let her know about this. The man who answered said she was out and he didn't know when she'd be back. I left my office number with an urgent message to call me. Given the level to which I believed police were involved, I wasn't going to talk to anyone else.

Now what? Betty would jump on this story. I dialed her number, and got a busy signal. Damn. Oh well, it was still early. I'd call her from my office. She could come there to review and sign a cover letter before Ricardo faxed it to every media outlet in the City. For that matter, she could stay home and we could fax drafts of the letter back and forth. God, I loved technology!

First we'd go to the straight media, TV and the daily papers, for immediate, bright-light scrutiny of the list. Then for insurance, and some analysis of why this was happening, the gay and independent liberal newspapers, which all hit the streets on Wednesday nights. Maybe we could get one of them interested in an exclusive interview with Betty or Stephen. The media-loving Lynnette might be the best choice to get reporters' attention, which was what counted most. I couldn't wait to get to the office to start faxing.

Chapter Thirty-Three

I showered and threw on my emergency outfit, in case I needed to see anyone from the press in person. Everything I'd brought home with me, including my report to the Pride Club leadership, was in the tote bag ready to return to the office. I hadn't even taken it out of the bag. I rummaged in the pantry for the ancient stainless steel thermos my granddad used to take hunting. It's not for backpacking—it weighs a ton—but it keeps the coffee hot. I dumped in the remains of the morning's brew, put the thermos and some muffins from the freezer in a plastic grocery store bag, and headed out the door.

Burdened with a bag on each arm and a purse, I dropped my keyring and then tried the wrong key on the lock. As I fumbled for the right one, there was a rustling behind me. I started to turn, but a fist met my head and I was shoved hard against the door, so hard it felt as if my nose was broken. Cold metal was jabbed sharply into my ribs.

"Keep your face to the wall and don't even think about screaming." The harsh whisper was unfamiliar, male. He was so close I could smell the sourness of his breath. "If you see me, I'll have to kill you. Give me the notes the girl gave you. I know you've got 'em."

"It's too late. I've already made a dozen copies and sent

them to the press."

"You're lying, bitch. I know every move you make." He gave me a sharp poke with the gun.

"Do you think after what happened to Miranda and Geoffrey that I'd just carry around the only copy in my purse?"

"Yeah, as a matter of fact, I do." He tore the tote bag strap off my shoulder. The strap broke, and the bag fell to the ground, spilling out the papers it held. A light breeze lifted the papers with a riffling sound.

"Is it one of those? Don't look at me!" He was almost shouting now. "Is that it?" He jammed the pistol behind my ear.

"It might be, I don't know—let me get it before it's gone."

"No, don't move!" I could hear him scrabbling after the papers, stomping on them to hold them down. On the other side of the door, Loba was barking furiously and scratching to get out. I prayed that Mrs. Lee would hear the noise and look out her window. Inside my house, I could hear the phone ring three times, stop when the machine picked up, then ring again a few seconds later. Too late, Diana.

Now he was back, with a fistful of crumpled papers. He tried to smooth them out with one hand while he held the gun on me with the other. The steel thermos in its bag had been looped over my left forearm while I locked the door, and I slowly worked the bag downward, to get a better grip.

When he had determined that none of the papers in his hand was the list, he cursed and threw them back to the ground in disgust. White pages fluttered at the edge of my vision. "All right," he said, grabbing a handful of my hair and jerking my head back sharply. "I've had it with you, bitch. Either tell me where you put those papers or I blow your face off!"

"I don't know! Please don't hurt me!"

Muttering another warning to me not to move, he bent to retrieve my purse, which he'd thrown down earlier.

I pivoted like a discus thrower and swung the thermos-weighted bag with everything I had. I connected with the side of his head. He dropped backwards and fell heavily to the ground. As he landed, the gun in his hand went off.

An explosion tore through my left arm. I don't remember hearing the shot. I do remember screaming and marveling that I could make so much noise. My assailant was lying, unmoving, in a heap. He seemed to be unconscious, but the gun was only inches from his hand. I staggered over to grab it, and finally got a look at him.

It was the man I'd followed from his clandestine meeting with Geoffrey Lawrence at City Hall, the one I had followed to the Castro. He'd been wearing a watch cap pulled low over his forehead, but his left ear was exposed and bleeding from where he was hit. He was breathing raggedly and stirred as I got near. My right hand was shaking so that I could hardly lift the pistol. My left hand wouldn't cooperate, and blood from the bullet wound was dripping onto the ground.

Mrs. Lee opened her back door and yelled that she was calling the police. I yelled back that she should call an ambulance too, and half sat, half fell onto the ground. Propping myself against the house, I braced the pistol against my knee. It was a .22 automatic equipped with a silencer. That was why the shot had made so little noise. I could hear Loba still throwing herself at the door and wished I had enough energy to open it and let her out.

After what felt like hours, four uniformed cops appeared around the side of the house and approached me cautiously, guns drawn. I passed out.

When I came to, I was lying on a stretcher covered with a

blanket, parked next to an ambulance. The paramedic, a very young-looking Black man, told me I'd missed a dramatic confrontation between the unfortunate cop who had opened my front door and an enraged Loba. The cop had lost it and pulled out his revolver, but a ranking officer, Sergeant Hoffman, had arrived and intervened. The paramedic had vastly enjoyed the encounter, and I overheard him retelling it with fresh embellishments for each new arrival. Too bad Loba was still on the scene; otherwise he could have said she was a timber wolf.

My arm ached and my nose felt as if it had been moved a couple of inches to the right, but I didn't particularly mind. Must be good drugs. My eyes regained the ability to focus in tandem and I saw Diana Hoffman supervising the dispatch of my attacker via a different ambulance. Mrs. Lee had her arms around Loba and was murmuring something soothing in Mandarin. Loba sat wagging her tail but keeping a watchful eye on me, poised for the next onslaught. It had been a hard week for both of us.

Diana Hoffman picked up my thermos slingshot and looked in my direction with a smile that could have many different interpretations. I chose to read it as relief that I was still alive, even if I now had a lopsided face and daylight could be seen through the hole in my left arm.

The hours that followed are a blur, which is fortunate, because I spent them at the Emergency Room at San Francisco General. Ricardo's cousin Graciela works there as an R.N., and she undoubtedly smoothed the way for me. The bullet had passed cleanly through my arm, and the wound was minor by Emergency Room standards. When it was dressed and I got a cervical collar and a prescription for pain, I was released to Jessie's reproachful care. I had to argue with her for half an hour and eat a bowl of vile squash soup before she gave in and let me use the phone. First I called Ricardo at his house.

"Maggie, all the exciting stuff happens when I'm not there," he complained.

"Maybe we can switch places for awhile and let the stuff happen to you. You're young and tough, why not? Anyway, I have something exciting for you to do."

"Not more background checks!"

"No, ungrateful one, this is real spy stuff. First, lock your door and don't let anybody except Betty Hastings inside. She'll give you a ride to the office. Take along the originals of the list and Miranda's notes. Betty will write a cover letter, and then you're going to fax it with the list and the notes to every TV and radio station and every newspaper in town!"

Next I called Betty. She was raring to go, as I had known she would be. When I told her about the Mayor's involvement, she yelled, "Let's get that blood-sucker!" We collaborated on the wording of a cover letter to grab the attention of the media. She promised to take Ricardo to the office and supervise the media blitz.

And so it came about that, during an otherwise slow news week, ratings-hungry TV journalists vied with newspaper reporters to get through to Mayor Rawlings and to Martin Cox, the Mayor's hand-picked Police Chief.

Jessie and Tate moved their TV into the guest room where I was bedded down, and we spent the evening watching events unfold. The five o'clock news announced that police were reopening the investigation of Miranda Post's death because of "new information" received in that case.

By six-thirty there was a live broadcast from City Hall. An on-the-scene reporter stood jostling other stations' on-the-scene crews and announced an impending investigation of the Mayor himself. The Mayor's whereabouts were said to be unknown even to his staff. Lou Tanner, a.k.a. Melvin Rawlings (rumored to be the Mayor's brother), who had been arrested that day in an assault with a deadly weapon, was being questioned in connection with other crimes.

I called Betty Hastings' house and left a message letting her know I'd have to miss the Pride Club's showdown meeting on Saturday—doctor's orders, true, but ruthlessly enforced by Jessie.

At the eight o'clock News Brief, the Channel 5 anchor reported that gunman Lou Tanner had refused to admit or deny that his stepbrother, Mayor Rawlings, had anything to do with the near-fatal attack on a private investigator.

TV had never been so exciting. I jumped out of bed. "I can't believe this! That goon is the Mayor's brother. Who wants to bet me that he sells out his little brother?"

"Not me. The Mayor's good will isn't going to be good for much, is it?" drawled Tate.

The ten o'clock news focused on the contents of the list. Through the cooperation of individuals from the Pride Lesbian and Gay Democratic Club, "a web of bribery and corruption extending to the highest levels of the City Administration" had been uncovered. Geoffrey Lawrence, who was described as a "power broker" for the Mayor, had used the Pride Club for money-laundering on behalf of the Mayor, Police Chief and others not yet disclosed to the media. Further arrests were expected. In a related story, police were following up on new evidence in what had previously been considered the murder/suicide deaths of Geoffrey Lawrence and "his companion." Unnamed sources in the police department now were calling their deaths a double homicide.

Ricardo dropped by to bring me flowers from his family,

and a manila envelope. Jessie pressed dessert on him. He apologized about the results of his research as he consumed ice cream covered in chocolate-sauce.

"Nothing exciting," he said. "I was hoping one of these people would turn out to have a record, at least, but they're really boring. I still don't know one way or another what a couple of them did on Wednesday night, but I'm working on it."

By eleven o'clock, the news update featured a special "City in Crisis" logo of the sort usually reserved for an earthquake, major fire or hostage taking. It included a short report on a press conference held by Warren Coleman and Lynnette McSorley of the Pride Club to decry the actions of Geoffrey Lawrence and Joe Leslie, reveal bribery and corruption at City Hall and the Hall of Justice, and point fingers in every direction except internally. Okay, there was still work to be done here. Lucky thing they had Betty and Stephen.

Liam called from Chicago. He had met a new man at the fundraising workshop. Ahmed was blind, and hence valued Liam for his true self instead of his pretty face. The upshot was that Liam was staying over an extra day. He'd become just a bit worried about me, since the City Hall murder/corruption stories had even made the news in Chicago, "and for this city to notice either killings or money-laundering, it's got to be pretty impressive. You are taping all this for your video memoirs, I hope. By next month, Fox will have it all dramatically re-created. I can't wait to see who they have play you!"

Chapter Thirty-Four

Most of Saturday I slept, dosed with pain medications and undisturbed by the phone. During one of my lucid moments, Tate gave me Betty Hastings' message that the Pride leadership had agreed to wait until Sunday for their meeting, so I could join them. I felt mixed emotions about this.

I opened the envelope Ricardo had brought me the night before. He was wrong—the envelope contained some valuable pieces of information. Jessie made me promise to go out with the very next woman she found for me before she'd bring me the phone. All for nothing. Ricardo was out, not surprising on this beautiful Saturday afternoon. I left a simply worded message about one more detail with his prissy twelve-year-old sister Estela, and went back to being a full-time invalid.

Jessie limited my TV consumption to a half-hour while we ate dinner Saturday evening. "You got too excited last night and you didn't sleep at all!" Jessie needs children to push around. Of course, I chose the news for my half-hour of viewing.

An on-the-scene reporter was recapping the event of the day. Two hours earlier, Police Chief Cox had announced his early retirement for health reasons, and presented his resignation to Vice Mayor Morton Fielding (the Mayor himself was still out of the City on undisclosed business). This news came as a complete surprise to everyone the reporter interviewed. Lou Tanner, a career criminal under arrest for attempting to kill a private investigator, was now alleging that he'd been acting on behalf of the Mayor to prevent an independent investigation of Pride. The Mayor had feared disclosure of his use of the club for money-laundering activities. Although Tanner was denying the murders of Miranda Post, Geoffrey Lawrence and Joe Leslie, it was believed that he would be charged with all of them.

Jessie and Tate brought me home early Sunday morning on their way to a baby shower for a lesbian couple we all knew. I'd chipped in on a ridiculously expensive pair of miniature Oshkosh B'Gosh overalls and booties that looked like tiny combat boots.

Jessie insisted on checking for assassins in every conceivable hiding space and several inconceivable ones, refusing to believe that I was out of danger. Tate pretended to help but mostly watched Jessie's progress with loving amusement. There were multiple messages on my answering machine. Two were from Sergeant Diana Hoffman (the second referring to herself simply as Diana). I caught Jessie watching me closely as we listened to those.

I made it as far as the couch, collapsed, and was asleep before Tate and Jessie got out the door. Although Tate had fed the animals and walked Loba, by noon the animals were in open revolt for attention. Loba kept barking in pretend alarm at routine street noises and the cats staged a hissing, yowling war game with the top of the couch as the disputed territory. This was fine. This kind of conflict I could handle.

Stretching produced pain in parts of my body that had no right to hurt. I surveyed the wreckage of my cottage. The cats and Loba had reacted to my desertion by shedding big-time, and no one had cleaned for days.

Under a soft cloud of cat and dog fuzz, the answering machine light was blinking. Before leaving, Jessie had dictated an outgoing message to the effect that, having saved the world, Ms. Garrett was now taking a brief rest; if one must, one could leave a message. No one appeared to have been discouraged by this. I had a tape-full of messages. An enterprising reporter had managed to get my name and had left his number—three times. Ricardo told me excitedly that I'd guessed right about Wednesday night. Kristin left chilly regards and the comment that my recent activities highlighted our incompatibility. Marc mumbled something that might have been "thinking about you." Betty bragged about the press coverage Pride had received, and passed along a request from Larry that I pick him up a milkshake at Double Rainbow on the way to our meeting, since only I knew how he liked them.

Just listening to all these requests, pronouncements and outpourings of emotion exhausted me. My arm was throbbing, and after toughing it out for a half-hour, I took another painkiller. All the creatures were walked, fed and watered according to their needs, and I had hours before the Pride Club current and alumni leadership meeting. I picked up the mystery novel Tate had loaned me and read maybe a paragraph before I passed out.

Lynnette woke me by nearly kicking in the door. It was two-thirty. "I came to give you a ride to the meeting. Why aren't you ready? I've been trying to call you for hours."

"I'm sorry, I guess my pain medication knocked me out, and I forgot to turn my phone back on."

Lynnette held the animals at bay, checking her watch every thirty seconds or so with a great put-upon sigh. I splashed water on my face, threw on jeans and a t-shirt, and poured some of the cold contents of my coffee pot into a commuter mug. I crawled painfully into her Honda, hoping she was angry enough to give me the silent treatment. No such luck.

"I heard about Tanner almost getting you yesterday. How come you don't wear a whistle?"

I mumbled some response. Lynnette continued, "Betty is so happy that our sleazeball Mayor *and* Chief Cox are in trouble that she's decided this whole investigation was her idea. Do you realize that this will be the first time all these Pride officers have ever been in the same room at the same time? Maybe we should've tried to get somebody from the press to take pictures. Do you think it's too late now?"

Since nothing she said, including the questions, required answers, I managed to doze for a bit. I suddenly started awake: "Larry's milkshake!" Over Lynnette's fuming objections, we detoured to Double Rainbow.

Larry had managed to take over the hospital sun room for the Pride meeting. When we arrived, Betty, Stephen, Warren and Larry were all seated at a table. Larry was in a wheel chair flanked by his IV pole. They were pointing at figures in the spreadsheets Judy Willis had produced, disputing dates in club history and charting discrepancies. Miguel was drawing an elaborate diagram that looked like a football play on an easel display board. Marc Romano and Mavis Baker sat a few feet apart, each alone. David Lindley and Tom Ng paced in non-intersecting circles near the French windows.

Warren Coleman was giving a detailed history of the authorized check signers in Pride for the past five years in response to Stephen's theorizing that anyone who was a signer must be part of any shady deals. Warren made it clear that a dozen people of impeccable reputation had been signers. "Stephen, you were an ACT-UP! street fighter then," he said, chuckling. "Did you even know there was such a thing as the Pride Club in those days?" He leaned back in his chair and stretched out his braces with his thumbs.

"Face it, Stephen, you've shown over and over that numbers aren't your specialty," said Miguel, flipping his marker into the air and catching it.

Betty took Warren and Miguel to task for baiting Stephen, and Larry turned to Lynnette and me. "It's about time! We're a third of the way through this mess. But, you did bring the milkshake, you good girls! All is forgiven. We've got markers in nine colors, and we're going to mark these sheets up with all the facts—all the facts." He paused to take a long sip of the milkshake.

"Amen to that," said Betty. "Even if Geoff and Joe end up taking the official heat for all this, the club members deserve to have an honest leadership."

"It's a waste of time for me to be here," grumbled David, from across the room. "I don't understand those spreadsheets."

"You've been in the club longer than almost anybody," Stephen reminded him. "You can help us put dates and names on the figures. Come see what we've got so far."

I sidled over to Larry. "Any confessions yet?"

"No, but if these boys don't shape up, there may be a new crime," he answered, rolling his eyes. He looked feverish, but his smile was radiant.

I sat where I could see everybody, in a deep chair that supported my arm. I tried to catch Marc's eye, but he was staring out the window. I followed his gaze to see what was holding his attention. The only view was of overcast sky

Mavis was methodically making her way to the bottom of a family-sized container of Chinese takeout, her eyes never leaving the food.

"I don't see the point of having Mavis here if she's not going to help," said David.

"Well, she is a former Executive Committee member, like Marc and Larry," Betty said patiently. "She's giving up her weekend just like we are, and I think we should be grateful. She may be able to settle questions for us."

"What can it hurt to have her here, if she can help put the pieces together?" Tom said, from across the room.

"Why not share the thrill of discovery, since we're all going to catch our share of the blame one way or another?" Larry observed.

"Because all she'll do is cover her own tracks," said Lynnette. "Mavis always sees to it that other people take the blame, and she gets any credit!"

Warren nodded. "I don't blame anyone for feeling unsafe with Mavis here. She's used strong-arm tactics in the past, why trust her to act in a principled fashion now?"

Everyone turned to Mavis. She was subdued, completely unlike her usual Sherman-tank persona. When she spoke, it was to Larry.

"I found out about the 'special funds' that Geoffrey was setting up after I'd been treasurer for a few weeks. I come from a long line of crooked politicians and I know money-laundering when I see it. Geoffrey was sure that if he helped pay off the Mayor's campaign debts, his career would be made. When I called him on it, he showed me some papers for a real estate deal I put together years ago, that, well, if the details got out, I wouldn't be a realtor anymore. Who knows how he managed to get his hands on them? It was enough to make me shut up."

"But then you quit being treasurer after just a few months. Did Geoff force you out?" I asked. Mavis humbled was difficult to watch.

"He told me to quit, but I didn't put up a fight—I was happy to get out, because I was afraid he was setting me up. As a matter of fact, I think that was always Geoffrey's plan— to frame whoever was treasurer if the shit ever hit the fan." She looked pointedly at Marc, who turned even more pale.

"What about sending me the bribe money, and then the threats? And telling Jolie to kill my cat? Was all that because of Geoffrey's hold over you, too?"

"So Jolie told you? Huh." Mavis gave me a searching look. "Okay, well, I knew any real investigation was going to rub off on me, so Geoff didn't have to push very hard to get me to help. But he was just acting as a messenger boy. That's really all he ever was, only I never figured it out until this week."

"Please don't feed us that tired line about just following orders," Warren said. "It's easy to say that now, when Geoffrey and Joe are dead and unable to defend themselves."

"A lot of things are easier to say now that they're dead," Mavis retorted, staring balefully at Warren.

"I still don't get it, Mavis. Why keep quiet all this time, and talk about it now?" I asked.

"Geoffrey had copies of those real estate deals in his safe, and they turned up when the cops searched his house after the murders. I'm trying to work out a deal with the D.A. to have charges dropped in return for cooperating on the Pride stuff. So I don't have anything to lose." Her gaze was vacant. Could she be on tranquilizers? She picked up her fork and resumed eating.

"Wow, and we've hardly gotten started," laughed Larry,

draining the last of his shake. "Too bad we're not taping this. We could sell the video as true crime action and live off the proceeds for a year!"

"Let's cut to the chase," Betty said. "We have all this money-laundering going on for the Mayor and Police Chief. Was it all done through Geoff and the treasurers, with a little blackmail sometimes, like what Geoff pulled on Mavis?"

"No, he'd need help while he was in office," I said. "And then, when the rumors started and the current Executive Committee voted to investigate them, he had to have someone still on the inside working with him. More importantly, someone on the Executive Committee was working with the Mayor's man, Lou Tanner. Otherwise how could I have received those anonymous notes so fast? And how else would the men who attacked me Wednesday night know exactly when to go after me?"

"Well, did you figure it out, Ms. Thang?" Mavis looked genuinely curious.

"Shades of Miss Marple," said Warren. "We're all assembled in the library for the dénouement. Do tell us who the guilty party is."

"Why it's you, of course, Warren," I said.

"That's a spiteful thing to say, Maggie," Warren said, his face sorrowful. "I know how much you resent people with money, and that you've been milking this case for all it's worth, but I didn't think you'd resort to making up lies about us. As anyone who knew Geoffrey could tell you, he always chose his helpers from among his lovers, who, as we know, were legion." He flicked a glance at Marc. "And of course those like our Mavis, who had financial need. I neither shared Geoffrey's bed nor needed any crumbs he might toss me. Tom and Geoffrey used to be an item. He's the only one on the

Executive Committee with that distinction."

Everyone turned in Tom's direction. He looked miserably embarrassed.

"Tom also has the distinction of an alibi during the Executive Committee's snack break Wednesday night. He spent the whole time in his new boyfriend's car. The manager of the building across the street from Lynnette told my assistant pretty much everything they did. The man claimed to be utterly disgusted, but you have to wonder, given the details of the report he gave to Ricardo." Tom still looked embarrassed, but slightly less miserable.

"Warren, the police will want the name of the gas station you went to on Wednesday night," I said. "I doubt you have a credit card receipt. Do you?"

"That doesn't mean anything."

"My hard-working assistant showed your picture to gas station attendants all over the vicinity. No one remembered you from Wednesday night. Maybe you can send us to the right place?"

"This is ridiculous. Why don't we get back to the real reason we're here, instead of engaging in irresponsible attacks—"

"I've been meaning to ask you where you got those elegant braces, Warren? I'm told they're very expensive, and according to your credit record, you're seriously overextended."

"How the hell would you know my credit status? The braces were a gift, not that it's any of your business."

"They're exactly like a pair that belonged to Geoffrey. His initials are on the inside facings, did you know that?"

For the first time Warren's composure slipped a notch. He tugged at his jacket, which fit rather snugly.

"Were the braces the only thing you took from Geoffrey's closet? How about that jacket? Did you try them on while you waited for the drugs to take effect?" There was a collective gasp around us. I focused on Warren.

"Did you help kill Miranda, too?" I asked. "Or did you just help set her up? You should have bought those stickers yourself, you know. No one would have thought twice about it. But the clerk will remember that goon."

"Isn't anyone going to stop this?" Warren turned to his fellow Executive Committee members. None would meet his eyes. "Well, I don't have to take it!" He headed for the door.

"Did you think Geoffrey didn't tell me about you?" Mavis stood and glowered at Warren. "He knew you wanted everything he had—the money, the easy-breezy way he had of charming people. You wanted to *be* him! And he played you with it. But he underestimated how much you wanted to take what he had, didn't he?"

Warren kept moving. Mavis caught up with him and effortlessly lifted him off the floor. Shaking him like a Great Dane with a rat, she bellowed into his frightened face. "Did you think I would just quietly take whatever rap was left?"

I staggered out of my chair, and realized that I'd be unable to stop Mavis. I turned to Betty. Somewhat reluctantly she got Stephen to help her intervene. Together they persuaded Mavis to drop Warren. He sat on the floor, somewhat hunched over.

Miguel dialed the police, and Stephen and Mavis flanked Warren while we waited for them.

"Did you think I didn't know about you, Warren?" Mavis said. She'd recovered at least some of her old crocodile smile. "This condescending s.o.b. was the brains behind the phony canvass and marking up the printing by five hundred percent."

"So you say. You have no substantiation for your claims."

"It's just a matter of time, now that we've got everyone here in one place," I said, making another attempt to stand up and then thinking better of it. "I think you'll be surprised at how many people will believe Mavis, given the paper trail we've got here."

Mavis laughed. "Yeah, Maggie's been nipping at your heels on the printer and canvass scams. Did it make you nervous, Warren?"

"No, but it's pretty uncomfortable down here. Mind if I stand up?" Warren rose, somewhat unsteadily, and straightened his clothing. There was a curious bulge under his left arm.

I caught Marc's eye and signaled him about my suspicions. He moved in fast behind Warren and twisted his right hand behind his back.

"Quick, he's got a gun!" Larry called out, not having missed a beat. Mavis pulled a .38 out of its holster and pushed Warren back onto his knees.

"I think we'd all be more comfortable if you were down there," she said.

"I'd testify against him," Marc said. Disarming Warren had been his only participation, and I was as startled as everyone else by his comment.

"You do, and I'll see to it that you serve at least as much time as any I do!" Warren hadn't given up yet. "I think you're in a poor position to be acting self-righteous."

"What was your story, Marc?" Lynnette was trying to stir up some more drama. "Don't tell me Geoffrey was blackmailing you, too? Or did good old-fashioned love do the trick?"

"I don't even have a college degree, let alone a master's. I'd lose my job at CAP if it came out. I told Geoff about it while we were lovers. The only part of the scam I came across was Warren and the phony canvass. I guess some part of me just didn't want to see the rest of it. When I told Geoff that I wouldn't cover for him and Warren, he broke up with me and kicked me out of the club leadership. Then he blackmailed me with what I'd told him about not having a degree. I know it sounds like a lousy reason to keep quiet about what he was doing, but I told myself that I was doing important work at CAP and nobody was getting hurt."

"Except the club and the agency that hired you, believing you've got a degree. I can't believe you were so selfish," said David.

"Well, you're our expert on self-centeredness," Betty spat at him. "Marc, why the hell would you need a master's degree to be a fundraiser, anyway?"

"It's in the agency's contract."

"So work it out with them that you'll go back to school! Then come back to the club." Betty flashed him one of those rare smiles. "I think you owe it to us."

Two uniformed officers entered the room. Warren had recovered his composure and eloquently protested his innocence. The cops might have been swayed except for the unlicensed revolver. That convinced them to take Warren into custody. He continued to work on them, however, and we heard him telling about his City connections until the door closed on them. A silence settled over us for a couple of minutes.

"Maggie, how could Warren have time to attack you on Wednesday and still get back to Lynnette's on time?" Stephen asked. "That was a big risk."

"He must have been pretty desperate to get rid of me

before you received Miranda's list, and for all he knew I'd be turning over her notes, too. Having the Mayor and Police Chief leaning on him wouldn't help any. But you all made it a whole lot easier for him." The Pride leadership were unified for once in their appalled exclamations. "Think about it. You have a pattern of taking off to get snacks or run errands during your breaks and coming back late. Warren and Tanner must have counted on getting Loba and me on the first pass. That would have given Warren plenty of time. He could have even bought the gas he said he was going to get."

"But it would look awfully suspicious for you to get killed on your way to our meeting," Tom insisted.

"The plan was to kill me in a way that looked like another gay bashing, and Police Chief Cox would ensure that it got treated as one. Would anyone in this body have questioned the fact that Warren was a little flakier than usual by getting back to the meeting late?"

We spent another hour figuring out how much was siphoned off, and when. It wasn't difficult once everyone was being forthcoming and sharing what they knew.

While we were drinking up the last of the Cokes afterward, Larry asked me, "When did you figure out that it was Warren?"

"What caught my attention was learning that although he comes from a poor family and only gets ten or fifteen hours of work a week as a free lance computer tech, he spends in the same league as David or Geoffrey. When I saw him on TV wearing those braces, I knew he'd lifted them from Geoffrey."

"How did you know Geoffrey's initials were on them?"

"I made that up. Engraving his name on his braces just seemed like the kind of thing Geoffrey Lawrence would have done, don't you think? Now I have a question. Who talked to Morris Drake in the first place?"

Larry laughed. "I'm disappointed in you, Maggie. I thought you'd have guessed. I was all of the unnamed sources. Morris lied in his article about it being several people, so he'd come across as more authoritative. That's why he clammed up about 'his sources.' Standing up for First Amendment rights sounds so much more impressive than covering up for making up a story. And now, my friends, I need to thank you for the lovely, lovely party. What fun we had! Unfortunately, I find that I am becoming very tired. Go home!"

Chapter Thirty-Five

Lynnette drove me home, with the transparent expectation of sharing an hours-long postmortem. I faked sleep in the car and tried unsuccessfully to prevent her helping me inside.

As I struggled with the keys, she asked, "Could you heat up some of that coffee with some milk, and maybe some chocolate?" God help me, I moved to do it. The animals rushed Lynnette as soon as she sat down, and I let them keep her distracted while I put milk in the microwave and checked for calls.

The answering machine was full of messages again, and I gave most of my attention to them, Lynnette's monologue providing a steady background noise. Jolie said she'd decided not to let anyone push her around anymore, but that meant staying sober. She said she might call me when she got out of the substance abuse/sexual addiction treatment center her parents had found for her in Oregon. My old band manager asked if I was free for a major gig with the group—that night. Jessie praised me for not answering and invited me to attend church service at MCC with her and Tate the following week. There were two single sopranos in the choir she wanted to introduce to me. "You meet the most interesting women at church. . . ." My dad wanted to know if it was me that the

Hudiburghs from down the road had heard about while they were visiting their daughter Marva in the City—something about smacking a man over the head with a thermos bottle? Ricardo complained that Betty had drunk all the coffee in the office, and could I buy some because he was broke?

"Do you think Mavis is going to take a lot of heat for covering up for Geoffrey? Maybe if she cooperates they'll go easy on her." Lynnette spoke louder so I wouldn't miss anything. "Don't even think about getting on my lap!" This last to Fearless, who was weaving her way between Lynnette's booted feet. I sloshed two cups of nuked coffee onto the table.

Lynnette had turned on the TV and settled into my favorite chair. By five o'clock at least one of the stations had preempted regular broadcasts in favor of "City in Crisis—Day Three." The news anchor announced the arrest of former Chief of Police Martin Cox. Lou Tanner, having made a deal, had admitted to participating in the murders of three people, Miranda Post, Geoffrey Lawrence and Joe Leslie, but only as an assistant to Warren Coleman, a local mover and shaker in San Francisco politics. More on "the unfolding drama of the fall of a city government" after these important messages.

During the commercial Lynnette made some calls. She came back ready to share the latest.

"Betty's friend Anita told her that the Mayor's brother is rolling over on him. He's saying that he and Warren made Geoffrey swallow three kinds of downers and Scotch, then held the gun in Geoffrey's hand and made him shoot Joe, so Geoffrey would have the gunpowder on his hands. Then Warren wrote the phony suicide note on the computer—Tanner wouldn't even know how to turn on a computer—while they waited for Geoffrey to die! She also said that Chief Cox ordered a tap put on your office phone, Maggie. Think of the conversations he probably heard . . . You'll never believe what David is going on about now. With everything that's happening, and you nearly getting killed twice, he's worrying about the money Mavis left for you to get off the case. He says he 'really feels' it should be deducted from your fee. As if there weren't enough other things to worry about!"

"Tell him it'll be needed as evidence. It'll become Exhibit Fifteen and I'll never see it again," I said, wearily. I knew Lynnette would find a way to dock me for it.

The answering machine made its clicking, whirring noise. I'd forgotten to turn the phone back on. I jumped to answer it. Anyone would be a relief from Lynnette. It was Diana Hoffman. Relief indeed.

"Hello, Maggie, I've tried to call you several times, but I kept getting your machine, and then your line was busy. I was starting to be concerned about you."

She was concerned. Was this a professional, cop concern or something more personal? "I was dead to the world or pain meds, then meeting with Pride Club officers." I told her about our confrontation of Warren and his arrest.

Lynnette was continuing unabated, unfazed by my phone conversation. "While you were in the bathroom, Larry told David if he didn't stop whining, he'd strangle him with his IV tube! Let's see, what else happened while you were in there?'

From Diana: "That was a close call you had with Tanner. He's wanted in L.A. and San Diego for several hits. I was so glad to see that you'd managed to out-smart him." This was more than professional courtesy. There was a new warmth in her voice. Were those stars I saw or just the sunset on floating cat hairs?

Lynnette raised her voice another few decibels. "You know we've lost a quarter of the Executive Committee through all this. Since you know so much about the club now, you might make a good acting member. We're also going to recommend to the club membership that we bring Marc back as treasurer. I kind of think he and Stephen may become an item . . . ."

I tried to ignore her and responded to Diana. "It was a closer call than I ever expected. Thanks for keeping that guy from shooting Loba."

"That was my pleasure," she chuckled. "Poor Larsen is going to hear that story repeated for years! Maggie, I wanted to thank you for not giving up on Miranda Post's case. I can't officially approve of what you did, but you should know that the rank and file are grateful for how it all turned out."

She must have heard Lynnette harumphing and crashing around a few feet away, because she suddenly sounded unsure of herself. "Am I—uh, am I interrupting anything? I was—um, on my way to get some takeout food, and thought you might like some, too. I could, uh, bring enough for two of you if, um . . . ." She'd even stammered. I thought it was adorable.

"I was just wrapping up the last of my responsibilities with the Pride Club, but I'll be finished in two minutes. I haven't had a chance to tell you about what happened Wednesday night." I smiled as I thought about telling Diana the full story of the Valkyries in bathrobes.

Lynnette gasped incredulously and drew herself up to her full 5' 4 ½".

"But you haven't told me half of what I want to know. We're not done yet, Maggie!"

"Oh, but we are, Lynnette, we are. I'll send you a final bill!" I hustled her to the door.

About the Author

Jean Taylor is a proofreader at a major San Francisco law firm. Before that she was a secretary, kitchen helper, volunteer co-ordinator, seamstress, emergency room clerk and full-time cadre in a Marxist/Leninist party. She sings soprano in the Metropolitan Community Church Choir and lives in San Francisco's Mission District with Tigey and Fearless, models for the cats in *We Know Where You Live*. They make no other contributions, literary or otherwise. Jean is completing her second Maggie Garrett novel, *The Last of Her Lies*.

Mysteries from Seal Press

The Jane Lawless Mysteries by Ellen Hart. The Twin Cities are turned upside down in these compelling whodunits featuring restaurateur and sleuth Jane Lawless and her eccentric sidekick Cordelia Thorn.
HALLOWED MURDER. $8.95, 0-931188-83-0.
VITAL LIES. $9.95, 1-878067-02-8.
STAGE FRIGHT. $9.95, 1-878067-21-4.
A KILLING CURE. $19.95, cloth, 1-878067-36-2.
A SMALL SACRIFICE. $20.95, cloth, 1-878067-25-7.

The Meg Lacey Mysteries by Elisabeth Bowers. From the quiet houses of suburbia to the back alleys and nightclubs of Vancouver, B.C., divorced mother and savvy private eye Meg Lacey finds herself entangled in baffling and dangerous murder cases.
LADIES' NIGHT. $8.95, 0-931188-65-2.
NO FORWARDING ADDRESS. $10.95, 1-878067-46-X; $18.95, cloth, 1-878067-13-3.

The Cassandra Reilly Mysteries by Barbara Wilson. Globetrotting sleuth Cassandra Reilly gets herself into intriguing situations no matter where she is—from Barcelona, Spain to the Carpathian mountains of Transylvania.
GAUDÍ AFTERNOON. $9.95, 0-931188-89-X.
TROUBLE IN TRANSYLVANIA. $10.95, 1-878067-49-4; $18.95, cloth, 1-878067-34-6.

The Pam Nilsen Mysteries by Barbara Wilson. Three riveting mysteries, featuring Seattle sleuth Pam Nilsen, take us through the worlds of teen prostitution and runaways, political intrigue and the controversial pornography debates.
MURDER IN THE COLLECTIVE. $9.95, 1-878067-23-0.
SISTERS OF THE ROAD. $9.95, 1-878067-24-9.
THE DOG COLLAR MURDERS. $9.95, 1-878067-25-7.

STILL EXPLOSION by Mary Logue. $9.95, 1-878067-48-6; $18.95, cloth, 1-878067-29-X. A gripping mystery featuring the sharp-witted journalist Laura Malloy and the timely subject of abortion.

SEAL PRESS has many other feminist titles in stock, including fiction, international literature, self-help and health, sports and the outdoors and women's studies. Order from us at 3131 Western Avenue, Suite 410, Seattle, WA 98121. Please include 15% of the total book order for shipping and handling. Write to us for a free catalog.